ASK ME ANYTHING

Also by Bethany Rutter

Slowcoach
Melt My Heart
No Big Deal

ASK ME ANYTHING

BETHANY RUTTER

First published in the UK in 2025 by
HOT KEY BOOKS
an imprint of Bonnier Books UK
5th Floor, HYLO, 105 Bunhill Row,
London EC1Y 8LZ

Copyright © Bethany Rutter, 2025
Cover illustrations © Sarah Long, 2025

All rights reserved.
No part of this publication may be reproduced, stored or transmitted
in any form or by any means, electronic, mechanical, photocopying or
otherwise, without the prior written permission of the publisher.

The right of Bethany Rutter to be identifiedasauthorofthiswork
has been asserted by her in accordance with the
Copyright, Designs and Patents Act 1988.

This is a work of fiction.Names,places,eventsandincidentsareeither
the products of the author's imagination or used fictitiously.Any
resemblance to actual persons, living or dead, is purely coincidental.

A CIP catalogue record for this book is available from the British Library.

ISBN: 978-1-4714-1936-2
Also available as an ebook and audio

Typeset by IDSUK (Data Connection) Ltd
Printed and bound in Great Britain by Clays Ltd, Elcograf S.p.A.

The authorised representative in the EEA is
Bonnier Books UK (Ireland) Limited.
Registered office address: Floor 3, Block 3,
Miesian Plaza, Dublin 2, D02 Y754, Ireland
compliance@bonnierbooks.ie
bonnierbooks.co.uk/HotKeyBooks

*For Billy Lindon, Emma Hughes and Laura Kay,
who made all the difference*

THE AUTUMN TERM

CHAPTER 1

I am Mary-Elizabeth Baxter, and I can do anything I put my mind to. I can make a great soufflé, I can apply red lipstick on a moving bus without a mirror, I can ace my A levels and get into the most competitive art history degree in the country, I can perfectly calibrate the amount of bleach and dye needed to achieve my trademark candy-floss hair colour. And this year, I'm putting my mind to having sex with Felix Balfour.

He's over there, actually. That guy – no, not that guy; come on, he's so not my type – yes, that guy. The one with the swishy blond hair flopping back from his face and those light-blue eyes and the stupidly full lips and the rather stern jawline and the tight, white T-shirt and the bell hooks tote bag. Him. He of history's most rakish smile and the editor of *Quad Magazine*, the mag for students of Queen Anne's College, London.

I gaze at him across the top of my single glass of rosé, simultaneously hoping he doesn't catch me looking, but also knowing that if he does then maybe that can be a nice little gateway into . . . something. I let my crush marinate, simmer, if you will, all throughout my first year – a little flirting here, some highly charged eye contact there, a bit of very close dancing in the club on magazine nights out – but didn't convert the potential into anything more than that. I wanted to get my feet under the table at the magazine, establish myself as a Talented Person on the staff, before crossing that particular sexual bridge. And now? I'm ready to cross.

'This is kind of weird, right?' Patrick says to me, nudging his hip gently against mine, snapping me out of my Felix-flavoured daydream.

'Hmmm?' I ask, tearing my eyes away from Felix.

'Like, having us all in one place.' His eyes scan across the room, where there are very much two camps: the newspaper people and the magazine people. I feel if you didn't know there were two camps, you would still be able to tell. It's not that the newspaper people are dry, per se, it's just . . . they're not as stylish as the magazine lot. Don't quite have the same élan. More serious. Less fun. So we generally keep ourselves to ourselves, but for some reason Jack Sampson, the president of the Quad Media organisation, decided we had to kick off the new academic year by mixing. Or, more likely, he didn't want to spring for two separate events, so here we are, the week before term starts, pretending that we're going to mix!

'Yeah, it is a bit,' I say, taking a sip of my drink. 'Well, they tried, I suppose!'

'Two households, both alike in dignity . . .' Patrick says drily.

'Ha! Try saying that to one of the newspaper lads. I don't think they consider us magazine lot very dignified.'

'What's not dignified about arts and culture and lifestyle and fashion?!'

'And advice columns!' I add. Naturally, I think my advice column is very important, and so do the students of Queen Anne's College. I started it halfway through last year when I was a mere fresher, just a little baby fish swimming in the great pond of London's biggest interdisciplinary university, because last year's editor, Emily Daly, was also a cute, chubby gal with great taste so basically let me write what I wanted.

'And advice columns,' Patrick reassures me. He's the deputy editor, Felix's right-hand man, having graduated to that position after being last year's film editor. Patrick is notable for being one of the Hot Gays – conspicuously good-looking and, well, gay. 'I'm going to get another drink – do you want something?'

I shake my head. 'No, I'm all right, thanks, Pat.'

'You sure?' he says, glancing at my nearly empty glass.

I shrug. 'I'm not much of a drinker.'

'Very wise,' he says before disappearing into the throng.

Instead of joining Patrick at the bar, I make a beeline for the jewel in the crown of the Queen Anne's College student union: the jukebox. An actual, old-fashioned jukebox that's somehow been rewired to operate digitally and contains about one million tracks, give or take. I weave my way through the crowd, making a very concerted effort not to look at Felix again, instead bumping my hip against Tyler – my beloved music-editor buddy – as I pass. They wink at me across the top of their beer bottle and go back to chatting to a girl I recognise from the newspaper – probably much deeper and cleverer than any of us magazine folk. And just as I'm about to reach my hand out and flip through the list of tracks ('From

ABBA to ZZ Top!' as the original faded lettering behind the glass top proclaims), another hand darts out in front of me.

'Wow!' I say, taken aback, looking up to identify the owner of the interloping hand, which is now pressing numbers on the machine.

The interloper hears me and looks over his shoulder. 'Oh, sorry,' he says, looking down at me. He's very tall and just generally quite large, like a bear. 'I didn't see you there ... not sure how, though.' He looks me over, presumably taking in my rather ostentatious hair, rather ostentatious make-up and rather ostentatious outfit. I raise my carefully plucked and filled-in eyebrows. 'What were you going to queue up, anyway?'

'"Fantasy" by Mariah Carey but you just –' I cut through the air with my hand in a swift gesture – 'snuck right in there.'

'Well, you could do worse than my choice,' he says, shrugging. 'Since "Genius of Love" by Tom Tom Club –' he begins, but I get in there first, not willing to let him think he's telling me something I don't already know.

'Is sampled on "Fantasy" by Mariah Carey,' I say, fluttering my eyelashes and smiling sarcastically. 'I'm Mary-Elizabeth Baxter, by the way.' I decide to be polite, but nonetheless try very hard not to instinctively start swaying my hips to the extremely catchy sound of the track he chose.

'That's a very sensible name for –' he begins before cutting himself off, instead moving his jaw from side to side.

'For what?' I ask, folding my arms across my chest. Or rather, slightly below my chest, because my chest is rather large. He doesn't say anything. 'For such a silly person?' I run my fingers over my 'M' necklace, feeling the comforting smoothness of the puffy letter against my fingertips.

He rolls his eyes. 'Well, you do have candy-floss hair. And are wearing –' he surveys my outfit – 'some kind of nightie?'

'It's a babydoll dress!' I protest. Why am I defending myself to this rando?!

'Babydoll dress,' he says, nodding. 'Got it. I'll remember that for next time I go shopping.'

'Anyway,' I say, flustered, 'who are you? I bet you've got a very silly name for such a sensible person.'

He exhales. 'Laurie O'Donnell,' he says flatly, holding out his hand. It's big and fleshy and looks pleasingly warm. I extend mine, not dropping my gaze so he doesn't think I'm intimidated by him. Instead of shaking it, he picks up my hand and looks at my nails. 'Of course,' he says with a smile.

'Of course what?' I ask. But I know. I know it's going to be something about the lilac glitter gels that I've got on my long, oval nails.

He drops my hand. 'Of course nothing,' he says. 'Ignore me.'

'Oh, believe me, I will,' I say, narrowing my eyes. Who is this guy? I mean, beyond being Laurie O'Donnell.

'I take it you're on the magazine?' he says.

'Why, because I'm so frivolous?'

'Because I don't know you,' he says, exasperated, as if he hadn't just been intensely judging me for my frivolity. 'I'm the research editor on the newspaper. I . . . well, I report on the research the different departments of Queen Anne's are carrying out.'

'Very noble,' I say. 'I'm the advice columnist for *Quad Magazine*.'

'Delightful.'

'It is, actually. I'm extremely delightful.'

'And what kind of advice do you dispense?'

'Wise advice about dating and relationships.'

'And do you have a lot of experience in that field?' I can't quite tell if he's asking if I'm a slut, but he might be.

'I suppose you could say that,' I say, blinking slowly, unwilling to defend myself against his assumptions because I fundamentally don't think there's anything wrong with being a slut. 'But mostly just my own natural wisdom.'

'What kind of qualifications do you need to be an advice columnist?' he asks nonchalantly, sipping from his pint glass.

'None in particular,' I say breezily. 'I'm not exactly a marriage counsellor. Just a chatty gal with lots of opinions.' But then I second-guess myself. Want to defend my section, my little column. 'It's not as easy as it looks though. I know everyone thinks they could do it, just because they have opinions.'

'Oh, I'm sure it takes a special kind of person,' he replies.

'You should give it a go,' I say, giving him my best sarcastic smile.

'Maybe I will.'

The track is winding down and no one is going to get between me and the jukebox this time. 'Excuse me.' I gesture for him to move to the side so I can get to it. I type in the number for 'Fantasy' by Mariah Carey, which I know by heart. Laurie looks at me, a faint, amused smile dancing on his lips. Annoying. I turn and say to him over my shoulder,

'Anyway, I think the best version of "Genius of Love" is the live version with Mystic Bowie.'

'So do –' Laurie begins, but suddenly our little tête-à-tête comes to an abrupt end with the arrival of a gaggle of what I would be able to identify at a hundred paces as Newspaper People just by their artfully unstudied outfits.

A tall girl with lank blonde hair says very much to Laurie and very much not to me, 'We're going to head off to the College Tavern if you're coming.'

'Oh, I'm coming,' he says drily. A very dry person, isn't he?

'Well, it was a pleasure meeting you, Laurie,' I say sardonically.

'You too, Mary-Elizabeth,' he says, as if my name has air-quotes around it. Ugh!

And with that, he's gone! What a strange, infuriating little person! Well, not that little, I suppose. Quite big really.

Finally, my beloved 'Fantasy' by Mariah Carey blasts out over the speakers, and I rejoin my crew of mag lads, ladettes and those like Tyler who have decided the gender binary does not serve them. With the newspaper lot disappeared off to the pub, there's less of a sense that we somehow have to be on our best behaviour, and we dance and chat and drink in peace until there's only a few of us left.

'Love the babydoll dress,' Felix murmurs into my ear as he hugs me goodbye. He always says exactly the right thing. Let me state once again for the record: this year, I'm putting my mind to having sex with Felix Balfour.

CHAPTER 2

Ah! The first week of term. All those freshers scuttling around looking furtive and nervous but trying to style it out – I can't believe it was a whole year ago that I was one of them, and now I'm all grown up and handing out copies of the magazine to the sweet little baby students.

'We have a stand at the Freshers' Fair if you're interested in writing for the magazine!' I say brightly, handing a copy to a blonde girl through a cloud of vape. She smiles politely and takes the magazine but doesn't seem that interested. On to the next one!

Finally someone I recognise is heading my way. 'Leonie! Magazine?' I know she'll take it because I literally sat next to her in our French Modernism seminar this morning. And she does take it, so now my stack of magazines to distribute is almost gone and my work is so nearly done.

'Magazine?' I say, extending my arm towards a passing fresher in a very daring neon-orange sweatshirt.

'No, thanks, I've already got one,' he says, waving a copy of the newspaper.

'That's the newspaper! This is the magazine!' I explain

brightly.

'Oh.' He frowns. 'Are they different?'

'Yes! Completely different! Completely different teams! The magazine is much more fun,' I assure him.

He grudgingly takes a copy of the magazine and slopes off, leaving me with one solitary copy left to distribute, plus the one I shoved in my bag for my own perusal. I've not done a bad job today – most of the *Quad* writers and editors hate doing distribution, but I don't mind standing around convincing people to take a copy of a free magazine, probably because I'm very nosy and like an excuse to see what people are wearing, what they're doing, what's the vibe on campus and all that.

I hold out the magazine to every passing student, but the fact that I only have one left makes me look slightly odd and very unofficial. 'Please?' I all but beg a tiny blonde girl who surveys my outfit of a vintage pussy-bow blouse tucked into a sequinned pencil skirt with curiosity. But she takes it! And my work here is done!

I've got the first magazine meeting of the year in an hour, which means there's definitely time for a coffee first. The campus café, the Workshop, has had a sleek makeover since we were last here and has now been brought kicking and screaming into the 'aesthetic' age – everything is wood and cream with hanging plants everywhere. It's all a bit samey, but I can't deny it's an upgrade from how unloved it was looking in my first year.

With my iced mocha in hand, I take a seat at a corner table. Ordinarily this would be the perfect opportunity for people-watching, but I feel like I should probably flip through the magazine before our first official meeting tonight.

I have to say, Juliana has done a great job of designing my page. She's really got a good eye. Much like this café, *Quad Magazine* used to be a bit of a mess before Juliana started working on it. She just made everything look . . . tidy. Intentional. Obviously, Felix is going to do a great job as editor this academic year – he already is, in fact – but Juliana's input cannot be overstated. She found me the perfect retro-inspired font for my column, 'Ask M-E Anything', and has made the page look appropriately stylish. My first column of the year wasn't anything too tricky (which was nice, because my brain was very much in summer-holiday mode when I wrote it for the Freshers' Week issue), just a classic moral quandary for me to advise on.

> Dear M-E,
>
> My mate was going out with a guy she met in Freshers' Week last year. We'd often go out as a group with people from our halls, and I'd sometimes feel like he was flirting with me on nights out. I don't think it was all in my head, and I definitely fancied him back. They broke up after a few months, but whenever he saw me around uni we would chat, and I was definitely getting flirty vibes. I bumped into him over the summer, and we ended up hanging out, and at the end of the night we kissed even though I'd spent the whole evening telling myself I wouldn't or couldn't. He felt bad about the kiss and told

my mate, and now she's pissed off at me, but he wants to give it a go. They've been broken up for months now – am I being a dickhead for even considering it?

Confused and Conflicted

Dear Confused and Conflicted,

It's always such a tough situation when you've got feelings for someone that your friend has dated. I guess it just comes down to how strong your feelings are, for both of them. Are you super-close to this friend, or do you think this guy could be the One? It all depends on what you're more willing to let go of: the friendship or the prospect of a relationship with this person. Flirting and making out in the club is fun, but if it's not worth losing the friendship over, then you know what the right decision is. But if you really see a future with this guy, and you don't feel like your friendship with this mate is super-strong, then on balance maybe that's the right answer for you. In general though, I would always counsel against choosing a potential date over a friend. Flirtations come and go but friendships are more likely to last. Whatever you choose, be definitive and don't let things drag on with this guy in secret. Make a decision and pursue it with integrity.

With love from M-E

I think that's pretty decent and even-handed advice, right? I try not to be too prescriptive because I think most people already know the answer to whatever question they're asking, and I just want them to figure it out for themselves. I also think most people are fundamentally good but come up against these moral dilemmas more than we would like.

I glance at the big clock above the counter. Oooh, better dash off to the mag meeting!

There is a stack of *Quad News* by the door of the café, as well as a smaller pile of magazines, so I pick up a copy of the paper as I dash out.

With less enthusiasm than I read the magazine, I flick through the pages of the newspaper as I walk, being careful not to bump into anyone. Blah blah blah, important news, internal politics of the university, groundbreaking research, same old same old. I've just made it to the Quad Media office for our meeting and am about to leave the newspaper on a nearby coffee table for someone else to read when –

What. The. Hell?

Do my eyes deceive me? Or am I looking at . . . 'NO NONSENSE'? A new advice column. In *Quad News*.

Dear No Nonsense,

My mate used to go out with this guy and I really fancy him. They've been broken up for ages and I want to ask him out because he fancies me too. We kissed on a night out recently and then he told her because he felt guilty and now my mate is pissed off at me, but she was the one who dumped him in the first place. Am I being a dick or should I go for it?

Wannabe Girl Code Respecter

Dear Wannabe Girl Code Respecter,

Frankly, I wouldn't bother: the main problem here isn't whether you're allowed to go out with someone your friend went out with, but with the fact that it seems like he's using this situation to make his ex – your friend – jealous. Yes, it does sound like he fancies you, which is always nice and flattering, but the fact that he went straight to her to tell her that you two kissed, even though they've been broken up for months, speaks volumes. It sounds like a level of drama you could do without. Don't hold back because you respect the girl code, hold back because you respect yourself.

No Nonsense

I stand in the doorway, my eyes scanning over it as my fellow writers and editors enter and take a seat. My blood is absolutely boiling. There is no way this column is by anyone other than Laurie. After he was so amused by me at the drinks last week! Silly little me with my silly little column! And now he's basically taking the piss! All our copy lives on the same server, so all he would need to do is wait for me to upload mine for printing so he can see the problem I've answered and then write his mean little version!

'Urgh!' I burst out, slamming the door behind me now that everyone's duly assembled.

'What's up?' Felix asks.

'What's up is this bullshit,' I say, holding up the newspaper. 'This tedious guy I met at the mixer thing last week was so, ugh, dismissive of me and my column, and now a week later he's started his own fucking advice column in the newspaper!'

'Yikes,' Katie Jones, the lifestyle editor, says, adjusting the blazer that's elegantly draped over her shoulders.

'Big, rude yikes,' I say, finally sitting down. I don't want Felix to see me losing my cool – must project an air of nonchalance at all times – but this has really taken it too far.

'Which guy?' Olu, the fashion editor, furrows her brow.

'Laurie O'Donnell,' I huff.

'Oh, him,' Felix says, his lip curled dismissively but his interest clearly piqued in some way. 'Never trust a mathematician, that's what I say.'

'It's deeply unchic!' I fume.

'The newspaper stealing stuff from the magazine! This is the last thing we need,' Patrick says, exasperated. Felix shoots him a look. Uh-oh. What does that mean?

'What?' Tyler asks as murmurs go up around the room.

Felix exhales, disgruntled. 'There's . . . well, things are tight in the Quad Media budget. Tighter than ever. The cost of paper has gone up so much over the past few years, and there's been a lot of – I suppose you could call it discussion and negotiation within Quad Media about what that's going to mean for us. Anyway, long story short, our funding has already decreased for this year and there's a chance . . .' He trails off. Infuriating.

'A chance what?' I ask impatiently.

'A chance that only one of us will survive.' At this point, everyone starts to look nervous.

'And you know which one that'll be,' Patrick says, rolling his eyes.

'Fuck!' Olu bursts out. She said what we're all thinking.

'It might not be as bad as it seems,' Felix says calmly. 'We have no idea what's going to happen. I wasn't even going to mention it, but obviously I didn't have much choice.' He glances at Patrick again, who's looking slightly sheepish. 'But it's better that we know what's going on, given how much time and effort we all put into the magazine, on top of our degrees. And anyway, we've still got a magazine to produce, so, section editors, tell me what you've got going on this issue?'

The energy is slightly subdued as the section editors go around and list their plans for the next issue, but by the end of the meeting Felix has managed to rally the mood a little.

We go to the bar for a drink afterwards and I try to put the whole thing out of my mind. I need a Felix-shaped distraction, and lucky for me he's pulled up a chair right next to me.

'Do you ever drink anything that isn't pink?' he asks, glancing at my glass of lemonade with blackcurrant cordial, the dark of the blackcurrant so diluted by the clear lemonade it's become a pale pink.

I flutter my eyelashes at him. 'Not if I can help it.'

He smiles and takes a sip from his pint. We're sitting so close to each other that I can smell his aftershave, all expensive and heavy and woody. 'I'm sorry about the whole Laurie O'Donnell thing. He really is the worst.'

'It's starting to look that way,' I sigh.

'I was never a fan, I have to say.'

'Do you know him?'

Felix nods. 'We were at school together.'

I frown. 'That surprises me somehow.'

'Go on,' Felix says, a sly smile on his lips.

'I don't know, I just mean . . . you have a particular vibe about you. And he doesn't really have the same . . . vibe,' I babble inarticulately.

'Ha!' Felix bursts out. 'Don't get St Alfred's College vibes from Laurie? Might be the fact he was on a scholarship.' Naturally, Felix went to a very fancy school. And so, apparently, did Laurie.

I shrug. I don't know enough about this boy to decide what vibes he has at all. Only that he's got to me. A lot. I let us sit in silence for a moment before I burst, unable to contain my irritation any longer. 'So, him doing an advice column for the newspaper is even more annoying for me than it looked, right?' I say. 'If the magazine does get wound down and they try to merge us with the newspaper, if they already have an advice column then what is the point in me? What do I have to offer?'

Felix sighs. 'I know, it's pretty fucking rude of them. Definitely taking liberties.'

'Rude of him in particular. I know it must have been his idea.' I narrow my eyes and think of Laurie O'Donnell and his smug face and him choosing 'Genius of Love' on the jukebox last week.

'Look,' Felix says, laying a reassuring hand on my thigh, 'all you can do is focus on what you're doing. Not what anyone else is doing. Just keep doing your thing the way you want to do it, and he can just fuck off. And there's no point worrying what's going to happen to the magazine; that's something for me to figure out. All I can do and all you can do is try to control the shit we can control, right?'

I nod, feeling a little flutter in my chest as I see his hand on my thigh. 'Felix, you're so wise.'

'I am, aren't I? Maybe I should start an advice column,' he says, giving me a sly sideways look, before taking another sip of his drink. His hand is still on my thigh.

On second thoughts, maybe it won't take the whole academic year for me to get with Felix . . .

CHAPTER 3

'You up for staying out a bit?' Juliana asks half an hour later. 'We were going to see if anything fun was happening at the club tonight.'

I shrug. 'Why not? I think my flatmates are around as well.'

'Great!' she says, and I message Aleesha and Morgan to ask if they are out.

Morgan's just left to go to Luke's, and I was going to go home but if you're out I'll stay, says Aleesha.

We shuffle from the bar to the club, which is well populated for a Thursday night when there are other club nights in places not so far from here, in Soho and Fitzrovia. That's one of Queen Anne's best assets: even though it's based in Central London, it has an unusually thriving student union, with bars that people actually drink in, a club that hosts well-attended club nights and actually pretty famous live music acts (to Tyler's great joy). We're all in the mood to dance.

I hop from foot to foot on my patent ballet flats as we cross the threshold. 'I need to get this nervous energy out of my system.'

sure what to do with it. 'Anyway, I just wanted to tell you how much I love it.'

'That's super kind of you!' I say, but she's already gone.

'Look at our little celebrity,' says Tyler brightly, clearly not too offended by the suggestion that my column is the best thing about *Quad*.

Then Aleesha says what we are all thinking. 'Don't you think it's mad that, like . . . no one is dancing? Thursday night in the union and not a soul on the dance floor.'

Tyler shrugs. 'I mean, it's not like it's wall-to-wall tunes.'

'No, but it should be,' I say, annoyed by the lack of general merriment around us. I thought this was going to be an opportunity to grind on Felix, but he's deep in conversation with Patrick and Georgia Scott, the film editor, over a pint at one of the high tables on the other side of the floor. The DJ, a guy with lank dark hair wearing all black, seems unperturbed that he has a captive audience and yet no one is dancing. 'I can't believe they disconnected the jukebox for the evening for this.'

'Well, why don't you be the change you wish to see in the world and all that?' Tyler pushes their short blond hair back in a very charming and roguish way.

'How should I attempt that, oh wise one?' I ask.

'I can't imagine it's that hard to start your own night here . . . I mean, I could ask Mark who manages the union for you, if you want?'

I let out a laugh. 'Moi? A nightlife entrepreneur? Dare I say a DJ?'

'Oh, my days,' Aleesha says, grinning. 'I love this already!'

'Why not?' Tyler asks, bolstered by Aleesha's enthusiasm. 'You've got good taste, you've got style, you know a lot of people and a lot of people know you – you could definitely get bodies through the door.'

'And onto the dance floor, most importantly,' I say, narrowing my eyes at the DJ resolutely sticking to wordless bleeps.

I mean, Tyler's not wrong, but I can't say I've ever considered such a thing before. What do I know about DJing? Not a lot!

'Precisely,' they say. 'Plus, everyone fancies the DJ. Well, most DJs . . .' Tyler doesn't need to point out that the vibeless situation in front of us is slightly undermining their point.

'So what you're saying is that it could be fun for me, but also a vehicle for further adventures in romance . . .'

'That's precisely what I'm saying. Plus, I think it would be fun for me, personally.'

'Plus, think of the outfits.' Aleesha grabs me by my chubby upper arms. 'Are you thinking of the outfits? Tell me you're thinking of the outfits!'

'There's a lot of potential to serve looks,' I say, nodding thoughtfully. 'Which is, of course, the second most important part after the fact that everyone fancies the DJ.'

'Or third most important part, after bringing the vibes to the union,' Tyler reminds me. 'What's your USP? I assume it's not going to be . . . whatever beepy shit this is.'

'It most certainly is not!' I say, horrified. 'Do I need a USP?'

'In my expert opinion, yes.'

'Agreed,' Aleesha pipes up.

'Well, you are the music editor so I should probably take your advice seriously,' I say to Tyler before turning to Aleesha. 'And I always take you seriously.'

'Sharing a bedroom wall with you means that I'm very aware that you like pop music, so why not something poppy and fun?' Aleesha suggests, before cutting a dirty look in the direction of the DJ. 'The fun part is, like, really important.'

Tyler sips thoughtfully for a moment. 'What about vintage bangers?'

'I like it! But I need parameters for what counts as vintage . . .' I take out my phone to google when 'Hey Ya!' by Outkast was released. Apparently it was 2003.

'What about only songs released in 2003 and earlier?' I suggest.

Tyler laughs. 'That's quite specific.'

I shrug. 'You said I needed a USP . . . maybe my USP can be that I only play songs that were released before I was born.'

'I've definitely heard of worse parameters for a club night,' Tyler nods, their eyes narrowed as if they're deep in thought. 'You could call it ThrowBax . . . like the word "throwbacks" but, you know, with your name in it?'

'Tyler Shaw! Your mind!' Aleesha exclaims with delight. I suppose it is quite a good name.

'You are a true marketing genius,' I say. 'Anyway, why don't you have a club night if it sounds so fun and easy to you?'

They shake their head. 'Nah, too much effort.'

'Ha!'

'But you should definitely do it!' they add instantly, not wanting to deter me from my newfound mission to be Queen

Anne's greatest DJ. Or at least a better DJ than this guy. 'I'll talk to Mark at the union, put you two in touch so you can sort it out, but I'd be shocked if he didn't go for it.'

'Do you know what? I think this might be an excellent idea.' I can't believe how quickly a plan has come together! I might not have achieved my plan of escalating my flirting with Felix, but I do have a fun new thing to look forward to – assuming this Mark guy says yes to it – so all in all, not a waste of a night.

Tyler clinks their glass against Aleesha's and then against mine. 'I'll drink to that. Hey, in exchange for setting you up with a new career as a DJ, can I ask you a favour?'

'Anything for you,' I say, and I actually do mean it.

'Well, you know how I'm a neurospicy icon?'

I nod. 'I do.'

'Well, Felix doesn't, and I sense he'd be weird about it, but I could do with some help proofing my section . . . and you're so eagle-eyed and on it, I was wondering if you could help me out?' Tyler flutters their eyelashes at me.

'Is that it?' I ask, slightly disbelieving.

Tyler shrugs. 'Maybe it's not a big deal for you but it would help me out a lot.'

'I would be honoured. Agony aunt, DJ, proofreader . . . I kind of feel like I've got a lot going on this year!' I say, delighted at my good fortune. If you couldn't tell, I'm a person who veritably perishes without a lot going on.

But Tyler's idea is one I truly didn't see coming. Mary-Elizabeth Baxter: DJ of the future?

CHAPTER 4

'Look,' Mark from the student union sighs, wiping down the bar ahead of another night of thirsty students darkening his door. 'As long as you get people in, buying drinks, behaving themselves, we're pretty much up for anything. What kind of night was it you wanted to do?'

I describe the 'concept' of ThrowBax, which seems to satisfy him.

'It's different to anything else we have,' he says, shrugging, 'so worth a try. When were you thinking?'

'Oh! Um . . . I hadn't actually thought about the when of it all . . .' I say, furrowing my brow.

'Two Saturdays' time?' he asks hopefully. 'We've had a band cancel their gig because they couldn't get a visa to tour the UK, so we have an empty slot to fill.'

Many people would be intimidated at the idea of their DJing debut being a Saturday night. Not me. I nod decisively. 'Sounds good.' I only have eyes for the outfit opportunities. Well, maybe the flirting opportunities too.

'You going to make a flyer?' Mark asks.

'I hadn't thought about it, but I can do that!' I say brightly.

And I am struck with the fiendish plan to hand them out when I distribute copies of the next *Quad Magazine* the week of my club night. Everything is truly falling into place.

Mark seems slightly bemused by my perky demeanour. Many people are; I'm used to it. 'Right, well, if you've got any questions, you know where I am, otherwise I'll add it to the schedule and put it on the published listings for that weekend.'

I salute him. 'I won't let you down, Mark from the student union.'

He just nods, a baffled smile on his face, and I head back to my little nest in Tufnell Park.

* * *

On the bus home, I check my 'Ask M-E Anything' email address and am delighted to find that I've received a couple of questions. I read them and settle on one for my next column, from a girl who's started seeing someone new and thinks she likes him too much. I even start scrawling down my response in my very chic little notebook from the fancy stationery shop in Covent Garden (that's what student loans are for . . . right?) and get so into it that I almost go sailing past my bus stop.

We only moved in right at the end of the summer, just before term started a few weeks ago, but already Aleesha, Morgan and I have developed a weirdly functional home life for three students. We eat dinner together whenever we're all at home, taking turns to cook. No instant ramen here!

'Morgan,' I say, very businesslike over our pasta alla vodka.

'Yeeeees,' Morgan says, raising her blonde eyebrows, knowing a request is coming her way.

Aleesha holds up a hand. 'Wait, let me guess.' She closes her eyes and places both hands down on the table like she's at a seance. 'You want Morgan to design the flyers for your club night.'

'How do you do that?!' I burst out.

'She's a witch,' Morgan sighs.

Aleesha is extraordinarily perceptive. Scarily so. It's almost impossible to lie to her, or evade telling the truth, and she often just knows what you're going to say before you say it.

'Says you!' Aleesha protests.

'We all have our little powers, don't we?' Morgan laughs. 'Aleesha knows what you're thinking, I always know what time it is without looking at a clock, and Mary-Elizabeth –'

'Can make anyone fall in love with her,' Aleesha says, nodding.

'With a bit of time, energy and persistence, I've never failed,' I say lightly, as if it's the easiest thing in the world.

'I think maybe of all of us, you've got the most useful skill,' says Morgan.

Look, I'm not saying it works on everyone, but I've found that if I fancy someone, even if at first they don't seem interested, if I put in the legwork, they will, at some point, develop a reciprocal crush on me. I can't explain why, or how. All I know is that it happens. Which is why I feel so confident about Felix Balfour.

'I'm right though?' Aleesha smiles broadly, knowing she's got me. 'About wanting Morgan to make you a cheeky little flyer?'

'You're right,' I say grudgingly. 'Morgan, what do you think?'

She shrugs. 'What's the point of studying fine art at one of the best art schools in the country if you don't use your powers for good?'

'Precisely,' I say.

I can barely draw a stick man, and was gently encouraged not to take art at GCSE, so it's kind of funny that I've ended up a fledgling art historian, but you don't actually have to be good at art to be good at reading art and thinking about art and analysing art. But Morgan on the other hand? She's got proper talent. And she's not wrong: the Powell School of Art at Queen Anne's is one of the best art schools in the country.

'So, what kind of thing do you want?'

'Nothing too extravagant!' I say, already feeling guilty about calling on her services. 'Just something basic but eye-catching, which has all the information about time, date, location and vibe.'

'And the vibe is, like, vaguely retro-flavoured?'

'Exactly.' I nod.

She turns around and grabs the unlined notepad and Sharpie that we use for writing shopping lists off the work surface behind us. 'Talk among yourselves.'

'You don't have to do it now,' I protest. I glance down at my phone. There's a text from my stepdad, Stephen. *Can you call Mum, please? She says she hasn't heard from you in ages.* Stephen is all right. He's not, you know, an evil stepparent from a fairy tale, he's just a bit useless. A bit wet. A bit bumbling. Which I suppose suits my mum just fine, because then she gets to be the boss. Her and my actual dad got divorced when I was about five – old enough to know I used to actually have a dad who lived with us, but not old enough to have built up loads of bucolic childhood memories. Now he lives in Hong Kong with his new family and visits once a year. Or thereabouts. I mean, he's busy and has a really important finance job, so it's not that surprising he doesn't come back that often. And there's such a big time difference, isn't there? It's just hard for us to talk on the phone or on Zoom when he's going to bed and I'm waking up.

'Ssssh.' Aleesha presses a finger to her lips. 'The genius is at work.'

Morgan rolls her eyes but smiles. 'I'm not exactly a genius.'

Aleesha and I do as we're told and talk among ourselves as Morgan scribbles away at the rickety kitchen table. But I'm distracted – I have another column to write for the next issue and I can feel bloody Laurie's bloody rival column hanging over me like a dark cloud. Maybe it was a one-off. Maybe he'll be bored of it by the next issue, will have forgotten about it and given up. All I can do is exactly what I've always been doing. I can't let him distract me. Then he wins.

'It feels like shit's even more intense than last year already,' Aleesha says, grimacing. Not to play into the cliché that humanities are 'soft' while STEM subjects are 'real', but it does always sound like Aleesha's natural sciences degree is just a little bit more hard-going than whatever me and Morgan are getting up to.

'You smashed the end-of-year exams though,' I remind her.

'But now I know I should be operating at that level, man,'

she says, shaking her head, her braids swishing in a very satisfying way.

'Don't put too much pressure on yourself,' I tell her. 'Nothing good is going to come of that. Obviously, it's great to know you've got the potential to achieve amazing things like you did in your first year, but it's fucking tough – such a tough degree – and there's no point psyching yourself out about it and getting inside your own head. You're exactly where you're meant to be.'

She swallows. 'I hope so.'

'Hope?! Hope didn't get you here, baby girl! It was hard work and determination!'

Aleesha instantly bursts out laughing. 'I feel like you need to monetise your pep talks,' she says, shaking her head.

'Did I take it too far?' I ask with a smile.

'Nah, just the right amount.'

Uni is so expensive these days that there's this added layer of pressure that just permeates everything we do. It was kind of a foregone conclusion that I would go to uni, but that's not the case for everyone, which means it's a constant tightrope-walk of trying to have fun and live our best lives, but also not waste this incredibly expensive opportunity to . . . ugh, improve our prospects. Grim.

Morgan slams the Sharpie down on the table. 'How's that for a first draft?' She holds up the pad and displays a riotous, eye-catching flyer that borrows the aesthetic of a Nineties DIY zine.

I gasp with delight. 'I love it. It's perfect. Don't change a thing. I'm going to take it to the magazine office tomorrow and illegally scan a hundred copies.'

Morgan beams. 'Happy to be of service! But you know, I can do better than this, right? It's just a brain dump.'

'I won't hear of it,' I say. 'I value your artistic labour. Hey, if I make any money on the door, I'll give you a cut as compensation.' My dad sends me an 'allowance' every month to compensate for his absence, and I think he thinks it's paying my rent, but really it's not enough for that, so I keep trying to come up with creative ways to make money. Selling my mum's friends' old clothes online and taking a cut . . . phoning Queen Anne's College alumni in university fundraising drives . . . I even did flu camp last year, which made me so sickly I can't face doing it again. And now, DJing? Anything to prevent me having to get a sensible part-time job like anyone else. Still, I can swing some Morgan's way for her work.

She shrugs. 'If you insist.'

'It really feels like things are coming together!' I clap my hands, delighted. 'I can't believe that two days ago this club night wasn't even a thing and now it's got a date and a flyer!'

Aleesha smiles wryly. 'This is classic Mary-Elizabeth Baxter though. Always up to something, always making something happen.'

'Like your column!' Morgan chimes in. 'One day you were doing wise advice over hash browns in the Anselm Hall dining room, the next you were making your case to Emily Daly to be *Quad Magazine*'s next agony aunt.'

'I guess I do like making things happen,' I say, blushing. In a world that seems to value apathy and coolness, is it a bit cringe to be a person who likes to do things? Maybe. But I have to own my cringe. It's too late to change; my enthusiasm and zeal are baked into me like chocolate chips in a cookie. I am what I am.

'Speaking of making things happen,' Morgan says smoothly. 'What's the situation with your current crush? That blond boy?'

'She's locked in – the crush is deep and official,' Aleesha says. 'He was feeling up her thigh last night.'

'So things have escalated,' Morgan says, nodding.

'I don't know if I would go that far. But they're definitely escala*ting*.' I don't want us to get ahead of ourselves here.

'I noticed Tyler didn't seem to be a fan when we were chatting last night,' Aleesha says, getting up and switching the kettle on to make tea.

'So what's the beef?' Morgan asks.

I shrug. 'I guess there's an argument to be made that Felix is just a tedious little posh boy, but . . . the heart wants what the heart wants.'

'Oh, so it's your heart now, is it?' Aleesha looks at me with intense scepticism mixed with deep affection.

'Fine, my swimsuit area.'

'That's more like it.' She tips three teaspoons of instant coffee into mugs and pours the boiling water over, stirs in some whole milk.

'As long as you know he's a tedious little posh boy.' Morgan shrugs.

'I think he's all right,' I say, once again feeling myself blush. I just fancy him. This is purely about riding him like a pony, not falling in love. I want to keep all of this in the realm of lightness and fun, and revel in his delicious hotness, so feeling any urge to defend him from criticism is . . . unwelcome. 'He can be my tedious little posh boy.'

'Is he going to come to your club night?' Morgan asks, accepting a steaming mug from Aleesha.

'I hope so,' I say coyly. 'I feel like it could be the perfect opportunity for . . . something.' I take a sip and sigh. 'Aaah. Lovely, horrible milky coffee,' I say, savouring the comforting taste of instant.

'Did you start a whole club night just to give you a vehicle to get with your crush?'

'I know that sounds exactly like something I would do, but on this occasion I'm pleading innocent. It was in direct response to how vibeless the DJ at the union was last night – I'm not lying, am I, Aleesha?'

Aleesha shakes her head resolutely. 'Nope. Very much not lying.'

'Well,' Morgan says, sipping her coffee, 'vibeless is one thing you could never be accused of. The vibes are strong with this one.'

'I suppose I'd better google how to be a DJ.'

CHAPTER 5

There I am, minding my own business, doing a final proofread of Tyler's section and mine in the *Quad* office before the new issue gets sent to the printers when my phone rings. The screen is illuminated and the word 'MUM' glares up at me.

'Ugh,' I say aloud to the empty office. I take a deep breath and answer. If I don't answer now, I'll only have to ring her later.

'Hello?' I say cautiously.

'Hello, darling!' she says exuberantly.

'How are you, Mum?'

'Oh, I'm fine! I just hadn't heard from you in ages, and I just got home from one of my classes so I thought I'd give you a ring.'

'How was the class?' I ask.

'Oh, darling, it was wonderful, just marvellous. One of my regulars got into crow pose for the first time ever! Truly remarkable. She was completely effusive, said it was all down to me! Isn't that lovely?' I wonder if this is the only question I will get asked in the course of this conversation.

'Mmmm,' I say. My mum's new life as a yoga teacher is

simply wonderful for her, a source of great pride and joy, not to mention attention. I've just never been able to figure out why she had to do her 200-hour training a) in India and b) at the precise moment I was doing my A levels. As if bloody Stephen of all people was going to be any kind of help to me in a time of high stress. About as much use as a chocolate teapot. But that's Alana Baxter for you. If her name sounds familiar to you, it's because she used to be a model. Yes, a proper model, like on catwalks and in adverts. On the peripheries of the Nineties 'supermodel' scene, one of the lesser stars but a star nonetheless. Her trademark was her halo of curls and her doll face, all high cheekbones, pointy little chin and heart-shaped mouth. Is she the reason I'm a hottie? Maybe. Is she also a bit of a demon? Definitely.

'Darling, I was just looking at my diary and I realised we don't have any plans to see each other,' she says dramatically. I can picture her now, sitting on the sofa, looking at her enormous hot-pink leather Smythson diary with the gold sprayed edges – extremely Alana Baxter – filled with various appointments and commitments in her huge, looping scrawl. 'And that simply won't do, will it?'

'I suppose not,' I say, softening a little. She's my mum. She loves me. She literally gave birth to me. We've just got this nineteen-year-long skirmish going on where we wind each other up for no discernible reason. You know how it is!

'Well, I don't want to disrupt your studies on a weekday so I was thinking of having a little look around the shops one Saturday and we could meet then? Does that sound good?'

'Of course,' I tell her.

'Wonderful! Ow!' she says indignantly.

'What?'

'I just tripped on a pile of floorboards. Nothing to worry about, sweetie.'

I try to suppress a groan. 'Why is there a pile of floorboards lying around?' I suspect I know the answer.

'I'm redecorating the living room! I wanted to give it more of a cosy Moroccan-riad vibe, you know? All deep-saffron walls and throw pillows, big leather pouffes absolutely everywhere.'

'Didn't you just do the living room?' I ask, but I know it's useless.

'I never felt quite at home in that spartan, Japandi space . . . too much pale wood,' she says as if it's a regrettable fashion decision from years gone by, which, I suppose to her, it is. 'Hence taking up the floorboards.'

Look, if it wasn't the living room it would be another room. It took me a long time to realise that other people's parents did not redecorate rooms on a biannual cycle, that this was very much a my-mum thing. It feels a bit ridiculous, the idea that this thing, or the next thing, is going to be the change that transforms her life.

I take a deep breath. 'I'm sure it's going to look gorgeous when it's finished.'

'I'll have it done by Christmas, darling, I absolutely promise,' she says emphatically, to reassure me we won't have a repeat of the year she was so deep into her unnecessary kitchen renovation that we had to eat Christmas dinner off our laps because she'd decided the dining table was utterly passé and had to be sold on Gumtree post-haste, and hadn't read the product description for the new dining table properly so was unaware it involved a four-week wait. Classic.

'All right,' I say a little sceptically. The door to the office opens and Felix slinks in, giving me a charming little head tilt and a knowing smirk. 'Text me the Saturday you want to meet, and I'll make sure I'm free.' I pause. 'I love you.'

'I love you too, sweetie,' she says before hanging up.

'Who was that?' Felix asks, the smirk still dancing on his lips. He takes his glasses off and rests them on the top of his head, pushing away his big, thick sweep of blond hair.

'My mum,' I say, trying to get back to my work.

He nods, clearly wondering whether to ask more or let it go. I know which one I'd prefer.

'Are you two close?'

'Not really,' I sigh. 'She'd love you though.'

'Oh, really?' he says, his interest piqued. 'Why's that then?'

'She's always flirting with good-looking men,' I say, rolling my eyes at a lifetime of irritation.

'I'll take that as a compliment,' he says, tapping the side of his pen on the edge of the desk, a lopsided smile on his face. But for once I'm not in the mood to play the game. When I'm at uni I try to put some distance between me and my mum, and whenever that gets disrupted I always feel a bit . . . invaded somehow. Like my little safe uni bubble has been burst. It's not that there's anything majorly wrong with my mum, it's just that things are always a bit difficult between us. I think she sees me as a Mini-Me, whereas I, naturally, want to believe I'm my own whole person, not an extension of her. 'Anyway, what are you up to?'

'Just a cheeky proofread.' I shrug.

'You've only got one page – surely it doesn't take that long?'

'I check another section too,' I say lightly, trying to get back to my task.

He frowns. 'Why?'

I swallow guiltily. 'I mean, I'm just checking another section today because the section editor's busy ... I don't, like, do it habitually.'

Felix nods slowly. 'I don't know, man, feels kind of like you're lying,' he says, trying to keep his tone light but clearly annoyed that I'm keeping something from him.

I shrug again. 'Not everyone is amazing at spelling and grammar. Some people are dyslexic. I figure I might as well help out where I can.'

'Who?' He frowns, curious.

'I'm not going to share people's medical information, Felix!'

'It's not that,' he says. 'It's that everyone's meant to take responsibility for their own sections, not get other people to do the work for them. I'm trying to save you a job!' he adds defensively.

'Well, I don't mind,' I say, so sharply that it officially marks the matter as closed.

You can fancy slightly bad people, can't you? I mean, it's not illegal to fancy someone a bit awful as long as you know they're a bit awful?

Tyler's section out of the way and Tyler's (anonymous) honour duly defended, I move on to my own page, the advice column I started hastily answering on the bus home from the union. I think I've done quite a good job with it, you know?

Dear M-E,

I recently started seeing a new guy and I'm worried I like him too much and it's ruining my life. Is it normal to like someone this much? Any time I don't spend with him feels like wasted time, and I find it hard to think about anything other than him. It's scaring me! Or should I just enjoy liking someone this much?

Hopelessly Devoted Girlie

xx

Dear Hopelessly Devoted Girlie,

I always think having a crush is just the best thing in the world. That fizzy excitement at knowing there's a person you're excited about is one of the main reasons for getting out of bed in the morning! If that feeling is continuing now you're in a relationship then I would just lean into it and enjoy it. Life can be hard and long and boring (eurgh), and going out with someone you really fancy is a guaranteed bright spot, so don't look a gift horse in the mouth! Obviously, if you literally can't do anything other than think about him or spend time with him, maybe that's a problem, but it doesn't sound like you're going to break up with him even if you do acknowledge that it's a problem, so I say you might as well ride the wave of obsession while you're feeling it and expect that everything will mellow out in time.

Love,

M-E

Of course, me writing a column now means Laurie, or should I say 'Mr No Nonsense', has to make his opinions known, too. The very next issue of *Quad News* contains this little gem, which makes me regret picking up a copy of the newspaper after my lecture.

Hey No Nonsense,

I fancy this new guy I'm seeing, like, *a lot*. Everyone's all about playing it cool, but I want to act like I like him as much as I actually like him. Is that a recipe for disaster? Should I maintain an air of mystery?

Thirsty Gal

Dear Thirsty Gal,

God, that sounds like a horrendous feeling. Can't say I've experienced it myself. First things first: never overestimate the power of mystery. What's the old expression? Familiarity breeds contempt. So I would recommend keeping your cards close to your chest rather than letting him know how much you like him. The less you give, the more he'll want. The less available you are, the more desperate he'll be to hang out. That's just science, my Thirsty Gal. A little bit of playing hard to get never killed anyone, and in fact, probably prolonged more relationships than it ended. Every relationship has someone who needs it more, and if you – horror – are that person, you'd bloody better not let on. Always leave them thinking you could be out the door at any moment, that's what I say.

In frosty coolness,
No Nonsense

Ugh! That's terrible advice! Horrible, even! I throw the paper in the nearest recycling bin and wonder how people can even live like that, holding everything back, not wanting to feel the feelings, let alone express them. To clear my head, I walk down from Bloomsbury towards Trafalgar Square to visit my favourite exhibition. I saw it for the first time during the summer holidays and I go back every so often to see it again. If I'm in a city full of free art, I figure I might as well make the most of it. Once I make it to the Portrait Gallery, I head up the stairs and to the little tucked-away side room that's been painted a deep forest green, the perfect contrasting backdrop for the 450 portraits of Saint Fabiola, rescued from second-hand shops, flea markets and God knows where else by the contemporary artist Francis Alÿs and displayed here together. I can't explain why I love it so much, but I find it so calming to be in this room. The effect is so striking: it's not just that they're all paintings of the same person, but that the paintings are the same. The same side-view pose, the same red cloak, the same hood. It's like a meme: infinitely reproduced and reproducible, all springing from the same source. But they're inevitably all different, because they're all made by people. And not professional people – amateurs. People painting this saint because they needed her, or wanted to sell an image of her, or wanted to practise their art. Some are on canvas like a regular portrait, some on glass, and there's even one made out of painted sesame seeds. There's something so human about that. Imagine painting a sesame seed? It's the sort of stupid idea only a human could have. Maybe that's what I like about it: the humanness of it all, the subtle and not-so-subtle differences of each portrait speaking a little bit to the individuality of the person making it, even if they're all pictures of the same thing. And the humanness of collecting the portraits, the effort of scouring through flea markets, hunting for hundreds of the same thing. It feels like an act of love, to collect them and display them like this. It's a comforting thought, isn't it, that art and love are everywhere?

CHAPTER 6

'That's a very gorgeous coat,' I say as Jessica Bailey, my personal tutor and the lecturer for my Sculpture in Space course, slips on a cobalt-blue wrap coat after our seminar. I am the last one in the seminar room because I was, of course, too busy chatting to pack up my things and now I'm at risk of getting locked in by Jessica. There would be worse people to get locked in a room with – she's actually really cool, and not even that old.

She blushes. 'Thank you, Mary-Elizabeth. That means a lot coming from you. It's always fun to turn up to classes and see what you're wearing.'

'I aim to please,' I tell her perkily.

'Well, if you carry on the term at the level of your first essay, I'll be very pleased indeed,' she says, holding the door open.

'Oh! Yes, thank you for that!' I had been pleasantly surprised by how well I did on my first essay.

She turns to me over her shoulder as she locks up. 'Don't thank me, it was all you. I didn't think there were any interesting things left to say about Jeff Koons, but somehow you managed it. That's one of the reasons I stick around, you know? It's nice to be surprised by my students . . . sometimes you say things I hadn't considered before.'

'Always aiming to make life slightly less boring!'

'You know,' she says, just before we part ways so she can go out the front exit and I can weave my way through a series of corridors towards the back (a shortcut to the *Quad* office that lets me avoid the drizzle). 'I get the feeling you think you're a bit . . . I don't know, frivolous . . . and maybe you are, but you're also really sharp. A really good student. I never wonder if you're going to show up unprepared or turn in a bad essay. Even when you were a fresher I felt you had this real spark of curiosity when everyone else was just finding their feet.'

I feel warm with pride. 'That's . . . really kind of you,' I say awkwardly, running my fingers over my puffy balloon-letter 'M' necklace, and now it's my turn to blush. All through school, I felt like such an underachiever, always bewildered in science and maths classes, like I'd completely missed something that everyone else seemed to know. Concentrating in class and doing my homework and revising for exams felt like this big, grey headache. Or a bunch of cables all tangled up in my brain. But now I get to learn only about things I really want to learn, it doesn't feel like such an effort. I'm glad it's not going unnoticed. 'See you next week, I guess!'

'We soldier on!' Jessica says with the smile of an overworked person.

* * *

On Thursdays I am blessed with an hour's break between Jessica's Sculpture in Space class and Possibilities of

Portraiture, which I generally spend lurking in the Quad Media office since it's so close to the History of Art Department. When I arrive for my hour's time-wasting today, I find the office is already unlocked and my magazine colleague Olu, fashion editor extraordinaire, is beavering away at her laptop.

'What's up?' she says, glancing up at me quickly as I take a seat at the desk opposite her. Obviously, I always want to chat, but I can sense that she's in focus mode.

'Not much . . . I'll leave you to it, don't worry about me,' I say, sliding my laptop out of my bag so I can at least pretend to do some of my essay for Considerations of Curation.

'Come on . . .' Olu murmurs under her breath, almost through gritted teeth. I can tell it's not directed at me, but I'm too scared to ask what she's waiting for.

I tap away, wanting to get this essay started in good time so I can devote all my energy to a) my club night and b) my romantic aspirations.

'Did you see there's a new edition of the newspaper out?' she says absent-mindedly, nodding over to a pile in the corner of the office before going back to her work.

I saunter over and pick one up. 'Oooh, an interview with the provost about the new sports centre . . . how inspiring,' I say, casting a bitchy eye over the front cover.

Olu chuckles and shakes her head.

It's only when I open it that my worst fears are confirmed. No Nonsense is in there *again*. They haven't got bored of their silly little column. Ugh!

Listen to this, just listen, OK? Here's my column from the next issue of *Quad Magazine*:

Dear M-E,

My boyfriend broke up with me a few months ago at the beginning of the summer and I spent the whole holiday being completely devastated. Now we're back at uni, he wants us to get back together, but I'm wary. I was completely crazy about him and the break-up was so hard, and I was just about ready to think about getting over him. The fact is, I've just never met anyone else I feel so strongly about. He says he's had time to think and he regrets breaking up with me. Am I deluded for even thinking of going back there?

Love,

Dazed and Confused

Dear Dazed and Confused,

I think your heart is telling you to give it another go. Whether or not that's the right thing to do is another matter, but I can tell your impulse is to get back with him. You've seen what life is like with him, you've seen what life is like without him, and it sounds like you prefer it when he's around. Was he an otherwise decent boyfriend aside from the break-up? Is he nice to you? Does he make you feel important? Does he devote enough time to you? I don't know the circumstances of the break-up, but it's possible he did make a mistake and has learned from it, and that you can move on together, stronger in the knowledge that you're both really choosing to be there. I know it's scary to put your trust in someone again after they've hurt you, but I think you can tell whether he's really learned and grown since you were last together. Good luck in making your decision!

Love,

M-E

And now here's bloody Laurie's column in the newspaper:

Dear No Nonsense,

My boyfriend wants to get back with me after dumping me unceremoniously at the beginning of the summer holidays. What should I do? I've really missed him, but I'm cautious about trusting him again!

Help!

Dear Help!

It's pretty clear what's going on here: your boyfriend dumped you at the beginning of the holidays so he could go and sow his wild oats in Ibiza or Mykonos or wherever he went with his mates, and now he's back at uni and he wants that sure thing again. He's had his fun and now he wants steady, reliable Help! back in his life. Are you going to reward him for breaking your heart or are you going to stand firm in your conviction that he's a rat and a player, which you know deep down is exactly what he is? Dream bigger!

No Nonsense

'This fucking guy!' I say, staring down at the new copy of *Quad News*.

'What?'

'This! Fucking! Guy!' I repeat, emphatically slamming my hand down on the desk for dramatic effect. 'This Laurie O'Donnell! He's pulling some shit again and I don't like it one bit.'

'What kind of shit?' Olu leans back in her chair, like she's maybe grateful for an excuse to abandon her task, at least for a few minutes.

'The last three editions in a row of *Quad News* have had advice columns in, written by this Laurie O'Donnell character, answering questions that are very much just a lightly rehashed version of the questions I, Mary-Elizabeth Baxter, had answered in *Quad Magazine*! I know imitation is the greatest form of flattery or whatever, but he's clearly taking the piss out of me!'

Olu sighs, and looks very much like she's going to tell me I'm exaggerating or blowing things out of proportion, so I hold up a hand to pause any objections. 'AND,' I say, extremely emphatically, 'this all started after we met at that beginning-of-term soirée, and I felt he was quite rude and obnoxious. It's like he's doing it all on purpose just to wind me up and make me feel stupid.'

'Well, if he is, then he's a dick.' She shrugs and spins around in the office chair, which is a potentially dangerous move since all our furniture is on its last legs.

'That's the only possible explanation,' I say, throwing the newspaper into the paper recycling. 'He's trying to lure me into an out-and-out rivalry. Well, I will not be drawn into silly boy games. I'm much too clever for that.'

Olu spins back to face her laptop screen. 'Too right,' she says absent-mindedly, then all of a sudden she gasps and lets out a strangled, delighted scream.

'What?! What?!'

She scoots over to me on the chair, which nearly tips over in the process, and grabs my arm. 'They just sent out the emails with the year-abroad placements for next year! I got into the Sorbonne!'

'Oh my God, that's amazing! Even I've heard of the Sorbonne!' She honestly looks like she's about to cry, she's so happy. 'I'm really glad I was here to witness this happy moment.'

She's clutching her cheeks like they already hurt from smiling. 'I didn't think I was going to get in! I thought I'd spend the year teaching French to some little menaces in a random town in the middle of nowhere!'

'Hey,' I say, remembering something. 'Isn't Felix on your course?'

She nods.

'I wonder where he's going,' I muse faux-nonchalantly.

'I can tell you – the French group chat is on fire right now. Let me just do some scrolling . . . there!' she says, finally locating the message. 'Guadeloupe!'

'Guade-bloody-loupe?!' I say, a little outraged. 'That's so far away!'

'Why?' she asks with a sly smile. 'You going to miss him?'

'No,' I say firmly, crossing my arms over my chest defensively. 'Not one bit. Not at all.'

'He's hot,' she shrugs. 'I don't blame you. I'm sure he thinks he's going to decolonise the Caribbean,' she says, rolling her eyes. 'When actually all he's going to do is treat it as a glorified gap year and know he can come back and say whatever he wants about it because he's the only one from Queen Anne's who's going.'

'That sounds about right,' I say with a smile. Sure, Felix is kind of bullshit, but maybe he's my kind of bullshit.

'It feels like it might be a bad time to get into something with someone, right? Just before our year abroad, you know?'

I shrug. 'I know. I can handle it.'

'OK, if you're sure . . .'

'I'm sure. It's not like I want him to be my boyfriend or anything. I just want to sleep with him. Get in, get out, you know?' But I don't think Olu is really listening, she's too delighted with her good news about going to Paris.

Guadeloupe! Of course somewhere like Paris would be too basic for the likes of Felix, wouldn't it? Couldn't just go to Montpellier like everyone else. Lyon not exotic enough for you? No, it simply must be the Antilles! Just my luck. Just as there's some vague hope of getting with Felix on the horizon, he's shipping off to the Caribbean in a matter of months! Fate, why do you wrong me so?

CHAPTER 7

You win some, you lose some. Win: I'm distributing the magazine with Felix. Lose: we are distributing the magazine in the beginning phases of a storm. An actual, proper storm, with a name and everything. Storm Philippa coming to kick our butts.

I honestly don't know why we're bothering. No one wants to stop long enough to take a magazine, and even if they do, it's going to get soaked straight away. I've shoved ThrowBax flyers into each issue, but to be honest word has very much got around without the help of physical media. We should just dump the copies of *Quad* in the Workshop café and get a coffee. But no, Felix insists on doing his editor duties.

'God, you're brave!' comes a voice from outside my hood.

'Hi, Jessica!' I say with a grimace. 'Just doing our bit for *Quad Magazine*.' I offer her one, which she takes quickly and shoves in her bag so it doesn't get wet. 'This is Felix; Felix, this is my personal tutor, Jessica.' He gallantly holds out a hand to shake hers.

'Nice to meet you,' he says very politely.

She glances between us, a little smile on her lips like she can tell I have a huge crush on him. 'I've got to dash, some first years are waiting for me in the Duke of Wellington Lecture Hall, but I'll see you tomorrow? I feel like you've probably got something interesting to say about Sarah Lucas!' she calls over her shoulder as she departs; it's kind of her to make me look clever in front of Felix.

'She was nice,' Felix says brightly, but before I can respond, an extremely beautiful girl with big, round glasses and an edgy pixie cut wearing chunky, stompy boots holds out her hand for a magazine from him, glossy black nails gleaming and neat. Very chic.

'Thanks, Felix,' she purrs at him.

'Any time,' he replies smoothly.

'Friend of yours?' I ask, feeling the jealousy irrationally poke at me.

'Oh, you know . . . just a first-year thing . . . nothing serious.'

I want to ask him about all the girls he's been with at Queen Anne's because I'm nosy like that. I want to be able to see them all, compare myself to them, see if I fit in, see if I'm completely deluding myself that it could ever happen with him. That girl certainly had a strong look, which counts in my favour, but also she was very thin, wasn't she? Which doesn't really count in my favour at all.

'You want to know something funny?' Felix says, shivering, holding a damp copy of the magazine out to various passers-by, who just want to reach their destination and not be bothered by eager Quad Media members.

'What?' I ask, as a raindrop falls from my hood and drips onto the end of my nose. I'm wearing a very stylish shiny red raincoat, which Georgia, the film editor, said was 'very *Don't Look Now*'. I'm choosing to believe it was a compliment.

'My ex-girlfriend was called Philippa . . . I feel like being absolutely battered by Storm Philippa is her way of getting revenge on me.'

'Why, what did you do to her?'

'Oh, nothing in particular, I just suspect I'm not the world's greatest boyfriend.'

I look him up and down with exaggerated interest. 'Nope,' I say, shaking my head. 'Definitely not boyfriend material.'

It's like a spark has been lit in his eyes, a sly smile curling across his lips. He looks at me, holding my gaze as people rush past us to get out of the rain. For a moment, it feels like he's about to kiss me, but of course he doesn't. Instead, we just have a little stand-off, a mutual skirmish over whether to escalate or back down. In the end, the boring option is chosen.

Look, I may be a little bit silly but I'm not stupid. I know Felix is probably not a good idea. And I know he's not going to be the world's greatest boyfriend. But all of that is fine if I just accept the situation for what it is: pure lust leading to brief fling. He doesn't need to be a saint or even boyfriend material if all I want is to sleep with him a few times and then be on my merry way, right?

'Anyway, I'm sure you have other, more compelling talents,' I say finally, breaking the spell.

He holds eye contact with me for a moment longer as he passes a copy to someone who actually takes it, though it quickly becomes apparent that they took it to use as an umbrella. I can't help but wonder if this is a total waste of time, but I'm not going to say that and cut my time with Felix short. We're edging close to something and, well, as the supermarket slogan goes, every little helps. Even if sometimes you have to stand around in the rain giving away copies of a magazine that it seems nobody wants anyway.

'Speaking of talents, when's your night?' he asks, and my stomach does a little backflip. My goal for today was asking him if he wanted to come, and he's already walked right into my trap without me even having to do anything.

'Saturday,' I say nonchalantly.

'Aren't you going to invite me?' The rain has finally let up and he collapses his umbrella.

'Do you require a personal invitation?'

'I don't go anywhere without one.'

'You are cordially invited to my night. It's called ThrowBax. It's on Saturday. It's at the union.'

'That's it?'

'Why, what were you expecting?' I ask, fixing him with a very flirtatious look indeed.

He shrugs. 'I don't know, I was thinking it might be fun to have a little after-party.' A very pretty girl with wavy red hair and freckles heads down the path towards us. As she passes, she doesn't so much as look at me, her eyes drawn to Felix, who hands her a copy of *Quad Magazine*, which she, of course, accepts. She even looks back at him over her shoulder, but he's already turned back to face me, and it's as if he's drawn in by this feeling of unfinished business that's lingering over us, like he can't fathom moving on to someone else now I've piqued his interest. I feel all warm and light-headed, like I'm going to float away over the university like a balloon.

'After-party?' I ask very casually.

'Maybe we can go somewhere.'

'Who is this "we"?' I ask, not daring to hope.

'Me and you, of course.'

Oh, it's on. It's so very on.

'Unless you'll have loads of stuff with you? I don't know what the modern lady DJ needs to carry with her.'

'I'll travel light,' I say, maybe too quickly. 'Where do you want to go?'

'A Chinese social club round the back of King's Cross. Open late, does amazing food.'

'Really?' I ask.

'Really,' he says, holding my gaze. I look back at him, his light-blue eyes twinkling at me from behind those thick, fair eyelashes. 'Then we can see where the night takes us.' STRAIGHT INTO BED, THAT'S WHERE THE NIGHT IS GOING TO TAKE US!

'I'm in,' I say, shrugging as if it isn't the exact thing I've been wanting to happen since last year.

It's so close I can almost feel it! I'm positively dizzy with crush, all warm and my heart racing. The thrill of the chase is fun, but I'm all about the capture . . . and that's just over the horizon!

CHAPTER 8

Today is the day! Tonight is the night! And now it's time to take care of all the most important things for a discerning lady DJ. My hair? Re-pinked for the occasion. My body? Smooth and silky like a dolphin. My outfit? We'll figure that one out in the fullness of time . . .

'What if no one comes?' I say, throwing another dress onto the already teetering pile of clothes that I've dismissed as not quite right for ThrowBax.

'That doesn't sound like you.' Morgan frowns from her position on the end of my bed.

'I know! I don't like it! This whole thing is really messing with my head . . .' I say, refusing to elaborate on whether I mean my club night or the prospect of getting with Felix.

'People are going to come! No one's having a house party tonight that I've heard of, so you have, like, no competition. Who wants to go out on a Saturday night and spend actual London money?'

'No one,' I say firmly.

'That's right! You are providing a service. A fun, cheap place to go on a Saturday night – what's not to like?'

'But can you imagine how mortifying it would be if no one came?'

'It's not going to happen! Not with Patrick Denton coming. Pat's coming, right?'

'Yeah, he wouldn't let me down,' I say, reasonably sure that's the case.

'And me and Aleesha are coming, and Luke's coming because I told him to, and he's bringing his housemates. Anyway, why do I feel like what you're actually saying is: what if Felix doesn't come?'

'Rude,' I say flatly. But she's not wrong. I know people are going to show up. I've handed out flyers and told everyone that I've seen this week. Plus, it's literally one single English pound to get in. It's more expensive for people not to come, if you think about it. At this point it would take some kind of force bloody majeure to prevent a decent crowd from showing up. But naturally the most important person in the aforementioned crowd is Felix Balfour.

'So now we can move on to the question of why he wouldn't come in particular.'

I shrug. 'Because I want him to?'

'He's said he's going to! There's no point psyching yourself out about it when you should be having fun!'

'I know, I know,' I mumble. 'We're meant to be doing something after,' I tell her, very off-hand, like it's nothing.

'What, you and Felix?'

'Yeah.'

'You kept that one quiet, mate!'

'I guess I don't really believe it's going to happen.'

'Oh, it'll happen, I'm sure. The only question is whether . . . you know . . . whether it's a good idea?' she offers gently.

'Why wouldn't it be?'

'Maybe because he's a total player?'

'Everyone is trying to warn me off him, but I know what I'm doing! I can take care of myself! I'm a big girl, you know?'

Morgan throws her hands up in defeat. 'Fine! I trust you, baby girl.'

Finally, I pull a short, tight, sequinned dress out of the wardrobe and hold it up for Morgan's approval. 'This is the one.' I'm pleased to report that it's a second-hand sequin dress – ever since I found out how terrible sequins are for the environment I've had to curb my natural magpie tendencies. No new sequins for me! Strictly vintage.

'Definitely the one. Fit for a DJ,' Morgan beams.

My bedroom is quiet for a moment as I start hanging up my mountain of rejected outfits back in my wardrobe, but I sense there's something Morgan wants to say.

'You're a funny one,' she says finally.

I turn to look at her over my shoulder. 'What do you mean?'

She smiles at me a little sadly. 'I mean, you're so confident and fun and assertive, blasting through life, but underneath it all you're a sensitive soul. That's why I want to look out for you with this stuff, you know?'

I swallow. 'I'm not that sensitive.' (I am.)

'It's OK! You're allowed to have feelings! It's not a sign of weakness, you know? Like, it's perfectly reasonable to worry that the guy you like won't show up to your party!

That's a totally normal feeling. It's not something to be ashamed of.'

'Well, I hate it,' I say. 'I just want to be peppy and blasé and not burdened by big feelings. About anything. Ever.'

'Don't we all! But you are, fundamentally, a person. Just a sack of flesh with neuroses,' she says drily.

'Thank you so much for that beautiful image, Morgan.'

'My pleasure as always,' she smiles sweetly.

'And more to the point, I just want to sleep with Felix so I've slept with Felix, you know? Like I just want to have done it. Ticked it off my to-do list, so to speak. It's not like it has to have huge significance or anything.'

'You're the boss,' Morgan says, saluting me with a sceptical look on her face.

I check the time on my phone, already bracing myself for a flurry of messages from people saying they can't make it, but there aren't any. God! Morgan's really got into my head about feelings. I just want to deal with other people's feelings, I don't want to have them myself. Or rather, the only feelings I want to experience are 'joy', 'delight' and 'arousal'. Is that too much to ask? To have everything under control all the time, to never expose my soft, fleshy underbelly to the world? To never let a guy know that I might actually like him?

'I guess I should put my face on and think about going out as I have to set up,' I say, swallowing hard, suddenly faced with the reality that I actually am doing this.

'You got all your . . . cables . . . and . . . gadgets . . . and whatever?' Morgan asks.

I nod. 'Everything is under control.'

'Just the way you like it,' she says with a smile.

'Precisely, my friend.'

I take a seat at my 'desk', which looks more like a dressing table, covered in perfume bottles and pots of glitter and tubes of lipstick and little trinket dishes overflowing with cheap, shiny earrings, strung with fairy lights. 'What are you going to wear?' I ask Morgan. 'Wait, don't tell me ... something black?' I say, wanting to divert the conversation away from me and my anxieties around tonight.

Morgan smiles. 'What else would I possibly wear?' I don't think I've ever seen Morgan wear anything other than black. She has this deep belief that if she puts zero energy into thinking about what to wear then her brain has exponentially more creative space to make interesting art. A nice theory, but it doesn't bode very well for your old pal Mary-Elizabeth here, with my unstoppable attraction to baubles and shiny things, tulle and lace and high heels and heart-shaped sunglasses. Not that Morgan would ever judge me for my personal brand of frivolity. That's why she's my flatmate.

I get to work, applying different layers of skincare and make-up, picking up and then deciding against different shades of lipstick and eyeshadow, before settling on a mint-green glitter eye with a neutral brown lip.

'Fascinating,' Morgan whispers as I paint my face.

'You know I can do it to you, any time you want,' I say, barely moving my lips, locked into intense concentration as I draw on my winged eyeliner.

'I don't think it's very me, do you?'

'You won't know until you try!' I say, but this is a familiar dance: we are both locked into our relative positions on image.

And then I'm ready, and there is no more messing around left for me to do. It's time to head to the union and find out if anyone's going to turn up.

They'll turn up, right?

CHAPTER 9

Of course no one is there at the advertised start time. That is to be expected. Even I, anxious as I am about the event, am not allowed to get in my own head about the fact that no one is here yet. I choose my first track and hit play: I always knew the first thing I was going to play was 'Gimme Shelter' by the Rolling Stones. It really sets the mood, sets the scene, sets the tone. I take a deep breath and close my eyes and let the sound fill the room, saying a silent wish that tonight goes well and people show up and Felix is true to his word and takes me somewhere afterwards.

* * *

'This is fun,' Patrick says forty-five minutes later, approaching the booth to give me a big squeeze. We survey the room, which has filled up nicely (minus Felix), lots of groups dancing or chatting at the bar. The atmosphere, dare I say it, is quite banging.

'I think so too!' I say, letting the relief that people showed up flood through me.

'Here,' he says, handing me a drink. 'It's just a lime and

soda. I thought you might get thirsty.'

'Thanks, Pat. Got to keep my wits about me . . . and not get dehydrated.'

'Very wise,' he nods. 'You taking requests?'

'I wasn't planning to, but for you, I can make it happen,' I say, before pausing. 'Maybe. Depends on what you ask for. I can't make any promises – my reputation is on the line.'

'Cheeky bit of ABBA?'

'For you, anything,' I say, reassured that I can, in fact, fulfil this request on the grounds that it's not terrible.

'Thanks, babe!' he says, pecking me on the cheek before returning to his boyfriend and their group of friends who are *certainly* bringing the good vibes.

Not wanting to squander the goodwill of Patrick and his crew, I line up 'Gimme! Gimme! Gimme!' by ABBA next, and then I can return to my main pursuit of the evening . . . waiting for Felix. I scan the room for him once again and don't see his floppy blond hair anywhere. Instead –

What the hell is he doing here? Bloody Laurie O'Donnell has just walked in with Charlotte Sherman, the newspaper editor. Oooh, she always looks so severe, so serious, so very un-me. And the less said about Laurie the better.

Our eyes meet across the dance floor and his face falls when he sees who's behind the decks. Classic.

I flash him my most dazzling smile to show that I Am the Alpha Dog and he is in my territory. He can copy my columns all he wants, but in this situation he is but a guest at my club night and I am the hot, sexy DJ.

Ignore him. Just ignore him. I don't know why he's here

anyway. This is a night for fun people, not serious types. Fun people like Tyler, who I see is enthusiastically making out in the middle of the dance floor with a very pretty, very feminine girlie with a cascade of blonde hair. Gosh, what a beautiful thing, what an unintended consequence of starting this night – facilitating young love! Superstar DJ and inadvertent match-maker! If only Felix was here to see my absolute prowess. But no, my efforts are rewarded with Laurie and his little girlfriend instead.

Charlotte Sherman says something into Laurie's ear and walks off in the direction of the bathrooms, leaving him alone on the edge of the dance floor. Even though he's a tedious bore, something about the image strikes my sensitive little heart, and I will him to come over to the decks just so he's not on his own. And, because I must have some kind of power of mind control, he does come over. He makes his way through the crowd, so much bigger and taller than everyone, but so tentatively and shyly pushes through the mass of bodies flailing to 'Last Nite' by the Strokes and approaches my little podium.

'I thought I should say hello,' he shouts from the other side of the decks. I gesture for him to walk around to my side, which he does.

'Hello, Laurie,' I shout into his ear, which requires me to stand on tiptoes because he is Rather Large.

'Hello, Mary-Elizabeth,' he says flatly.

'And what are you doing here?'

'Oh, I assure you I'm not here on purpose.'

'I couldn't imagine you were.'

'I just . . .' He trails off.

'What?' I ask, curious.

'I just heard . . . music coming from here when I left the Quad Media office and wanted to see what was going on.'

'You heard music, did you? Coming from the union? And you had to investigate?'

He sighs. 'Fine, you win, I heard . . . good music coming from the union.' His pink cheeks look positively scarlet under the lights, and under the forensic examination by yours truly.

'That wasn't so hard, was it?' I say, cocking my head.

'You've got good taste,' he says begrudgingly.

'Good taste for a girl or something? Is that what you wanted to say?' I ask.

'No!' he protests, his dark brow furrowing. 'I wouldn't say that.'

'So, what was the track that lured you in? My siren song, if you will?'

Laurie rolls his eyes and huffs, but eventually summons the energy to answer. 'The Run-DMC remix,' he says extremely reluctantly.

'Certified banger,' I say, nodding my head sagely.

'You know he –' Laurie begins.

'Only got paid $5,000 for the remix when it ended up selling over five million copies? Yes, I did know that,' I say, twirling around obnoxiously. I will not let Laurie think he knows more about my shit than I do!

'Touché,' he says gruffly. 'Well, just thought I should say hello.' He turns and looks over his shoulder, catches the eye of Charlotte Sherman over by the bar, before turning back to me. I studiously ignore him while I get 'Like a Virgin' playing

(I wanted to play 'Like a Prayer' but that's an end-of-the-night, drunken-wailing kind of song, not a sexy little middle-of-the-night kind of song, which is exactly what I need right now).

It's a bit weird that he turned up, but given there's still no sign of Felix, I can't exactly complain about the people that did show.

I'm about to say something witty and devastating to Laurie when – gasp! Speak of the devil! My heart absolutely leaps with joy at the sight of Felix walking in. He spots me from across the room and raises his arm in greeting but frowns at the sight of me talking to Laurie. I wave back, slightly too enthusiastically, which makes Laurie turn his head to see who I am waving at.

'Oh,' he says, turning back to me.

'Oh?' I say very pointedly.

'You just seemed very happy to see Felix, that's all,' Laurie says, shrugging.

'Maybe I am, maybe I'm not.'

'Friend of yours?' he asks, before pausing. 'Or . . . is he your boyfriend?'

I blush and clear my throat. 'No,' I say, shaking my head. 'No one's my boyfriend. I don't really do that.'

'Well, that's something, I suppose.'

'What's that supposed to mean?' I say, taken aback at how confidently he disparages Felix.

But I don't get an answer. Charlotte Sherman returns and places a hand on Laurie's shoulder.

'Mary-Elizabeth, this is Charlotte. Charlotte, this is Mary-Elizabeth.'

'Oh, I know who you are,' Charlotte says with an amused little smile, like it's a private joke between them or something. It makes my stomach turn in knots.

I open my mouth to say something very memorable, when all of a sudden, the music just cuts out completely. No more music. No more 'Like a Virgin'. Just silence and confusion. The record-scratch freeze-frame that absolutely no one wanted, least of all me.

Instantly my stomach drops, a pit opening up inside me, and I wish the ground would swallow me up. Everyone turns to look at me, which makes all the blood rush right to my face, a hot wave of shame washing over me. I look down at the decks, look back up for a moment, lock eyes with Felix, who's making an awkward face at me from over by the bar. Why did he have to turn up about two minutes before this happened? Why couldn't it have happened before he showed up here? Why do bad things happen to moderately OK people? And what the hell do I do now?

I look around, panicked, but Laurie and Charlotte are no help. Charlotte is just grimacing awkwardly, like this is somehow inconveniencing her, and while Laurie does look a bit stressed on my behalf, he's not actually doing anything to help me, though right at this moment I can't actually tell you what that would be. Maybe I'm not quite DJ material yet.

'Ummm . . .' I say, swallowing hard, feeling the eyes of the crowd on me. The instant sickening silence has been replaced by awkward murmuring. I look down at the decks again, then think to check underneath. Genius! A cable that's very much meant to be plugged in is lying limply on the floor. I bend to pick it up, my silly little sequinned dress feeling tight and conspicuous all of a sudden, and jam the cable back into its port. I nearly vomit with pure relief when the room is once again filled with the sweet sounds of Madonna, and within a split second everyone is dancing once more, like it never happened. But my heart is doing a million beats per minute, and I've broken out in a cold sweat, so clearly it very much did happen. And in front of Felix as well! God! Just my luck.

'Well, thank God for that,' comes a smooth voice from the other side of the decks.

'Felix!' I say, almost without meaning to. Don't want to be too keen, do I?

No sooner has Felix materialised than Laurie and Charlotte are gone without so much as a goodbye. Can you say rude?

'Well, bye then,' Felix says over his shoulder to their backs as they make their way through the crowd to the exit. Good riddance, I say. 'Classic O'Donnell behaviour. Thinks he's better than everyone.'

The music is too loud for me to ask Felix what their story is, but it's clear there is a story, and if I don't find out what it is, I'll surely die.

'Thanks for coming,' I say, trying to put the embarrassment of the technical malfunction behind me.

He shrugs, walking round to my side of the booth. 'I wouldn't have missed it. You gave me a personal invitation, remember?' Felix slides a hand onto my shoulder, his fingertips brushing the back of my neck. Promising.

He nods over to a group of guys on the dance floor. 'I came with some lads from my course – they seem to be having a good time.'

'Well,' I say, blushing at the thought of the Loudest Silence Ever, 'barring technical difficulties, I feel like it's going quite well . . .'

'That sort of thing could happen to anyone, it's no big deal,' he says, which in a way makes me think it's even more of a big deal. 'You should be proud of yourself. And I'll see you after, yeah?' He looks me right in the eye as he says it. I feel a distinct fluttering in my chest.

I feel too overwhelmed with joy and lust to say anything so I just nod. I feel the urge to cut the interaction short, keen to keep the feeling of possibility and anticipation in the air.

'You should get back to your friends,' I say, looking in their direction. They really do seem like they're having a great time. God, maybe I'm actually good at this?! But if I was actually good at it then I wouldn't have had that absolutely gaping silence right in front of Felix, would I? So basically, it's too soon to tell. Maybe I should do another one in a few weeks just to make sure.

But first . . . I have a date with Felix Balfour to attend to!

CHAPTER 10

'I didn't really think this one through,' I say, looking down at my sparkly dress, standing out like a sore thumb in the decidedly more casual environment of the Chinese social club, a shiny silver pot of jasmine tea steaming between us, the tea cooling in little white cups without handles.

'I think you look great,' Felix says, that trademark smirk of his playing on his lips.

'You'd better.' I slide my foot forward so it brushes up against his. He doesn't move away, instead tilts his foot to the side so I can feel the pressure against mine. 'I turned down going to an after-party at Zach Collins's flat for this.'

'And Zach Collins does throw a good party,' Felix shrugs. 'But I think you made the right decision.'

'I think so too,' I tell him as an austere middle-aged waiter silently sets our food down on the table before stomping off. The meat is glossy and gorgeous, sitting like a prize on top of brilliantly white rice. We eat, chatting away, glancing up at each other every so often, the powerful spark of shared eye contact fizzing away between us.

We're quiet for a moment, which obviously is my kryptonite,

so I break the silence with the question I've been wanting to ask for hours. 'So, what's the story with you and Laurie? Just a classic schoolboy rivalry?' I ask, remembering what he'd said about them being at St Alfred's College together.

Felix leans back in his plastic chair and puts his hands behind his head. 'Something like that. He's just a bit of a dick, that's all. Or maybe dick is the wrong word . . . maybe creep is better?'

'How do you mean?'

Felix inhales sharply. 'Just some dodgy stuff with a girl in sixth form, trying a bit too hard, you know? Eventually someone had to say something, and things got a bit heated and everything escalated from there. But it's not really my place to go into it now.'

I swallow. 'Yikes . . .'

'Yeah, he's one of those guys,' he intones grimly. 'But enough about him.' Felix does an exaggerated stretch, looks around the café before fixing me with a very direct gaze. 'I think it's time we went home, don't you?'

I pause for a moment, almost letting myself think about how vague his explanation of his beef with Laurie was. But then I push it aside. Eyes on the prize.

'Sure,' I say, fluttering my eyelashes at him across the Formica table. 'Your place or mine?'

'Mine,' he says decisively. 'My housemates are away on a rugby trip and for once I've got the place to myself. Might as well make the most of it.' A smile creeps across his face that's so assured and alluring it makes my stomach do a backflip.

When we get back to the house he shares with his course-mates Oscar and Mitchell, the place is dark and quiet, as you might expect it to be at 4 a.m. Really dark. Really quiet. Really still. He flicks the light on, and it illuminates a surprisingly tidy living room. The only things out of place are the piles of books everywhere, which actually have a rather charmingly bohemian effect, because of course they do.

'This is nice,' I say, looking around. 'Very nice indeed. I mean, not that my flat isn't nice, it's just . . .' The more of it I take in, the fancier it gets. A lot of my uni friends live in houses, but they don't live in houses like this. Not cosy, well-decorated houses on quiet, pretty, residential streets. They live in huge, draughty, cavernous houses on main roads with, like, six flatmates and three wheelie bins in the front garden. Everyone has rickety dining tables grudgingly supplied by landlords or found in a skip, threadbare IKEA sofas or something uncomfortable in faux leather. Not Felix. His sofa looks like a gorgeous velvet cloud and his dining table is solid wood, something my mum would make Stephen drive across London to pick up from a vintage furniture warehouse as part of one of her domestic projects.

Felix shrugs. 'It was my parents' first house back in the day. They held onto it when they moved to Dulwich, just rented it out until I went to QAC.' Normal. 'When I was growing up I was always a bit perplexed by why they'd choose to leave here and move to the suburbs, like they'd deprived me of something, you know?' I'm not entirely sure Felix knows the meaning of the word deprivation, but whatever, I'm not going to interrupt the flow of the evening, am I? 'So it's kind of nice to be living here now, at last.'

'How did you know you would go to Queen Anne's and need the house at all?' I ask, amused.

'Oh, I knew I would be going to Queen Anne's,' he says, shrugging. 'My dad went here, his dad went here, his dad went here, et cetera. A family tradition, I suppose.'

'And what if you didn't get in?'

He looks at me as if I've just made a really good joke. 'Ha ha,' he says, and I realise what he means is that with a legacy like that, there's no question about whether he gets in or not. OK, so he's kind of annoying, but so am I! Aren't we all annoying in our own special way? And besides, I can't imagine not finding out what it's like to run my fingers through his hair or what his skin feels like against mine, and who am I to disrupt a plan so close to its execution?

Speaking of which! Felix reaches his arms out to me and wraps them around my waist. This is it! It's on! It's so on! 'Is this OK?' he murmurs before our lips meet.

'Very OK,' I say breathlessly. And then we kiss for the first time and it's everything I wanted it to be. Hot, steamy, sexy, full of the promise of more to come. I thought I would be more into it than him, but the way he kisses me, it's like he wants to eat me alive.

'Shall we . . . shall we go upstairs?' he offers, and I nod so quickly I think I might have given myself whiplash. But I can worry about whiplash later! Right now, I'm going to finally sleep with Felix Balfour!

CHAPTER 11

I did it! I did it! I slept with Felix! And it was hot! He was just so assertive, so commanding even, not like a lot of the nervous, fumbling boys I've been with before. This is what I'm realising: it's so rarely about what they actually do but how they make you feel, and Felix makes me feel excited and desired. All of which makes it hard to remember that I kept telling myself I just wanted to sleep with him to say I'd done it. That was more than doing it – that was loving it.

So . . . now what do I do? Find a new crush and move on? Or maybe just keep things going with Felix a little bit longer? I mean, now that I know I like his style? Now I know I like the way we work together in bed, the way he seems to find me and my body extremely hot. It's only sensible . . . Nothing serious obviously.

'So, was this just a . . . one-time thing, or what?' I venture in bed the next morning, trying to keep my tone incredibly casual. Like I don't care either way.

He props himself up on his elbow and leans his gorgeous face against his hand. He looks down at me in a very handsome way. 'I hadn't really thought about it. Why, what do you want?'

I shrug. 'I'm easy, I just like to know where I stand.'

'It was fun . . . I'd definitely do it again. If you would too, right?' He sounds almost like he thinks I might say no. I enjoy having the upper hand for about two milliseconds.

'Sure, why not?'

He nods, looks like he's thinking. 'The only thing is, I would feel kind of weird about it if everyone at *Quad* knew, you know? Like just . . . politically. I feel like it would be a bad look. I don't want to be accused of favouring you or making things weird in the magazine. Does that make sense?'

Without even meaning to – I swear – my face automatically arranges itself into what I know to be a look of such scepticism it could probably turn a man to stone.

'What?!' he says, laughing.

'Are you trying to tell me that I'm the only girl on *Quad* you've slept with?'

'Is that so hard to believe?' He looks at me with what I imagine he thinks is complete sincerity, eyes all wide, blinking those pretty eyelashes of his.

'Er, yes, abso-fucking-lutely.' I very much roll my eyes at him. 'Not that it would be a problem either way, what with this being a very casual thing and all. But I do write a dating and relationships advice column. You know that, right?' I give him my best, entirely innocent smile.

'I had heard something to that effect, yes.'

'So I am not naive. And I would appreciate it if you didn't treat me . . . thusly,' I say tightly.

He nods. 'OK, I don't think you're naive. I just don't like people talking about my business, and I want to retain some vague air of authority at *Quad*, even if it's . . .' He shakes his head and closes his eyes.

'What?'

'A sinking ship,' he says, but I really don't want to get into Quad Media politics at this particular moment in time. Not very sexy, is it? Obviously, it does affect me but . . . like I said, not very sexy.

'OK, I won't tell anyone at *Quad*,' I say finally. What does it matter? It's not like I wanted to get with Felix so I could tell people about it. I wanted to get with Felix because I fancy him, and now I want to keep getting with Felix because I like the way his hands feel on me, so confident and unafraid.

'Great, thank you.' He shifts his position a little and runs a hand up my thigh, as if to prove my point. 'And obviously, I'm going away next year so the timing . . . it's not great.'

'Oh?' I say, acting as if this is completely new information, and not something I learned from Olu in the magazine office.

'Yeah . . . got my year abroad coming up actually,' he says, like it's sort of a surprise to him.

'And where are you off to?'

'Guadeloupe – it's in the Caribbean.'

'I know where Guadeloupe is, Felix.'

'I mean, a lot of people don't! I've got used to having to explain it!'

'Well, that's wonderful, congratulations. I'm sure you'll have a great time.'

'But you see what I mean, right? The timing . . .'

'The timing,' I repeat.

'That's why it's best to keep it casual, you see that, right?'

'Totally,' I tell him, because I wanted to keep it casual too – it's just annoying that he beat me to the punch. Classic Felix.

'I just think you're really cool, you know? I think it would be hard for both of us if we got too close and then I had to go away.' The thing is, it sounds like he's actually being sincere. Maybe I'm being stupid or, heaven forbid, as naive as I just defended myself against being, but I do get the feeling that Felix might actually, you know, like me.

I head home and decide to tackle one of the problems that I picked up from my *Quad* mag pigeonhole earlier in the week. As well as the askmeanything@quadmedia.qac.ac.uk email address, we also offer a less embarrassing and more anonymised way of sending in questions the old-fashioned way. Just jot it down on a bit of paper and slide it into the pigeonhole and your old friend Mary-Elizabeth will pick it up.

Dear M-E,

How can I tell if someone likes me? I'm bi, and find that I always assume girls just want to be friends with me, even though I know there's a chance they might fancy me too, because I fancy them! I feel like I never know for sure and am too scared to put myself out there and find out. Or I'm scared to deal with a situation where someone likes me and I don't like them back? I find people so hard to read! Help!

Romantically Illiterate Babe xx

Dear Romantically Illiterate Babe,

I wonder if the key to solving your problem lies in being at peace with rejection. You use the word 'scared' not once but twice, both in terms of being rejected, and having to reject someone. But what are you scared of? Think through what actually happens when you get knocked back romantically. Think about when that's happened in the past. Sure, it was probably not pleasant in the moment, but how do you feel about that person now? Had you even thought about them until I just asked you to? Was it really that deep? (If it was, then apologies! But I suspect not!)

Being at peace with rejection is the foundation to having a fun and fulfilling romantic life, if you ask me (which you did). It allows you to keep picking yourself up and dusting yourself off, bouncing back more quickly, internalising fewer messages about yourself. And the more you can do that, the more you can feel comfortable with rejecting other people, in a kind and gentle way. If it didn't kill you to get knocked back, and you were able to just go on with your day, week, life, then the person you're so scared to reject will probably be able to do the same. It's kinder and more liberating than dragging someone through a mediocre back-and-forth in the name of sparing their feelings!

Now, as far as being bi and interested in girls goes, I'm going to need you to trust your gut here, and not always work on the assumption they want to be friends! Or at least be open to the possibility that they might want something else from you. You tell them they have a cool vibe, ask if they want to get a drink, and without being an absolute maniac, give as many signals as you can that you're flirting with them (I'm thinking engaging and, dare I say, SEDUCTIVE eye contact, and confident body language) and then as far as I'm concerned, you've done your bit. The rest is up to them and depends on whether or not they're interested in you romantically. And again, we meet our old friend rejection: what's the worst that can happen if they're not queer or not interested in you? Sure, it's a little bit uncomfortable and a little bit disappointing, but is it really the end of the world? And who knows, maybe they've never thought about their sexuality before and you're the person that gets them to start questioning it? I believe in you!

Love,
M-E

Oh! I do love writing my silly little column and helping people with their problems. I hope I get to do it forever.

CHAPTER 12

'Le Salon de Mary-Elizabeth is open for business,' I say with a bow, pushing open the kitchen door and allowing Aleesha and Morgan in.

'You're too cute,' Aleesha chuckles.

'Cute is my middle name,' I say, pulling out a chair and gesturing for the two of them to sit.

'Real ones know you don't have a middle name. Two first names is more than enough,' Morgan correctly observes.

'Right!' I clap my hands together. 'What services do the ladies require?'

Recently I've been feeling like all I've been doing is gadding about, chasing Felix, being a baby art historian, superstar DJ and agony aunt extraordinaire, and I haven't been paying enough attention to my flatmates and besties. So today I've baked a cake (Nigella's chocolate Guinness cake, because do you really need another cake when that one exists?), bought some fancy loose-leaf tea, which is now brewing in a cute teapot I found at a market and will be strained to within an inch of its life because I also bought a vintage tea strainer, and have set up various beautifying items on the kitchen table. A candle is burning away, the soothing tones of Classic FM are on the radio, and it's altogether rather cosy.

'I feel crispy, man,' Morgan says, shaking her head. 'Like, my skin? Crispy. My hair? Crispy. Do you have anything to de-crisp?'

'Say no more, my queen.' I turn to Aleesha, who's already holding bottles of nail varnish up to the light. 'A manicure?'

'Sometimes you have those nails with the little flowers on . . . can you do that on me?' Aleesha asks.

'If I can do it on myself, I can certainly do it on you, my friend. Let's get Morgan cooking and then I will work my magic on your nails. Cake?'

They both nod enthusiastically and I slice into my creation, which has turned out perfectly. I pour the tea into little china cups, hovering the strainer over the top and watching the glossy little leaves pile up. I spritz Morgan's hair with a spray bottle and comb through the conditioning treatment with my wide-tooth comb before clipping it up, and then applying a thick face mask to her skin.

'I feel like I'm in a spa,' she murmurs as I stroke it across her forehead. She's got her eyes closed and seems truly relaxed.

'A spa with delicious cake,' Aleesha says once she's swallowed down her mouthful.

'Nicer than a spirulina juice or whatever the hell you consume in a real spa,' Morgan murmurs.

'Can you imagine me serving you spirulina? I wouldn't even know it if I fell over it. Anyway, you just chill and enjoy the soothing tones of Debussy on the radio and let your skin and hair de-crispify themselves. That hair mask works magic – you know the absolute abuse I've put my hair through to stay pink for this long, and it still feels all silky and nice, right?' I hold it out for her to touch.

'Like butter,' she says, shaking her head in disbelief.

'And now, it's madam's turn,' I say, sitting down at the table across from Aleesha. 'I'm going to politely request you don't eat or drink while the nail varnish is wet so if you want refreshment, do it now.'

'Yes, boss,' she says, scarfing down the last of the cake and inhaling the tea. I don't just paint, I give her the full works, pushing her cuticles back, filing, massaging the cream into her skin, and then painting meticulous, thin layers of sheer pink varnish before taking my little metal dotting tool and, with the steadiest hand, creating sweet little daisies at the tip of each finger.

'You have beautiful nails – such long, elegant nail beds.'

'That's such a Mary-Elizabeth compliment, isn't it, Morgan?' Aleesha says with a smile.

'Ain't no one looking at people's nail beds except you,' Morgan agrees, her eyes still closed in relaxation.

'Well, may I be the first to compliment you on your nail beds; they are almost as beautiful as your singing voice and your calming vibe. And, Morgan, you have my favourite teeth on the planet, and your art will probably change the world. All of which is to say . . .' I add, painting a final layer of topcoat to seal in my handiwork, 'I appreciate you both so much and I know I can get a bit lost in the sauce and have all my little projects run away from me . . . whether that's, you know, DJ-ing or . . .'

'Boys,' they say flatly, in unison, before bursting into laughter.

'Well, exactly. But I just wanted to say I love you both and I'm sorry if sometimes I'm a bit absent or whatever. And that I am not unaware of it!'

'What would be the point of living with a social butterfly and then being shocked when she's always out?' Morgan shrugs.

'Exactly. But I have to say, this is nice . . . so if you feel inclined to have pangs of guilt more often, I wouldn't say no,' Aleesha says, reaching for the cake knife.

'Excuse you! Your nail varnish is still wet!' I chastise her, before carving off another piece and feeding it to her off a fork as she dutifully keeps her hands on the table.

Morgan peers across the table at Aleesha's nails. 'Shit, man, they're so good! They almost make me jealous.'

'I can do yours if you want.'

'Nah, I'll only wreck them with paint in the studio.'

'That doesn't matter to me though. I would still enjoy doing it for you,' I offer.

She smiles. 'Go on then. Are black flowers a thing?'

'For you they can be,' I say, settling down opposite her and getting to work, even though, as she says, they're going to get wrecked in no time at all. Because the process is the point. The act of doing something for someone else, who you love. That's the point of everything, I suppose, isn't it?

CHAPTER 13

It is so very gorgeous to wake up in bed with Felix! Things are, dare I say it, going . . . kind of well? I mean, he's not my boyfriend, of course, but I'm actually seeing him. Mostly in bed, which is fine with me, because if there is anything I enjoy more than rolling around sweatily with Felix and having my brain addled by the orgasm hormones then may I tell you that my brain is too addled to think of it right now.

'Do you want a coffee?' I ask him as seductively as I can manage at this time of the morning, fluttering my eyelashes at him and wondering if I should have started doing the 1950s housewife trick of wearing make-up to sleep in so you wake up looking glamorous.

'Do you have proper coffee?'

I shake my head. 'Only instant.'

He grimaces. 'No, thanks. I don't know how you can drink that stuff.'

'It's not so bad,' I say with a shrug. It's only the nicest, most comforting thing in the whole world, I do not add.

'Not so good either,' he says, sitting up in the bed and leaning against the headboard. His chest is bare, smooth and lightly tanned even though we're well into the chilly end of autumn. It's like he has a delicious year-round glow, because of course he does. He's Felix Balfour. If anyone's going to have a delicious year-round glow, it's him.

'What are your plans for the day?' he asks me. It's a cold, sunny Saturday and naturally I would like to spend it with him, but instead I've agreed to hang out with my mother.

'Meeting my mum,' I say, shrugging.

He squints at me, trying to remember our previous conversation about my mother. 'And you . . . don't like your mum?'

'It's not that,' I say quickly, the stab of disloyalty spearing me right through the heart. 'I love her. I like her. She's just hard work, you know?'

'All the best women are,' he says, flopping back on the bed and reaching his arms out to me. I climb on top of him and, oh, look, we are once again having sex. Who can blame me for wanting to stay here with Felix all day? But, unfortunately, I have places to be.

* * *

I'm only a little bit late to meet my mum in Covent Garden, but of course she's a little bit later than that, so I get to pretend that she's totally inconveniencing me.

'I'm sorry, darling, I didn't want to miss the delivery of my vintage leather pouffe!' she says, drawing me into a tight hug against my will when we meet in the piazza.

'It's fine, Mum,' I tell her grudgingly, and we begin our stroll around the shops.

When we're in the big branch of Boots on Long Acre, in search of the one specific volumising product that's the only thing my mother will use on her trademark curls, on the end of the Dior counter I catch a glimpse of their new campaign. I'm slightly surprised to see that instead of a sexy young actress, it's a sexy old model – Gina Simone, one of my mum's old model lot, but she barely looks a day older than her supposed heyday.

'Good for Gina,' Mum says when she spots it, but her words have an edge to them. 'I'll pay for this, and then shall we get a coffee, darling?'

'Sure.' I shrug.

She leads us to a café down a side street and we're blessed to find a vacant table. We sit down, and a good-looking young guy comes over to take our order. I let out an audible sigh because I know how this is going to play out, but Mum doesn't notice.

'Are you an actor?' she asks him after our orders have been duly placed.

'Uh, no,' he says, shaking his head, looking a little confused.

'A model then?' she ventures.

'Not that either,' he mumbles.

'Well, you should be, darling – beautiful bone structure.'

He turns a colour I did not know it was possible for a human to become. 'Thank you,' he squeaks out before scuttling off.

'Mum,' I whisper through gritted teeth when he's gone. 'Stop flirting with the waiter, it's mortifying.'

'Mortifying for who?'

'Him! Me! You! Everyone involved,' I tell her.

Mum just shrugs. 'Not for me. You need to lighten up.' She is possibly the first person in human history to tell me that, while everyone else wishes I was just a little bit more serious.

I let out a groan to signal my irritation but leave it at that.

Our coffees arrive, steaming and deliciously frothy. I take a sip and decide to be a grown-up rather than leaning into my tendency to get annoyed by my mum. 'How's the yoga?'

'Oh, it's just marvellous, darling,' she says, her eyes bright with enthusiasm. 'I've now got three classes! And to think, only a few months ago I had none!'

I can't help but smile at that. I am proud of her. 'That's great, congratulations.'

'It's only in the church hall at the top of the hill, but . . . it feels like people are really enjoying it, you know? A real place for connection and bonding. The yoga's going great, it's just . . .' She trails off.

'What?' I ask, suddenly seized with concern.

She sighs heavily, dramatically. 'Darling, you know that big campaign I did? The jeans ad?'

I resist the urge to a) pretend I have no idea what she's talking about and that I've forgotten all about it, or b) ask her how I could possibly have forgotten about it when she brings it up at every available opportunity. To say that the Sabor jeans campaign was her heyday would be an understatement. It was the heyday of a whole generation of models, of which she was one. I have to admit, the campaign is not just very cool but genuinely iconic.

Instead of trolling her, I just nod.

'Well, apparently it's somehow the thirtieth anniversary of that shoot coming up and they want to get us all back together for it, you know, to recreate it.'

'That's fun,' I say encouragingly, but I can tell by the way she's nibbling the skin on her lip that she's not excited about it at all. 'Isn't it?' I ask.

She tries to offer me a brave smile but her face falls. 'I just don't know if I can do it,' she says, shaking her head. 'It's not for ages, maybe the summer next year . . . I suppose they're making enquiries now because so many of us are still so in demand,' she adds with a sad smile.

'Why would you say no?' I ask, but I think I already know why.

'I just don't know if I want to be photographed standing next to them all . . . I mean, you saw what Gina Simone is looking like these days . . .' I can tell the Dior campaign is playing on her mind. Gina Simone looked completely sensational, sure, but she would have been airbrushed to shit, plus she is probably cosmetically enhanced to within an inch of her life!

'I did,' I say, nodding slowly. I can see why my mum would feel self-conscious in a line-up with the other models if they all looked like Gina Simone. It's a great source of shame for her that she's, to her mind, let herself go, but she's still so incredibly beautiful, in a way that no one else can compare to. At least, that's what it feels like to me. 'But she has nothing to do with you. You're not Gina Simone, you're you,' I say, wanting her to understand that she deserves to be there just as much as any of the other models. She doesn't have to be anything other than who she is.

But – surprise, surprise – it doesn't work. 'You don't need to tell me that, Mary-Elizabeth, darling,' she says a little shortly, and I can tell she didn't really understand what I was trying to say, which flares up a little flame of irritation in my chest. 'I know I'm not Gina Simone; I never was, and I never will be. I never got a Dior campaign back in the day, let alone now. I'll bet you anything Gina's not teaching yoga in a church hall,' she says a little bitterly.

'A minute ago you were so proud of what you've built! And now it's just nothing?' I ask her, trying to get her to see the insanity.

Mum picks up her coffee cup, exhales sharply through her nostrils. 'It's hardly a Dior campaign, is it?'

'I don't know what to say to you,' is all I can manage. But I don't want to let it go. I don't want her turning down the reunion shoot, because I think she'll regret it in the future.

'I suppose I could go on a diet or try one of those wraps where they cover you in seaweed and cling film – apparently you can lose inches doing that,' she says, bringing the cup to her lips, lost in thought of how she can possibly bring her body in line. 'But maybe it's my face that's more of the problem? I can lose weight, but I can't just magically make myself look twenty-five years younger, can I? Maybe it's time to seriously consider some interventions.' She sets the cup down and starts gently pulling at her neck to erase any sign of sagging, as if she was looking in a mirror.

'You don't need to do that,' I say as gently as I can, but it comes out more forcefully than I intend it to.

'Darling, you have no idea what it's like. You think you'll

be young and beautiful forever, but it catches up with you. You've got to be on your guard at all times,' she says, narrowing her eyes.

'I don't want to be on my guard.'

She shrugs. 'You don't have a choice. Time comes for us all.'

I want to tell her that I think she's the most beautiful woman in the world, that even though she's annoying and she's hard work and she's irrational, I love her just the way she is. But I don't.

'Fine, don't do the campaign then.' I throw my hands up in the air. 'No one's forcing you.'

'Well, I didn't say that,' she mumbles. 'I might do it.'

Don't say it don't say it don't say it don't say it don't say it. 'So you just wanted to complain about it but you're still going to say yes to it?' I say flatly, because I can't help myself. Oops.

'No, that's not it,' she says resolutely. 'I'll email them back now and say no.' She starts rummaging in her enormous Chloé tote bag for her phone.

I reach my hand out to stop her and knock over the glass of water on the table between us.

'What did you do that for?' Mum says, leaping dramatically to her feet to avoid the spill.

'It's just water, it didn't even go on you,' I say wearily, but the young, handsome waiter is already making his way over.

'I'm terribly sorry,' Mum says to him. 'My daughter is so clumsy, she spilled this water all over the table.'

'No problem at all,' he says, wiping it down with a cloth. 'Shall I get you some more water?'

'No,' I say quickly, 'I think we're leaving.'

Mum blinks at me, wounded. But I can't keep going with this ridiculous back-and-forth any longer. Plus, by knocking the water over, I may have inadvertently prevented her from turning down the reunion campaign.

This is what it's always like with my mum: even when I'm making an effort, even when I'm trying, it's like we're speaking at cross purposes, like we're speaking different languages, like all the baggage we're bringing to every conversation is too much to be able to just cut through it and see eye to eye.

I suppose the thing is, what actually worries me amid all my complaining about my mum is that underneath it all, I'm just like her. Not very original, is it?

After we part ways but before I get on the bus home, I stop by the Portrait Gallery to see my favourite room, sit with Saint Fabiola, all 450 of her. I might as well, since I'm here. It's a Saturday, so the gallery is heaving, but the little side-room housing this exhibition is almost empty. I sit on a bench in the middle of the room and let my eyes roam over the images, hundreds of them, all the same and all different, all collected by the same man and displayed here for my pleasure. When life gets annoying, there's always art, I suppose.

CHAPTER 14

I'm slinking around campus after my Possibilities of Portraiture lecture, sipping on an iced mocha from the Workshop, half wondering if I should go home, half wanting to just very casually swing by the Quad Media office to see if Felix is there. He's definitely been there at this time before, so the odds are good. Plus, I should check the pigeonhole to see if anyone's sent in another problem, so I really do have plausible deniability. And besides, it's a perfectly acceptable time to suggest a drink, and even busy magazine editors need a break with their cute little pink-haired girlie. It's settled. My work here done, I make my way out of the café and through the little courtyard towards the building that houses the Quad Media rooms. Coming in the opposite direction and walking inescapably towards me is Aaron Hayes, a pleasant but unremarkable fling from my first year. We make awkward eye contact, but I refuse to pretend we don't know each other so I cheerily greet him with a 'Hello, Aaron!'

'Hi, Mary-Elizabeth,' he mumbles, passing me before doubling back. 'I just wanted to say I went to your club night, and it was pretty great.' He's shifting slightly awkwardly from foot to foot as he addresses me.

'Oh! That's nice of you to say,' I reply graciously, feeling vaguely like minor royalty.

'Would you want to . . . get a drink sometime?' he asks, raising his eyebrows optimistically.

'Like a date?'

'Well . . .' He swallows and clears his throat. 'I don't know if I would call it that, but . . .'

I sigh. I truly only have eyes for Felix at the moment. Sometimes I have to live out the advice I dispense in my columns, and it feels apt that only this term I had to extol the virtues of rejection. 'I had a great time with you but I'm not really in a dating mode right now. But I'll see you around, and I hope you come to the next one?'

'Sure,' he says, blushing deeply. 'I'll see you then.'

The funny thing is, I couldn't get a scrap of attention from Aaron after we slept together. It was like as soon as he got what he wanted he lost all interest, and now I'm a bloody superstar DJ he wants to hop back on the Mary-Elizabeth hype train! Classic. Just as Tyler predicted!

When I make it to the *Quad Magazine* office, I can see the light is on through the glass panel at the top of the door, which means someone must be there. I push the door open and – yes! I have truly hit the jackpot! Not only is Felix here, but no one other than Felix is here! This is the best of all possible scenarios.

His head jerks up from his laptop, his floppy hair falling across his face. 'Oh!'

'Only me,' I say, setting my bag down on a chair and walking over to the desk where all his stuff is spread out.

'Were you coming to do some work?'

'No, I was just looking for you.'

'Why? What's up?'

The directness of the question takes me aback. Why wouldn't I be looking for him just because I want to see him? I shrug. 'I hadn't seen you in a while so thought you might be here.'

He smiles, but there's an air of impatience around him. 'Well,' he says, holding his arms out to me, 'that's very nice of you, but I've got a lot going on right now,' he says, before kissing me, which is nice, but also he is very much brushing me off.

'OK . . .' I say warily. 'It's not a big deal, I just thought I'd come by the office, don't worry about it.' I should have bloody gone out with Aaron Hayes instead, shouldn't I?

'I'm sorry, Mary-Elizabeth, it's just . . .' He shakes his head bitterly. 'You just don't get it, do you? How messed up things are here? How hard I'm having to fight so that the magazine doesn't just disappear? That problem hasn't gone away, you know, and it's my responsibility. It's a big responsibility! Having to make our case to the union for continued funding, having to explain what we do that's so . . . bloody . . . special and unique that the newspaper doesn't do, can't do, justifying the continued relevance of the magazine. They want to shut it down, or at least stop funding it. It's like we're in this silly battle with the newspaper, and the newspaper will always win because it's more proper.'

I sigh. 'I didn't know things were that bad.'

'Well, you wouldn't, would you? You have basically no responsibilities, you just do your column and that's it, but I'm the editor and it's all resting on my shoulders,' he says, exasperated.

'OK . . . well, if there's anything I can do to help . . .' I pick up my bag and go to leave the office. I mean, it's technically true that I have basically no responsibilities, but I don't like the way he says it.

He drops his head into his hands. 'I'm sorry. I'm just stressed. I didn't mean to take it out on you.'

I turn back, keen to stand my ground a bit. I shrug from the doorway. 'Whatever, don't worry about it.'

'No, wait, come back,' he says, stretching his arms out to me from his swivel chair. 'Come here.'

That's more like it! I casually stroll over to him, and he gestures for me to sit on his lap. I decide to be brave and not worry about the weight limit of the *Quad Magazine* swivel chairs. He wraps his arms around me from behind and leans his head against my back. 'I'm sorry. I'm just not in the mood today. Shall we do something nice soon to make up for it?'

I pause for a moment, wanting to make him sweat a bit. But finally I relent. 'Sure, why not?'

Because that's what I'm here for, isn't it? The *why not?* It's fun, it doesn't matter, it's chill.

CHAPTER 15

Look. I'm not stupid. I know I say that a lot and you could maybe tell your old pal Mary-Elizabeth that there's no smoke without fire, but I really don't think I am. Sure, I deliberately give myself candy-floss hair and have a penchant for clown fashion, but I am, at my core, an intelligent person. Queen Anne's Powell School of Art and Art History is a serious department and, like I keep mentioning, for reasons unconnected to the fact that I want to establish that I am a certified non-idiot, the art history degree is competitive and hard. All of which is to say that I know pursuing things with Felix Balfour is a bad idea. And if I know that, then it means I'm in control of my shit while I do it, right? I am owning the badness of the idea. I am empowering myself to make bad decisions. As long as I know what I'm doing, then everything is kind of OK.

I'm sorry about the other day, I was a total arsehole. Let me take you for cocktails tonight?

An unexpected date with Felix! What a delight.

I brush some mascara onto my eyelashes, swipe a bright, blue-toned pink lipstick over my lips and then I'm good to go. Oooh, I wonder if he'll come back to mine later. I do like sleeping with him, I have to say. Very fun. Very intoxicating. I do like walking the streets of Bloomsbury feeling a bit like I'm permanently drunk, when actually it's just the energising vibes of getting to sleep with someone you really fancy.

'Cheers!' I say, clinking my cocktail glass against his. I may not drink much, but when I do, I want it to be a very silly cocktail with a maraschino cherry, which this very much is.

'Cheers,' he says, looking at me over the top of his glass as he takes a sip. Gorgeous. Devastatingly handsome. And here on a date with yours truly.

'So, how are *Quad* things?'

'Exhausting but worth it,' he shrugs.

'All the best things are,' I tell him, fluttering my eyelashes at him.

'Ha! You know, I've never met such a flirt as you,' he says, shaking his head and smiling.

'It's what I do best.'

'Among other things.'

'Among other things,' I repeat after him. 'It's fun to be out with you.'

'Ah, you know, I just thought . . . why shouldn't we go out for a drink? You're doing such a good job of not making it a big deal within the magazine, and I thought let's chill out a bit.'

I nod. 'I'm glad, makes everything feel a bit more . . . normal.'

'Normal like how?' he asks, taking another sip of his Old Fashioned.

'Just normal like we're –' I stop myself. I want to say like we're properly dating, but I know that's the wrong thing to say. 'I don't know, ignore me,' I say, shaking my head.

But it doesn't derail the conversation for too long, and within moments we're back on track, chatting about uni and the magazine and some foreign film he went to see the other night (who with?) and how annoying his housemate Oscar's girlfriend is and the conversation just rolls on and on until –

In walk Laurie O'Donnell and Charlotte Sherman. And they seem to be wearing matching boring outfits, although I'm sure it's not intentional, just a product of being too serious to think about clothes. And anyway, are they ever apart? Are they joined at the actual hip? And do they ever smile? They always look so bloody intense! What does she see in him? Does she know literally zero other boys? Because even if I knew literally zero other boys, I would probably rather be single forever than decide Laurie O'Donnell is the best possible option. I'm so sick of this guy, just turning up everywhere all the time. I feel like I never used to see him and now I can't get rid of him. Like if the Baader–Meinhof phenomenon was a person. I really can't deal with them souring our evening. I down my drink. 'Shall we go?' I ask, smiling seductively at Felix from across the table.

He nods. 'Sure.'

'Your place or mine?' I hold his gaze, which has the dual effect of giving me the most delicious butterflies in my stomach and preventing him from looking in their direction.

'Either's fine with me,' he says, raising his eyebrows, the unspoken 'as long as . . .' hanging in the air.

'Mine then,' I say decisively.

As we walk along the side street from the bar to the main road, Felix slips his hand into mine and then both into his coat pocket. At first I think, Oooh, how cute, but then I start to wonder if it's so that no one can actually see us holding hands. God, stop being paranoid, Mary-Elizabeth. Get over yourself. We turn the corner to the bus stop, where the indicator board says we only have a two-minute wait, which is good news for me because I have the slight feeling with Felix that any minor inconvenience will make him disappear. Too long waiting for the bus will send him home on his own, not coming back to mine. After a few minutes, I do indeed see the bus cruising up Tottenham Court Road towards us, about to take me home to my flat with Felix. But he hangs back as I step forward to hail it.

'Babe,' he says ruefully, looking down at his phone, 'I've got to go, I'm really sorry. There's some big drama with the Quad Media society and they need me to help figure it out . . .'

'Now?' I ask, raising my eyebrows at him. 'Like, right now?' The disappointment is beating furiously away in my chest.

'I know, I know.' He hangs his head as if it's a great disappointment to him as well. 'The timing . . . it's just not the one, is it?' Echoes of what he said about our whole situation.

I shrug. 'I guess not.'

'I'll make it up to you though,' he says, putting both hands on my shoulders and looking me right in the eye. 'We'll do something fun, no interruptions. I promise.'

'I guess this is just the cost of doing business with Felix

Balfour, big name on campus, king of the Queen Anne media empire.' The bus departs without us on it.

He gives me a roguish smile. 'I'm not the king, that's Jack Sampson, and I can't really say no to him.' President of the Quad Media organisation, pretty decent guy, so if he needs Felix for something important then I guess I just have to suck it up, don't I? 'I feel like I've got to do everything I can to fight for the magazine right now,' he says, his smile falling.

'It would be a shame if it all just . . . disappeared,' I agree. We devote so much time and energy into making it actually good, actually fun, actually interesting, actually worth reading. I don't want to see it disappear any more than Felix does.

I can't help but feel like a bit of an idiot really for expecting better from Felix. But if I was writing an advice column to me, I would probably tell me to trust him and see where it goes. I can't help but laugh bitterly at the advice I know Laurie would give. Something like: 'Only an idiot would trust this prick.' Alone at the bus stop, waiting for another bus to turn up, I wonder if maybe on this occasion Laurie would be right.

CHAPTER 16

The thing about having your finger in many pies is that there's always something going on to distract you. Distract you from what, Mary-Elizabeth? Unfortunately, I have to confess that I need distraction from the fact that although Felix is precisely as gorgeous and delicious as I wanted him to be, the scarcity factor is taking up a lot of my brain energy. Is he going to suddenly disappear on me? Is he going to cancel our next planned hangout? Is he going to drop me unceremoniously at any moment? The latest: is he going to show up to my next night?

As annoying as that is, the fact remains that the next instalment of ThrowBax does require planning and preparation, which cancels out a little bit of the mental space I'm having to devote to being obsessed with Felix Balfour. I've got outfits to think about, not to mention playlists! Two things I do very well, if I do say so myself.

Morgan and Aleesha are still eating dinner when I leave to set up at the union, and in between gasps of delight at my silly little tulle dress with stompy boots, Morgan laments having to leave the night early to go to her boyfriend Luke's flatmate's birthday party at their place in Clapton.

'It's just rude, honestly,' she huffs. 'I tried to get them all to come to your night instead, but they were dead set on a house party.'

'I'm already fuming about having to leave early,' Aleesha says, twirling some spaghetti around her fork.

'I just appreciate you guys coming,' I say, thankful that at least two people will show up. For a bit.

'Wouldn't miss it!' Aleesha beams at me from the table, and I feel duly reassured for at least thirty seconds that it's not going to be a complete dead zone.

I'm on the bus, a little jittery with anticipation, full of hope that, once again, people will turn up and the first instalment wasn't just a blip, when my phone screen illuminates with an incoming call from my stepdad.

'Hello?'

'Er, just a quick one, but have you heard from your mum recently?' My stomach drops. This is not what I need right now.

'No,' I say, trying not to let my anticipatory jitters tip over into full-on hysteria. 'Why?'

'She's just not answering her phone. I'm not sure where she is. I'm sure it's nothing, though, so don't you worry about it.'

'Well, I am worried,' I say impatiently – even though I'm not really worried, I'm just annoyed at having this dropped on me when I was already stressed.

I hear Stephen sigh. 'She always turns up.' Which is true, and why I'm not actually that worried. 'Anyway, what are you up to tonight?'

'I'm DJing at the union,' I tell him, and start to feel a bit sick with nerves as I say it. God! I'm meant to be cool, calm and collected!

'Oh! Well, that's fun, isn't it?'

'I hope so . . .' The bus turns off Euston Road, which is my cue to get off. 'Well, I'm nearly there.'

'I'll leave you to it, then. And don't worry about your mum. I'll let you know if I figure out where she's got to.'

* * *

Once again, I didn't need to worry about no one turning up. Even with the rival birthday party going on at Luke's, the union is absolutely heaving by the end of the first hour. I'm making good choices, reading the mood of the room, sticking to the vague plan I had for the flow of the music but making little adjustments where I can sense a tendency towards one direction or another, maybe sticking with disco for a little longer than I'd anticipated before sliding into some Nineties hip-hop or some spiky Eighties pop. It's actually going well, I just wish I was more able to enjoy it. My brain is half there, with one quarter wondering where Felix is and another quarter wondering what my mum's up to. It would be much nicer if my brain could be fully there. No distractions.

My eyes keep scanning the room in search of Felix, and logically I know that any minute now he'll walk through the door just like he did last time, but it's still kind of distracting to have his absence feel so . . . well, present. But eyes on the prize! I've got work to do.

Maybe it's because it's so upbeat and exuberant, or maybe it's because Dolly is the patron saint of all that is good in the world, but '9 to 5' makes people lose their absolute minds. Ugh, I wish Felix was here to see this! Never mind.

Around 11.30 p.m., Aleesha approaches the DJ booth with her arms outstretched. 'Me and Morgan are heading to Luke's for Tommy's party now! See you later or tomorrow, I guess!'

Morgan bops her way over to join Aleesha, twirling ecstatically to 'You Make Me Feel (Mighty Real)'. 'Sorry we're having to bail early, but it doesn't look like it's going to make any difference to the vibe!' She looks back over her shoulder where everyone is reaching peak joy. 'Did Felix turn up?' Morgan cranes her neck to scan the crowd for him, something I've been subtly doing all night.

'Not yet!' I say as hopefully as I can manage.

'Boo!' Morgan gives an enthusiastic thumbs down.

'Boo indeed,' I say flatly.

'Have a fun night!' She leans into the DJ booth and kisses me on the forehead before the two of them disappear.

Just before the stroke of midnight, with two hours still to go until the end of the night, I check my phone, and to my surprise the screen is full of messages. The dopamine hit of correspondence mingles with the instinctive knowledge that multiple text messages from different people is probably not going to be all good.

MUM: *SORRY about Stephen bothering you earlier, he's so silly. I left him a note saying I was going to spend the night at Leila's in Margate because I felt like some sea air, but he didn't think to look in the fruit bowl where I left it* 🙈. *Apparently, I'm not allowed to turn my phone off for a bit of peace either!*

A likely story. I wonder what she's really up to. Probably off sneaking around with some inappropriately young guy that she's managed to hypnotise.

STEPHEN: *Don't worry about your mum, it seems she did leave a note! All good! Good luck with spinning those discs!*

Which leaves only one more. Ugh.

FELIX: *Really sorry but I can't make it tonight – some important issues have come up at* Quad *and I need to deal with it. All the fun of being the magazine editor! Hope the night goes well though.*

Again, I say UGH!

On the one hand, it makes me feel extremely miserable because now I know he's not coming, but on the other hand, knowing he's not coming means I don't have to spend any more time wondering whether he's going to turn up or not. Instead, I can devote that brain space to wondering what these important issues are and how they're going to affect yours truly, the protagonist of the universe. But for now, we dance.

I try to forget my troubles and twirl around the DJ booth in my silly little tulle dress, swishing around and letting my curls bounce to the music. I don't need Felix! I don't need anyone! I am fine on my own! I'm a DJ running a successful club night! People are dancing! I look gorgeous!

There's a steady stream of people wanting requests, which on the one hand I take as an insult to my superlative DJing skills, but on the other, it's actually kind of nice to feel like a special little princess that people have to wait around to speak to. I take flirty little sips through the stripy straw on my lime and soda between chats, because I've got to stay hydrated, and nod attentively at the people leaning into the DJ booth to ask for 'Edge of Seventeen' by Stevie Nicks, 'Toxic' by Britney Spears, '4 My People' by Missy Elliott.

And then, 'Hello, Mary-Elizabeth,' comes a low, flat voice I'm now annoyingly able to recognise without even looking up.

'Hello again,' I say impatiently. Of course it's Laurie, not Felix, nor even some cute potential new crush for me to flirt with. 'Did you just happen to be in the office and get tempted in by yet another tune or are you here on purpose this time?'

'Would you believe me if I said I was here on purpose?' he says, a slight smile dancing on his lips. 'Word got around to my coursemates that it was a fun night so a group of us thought we'd come together.'

'Who knew I'd be such a hit with the mathematicians,' I say, softening a little.

'How do you know I'm a mathematician?' he asks flatly. He's right, I don't think he told me that. Now he knows I've been talking about him, ugh.

'Well . . . I . . .' I frown, wrong-footed. 'Sometimes you just know these things. Sometimes you can just tell by looking at someone.'

'Ha!' he says, clapping his big hands together. 'I actually had a request, believe it or not,' he says, the smile returning. When he's not being all austere and dry, he has quite a sweet face, doesn't he? Annoying of him, to be honest.

'And what would that be?' I furrow my brows at him in an approximation of deep thought. '"Genius of Love" by Tom Tom Club? Because I've already played that earlier in the night.' I'm glad he wasn't there; it feels like I've got one up on him by playing it before he was around.

'Er, no,' he says, moving swiftly on. 'But sort of close actually. I was thinking about "Lazy" by X-Press 2 and David Byrne.'

'Huh,' I say almost involuntarily. 'Could be kind of vibey, couldn't it?'

'Vibey indeed,' Laurie says drily.

My gaze wanders over the room, to all of these people having fun, and I let a little flush of pride fill my chest. I did this! I made it happen! Even Laurie and his maths friends, somehow, seem like they're having a good time (I don't know what goes on in the heads of mathematicians). I take a final, long slurp of lime and soda and let out a sigh. I did it. I really did it again.

* * *

The clock strikes two o'clock, which is my absolute non-negotiable curfew set by the union, and I gasp with delight at the knowledge that I've made it to the end of the night with absolutely no technical issues! I did it! Sure, Felix didn't turn up and I kept thinking about my parents, but at least I didn't have a room full of hundreds of people staring at me in complete silence!

As soon as the lights come on, there's a mass exodus towards the big double doors of the main entrance, leaving only a few stragglers behind. None of them are Felix so I just busy myself with trying to pack my things away. Nobody wants to be hanging out under the rudely bright lights of the union – a classic tactic to clear a space at the end of the night – and as my friends file out, they wave at me and blow kisses towards the DJ booth. I wave back, but my hand feels heavy and I can't raise it properly. Which is . . . strange. If someone was chilling with me in the DJ booth, right about now I would turn to them and say, 'You know what? I feel a bit weird.' But there's no one there, so I just keep trying to pack up my stuff, winding a cable round my hand around . . . and around . . . and around . . .

All of a sudden, it's like I've been . . . like I've been . . . wrapped in a big, heavy duvet in a warm room, and it's time to go to bed . . . time to sleep. It's like someone has turned out the lights . . . dark . . . delicious . . . sleep . . .

CHAPTER 17

Awake. So I open my eyes. But it's hard to open my eyes. It's all just very . . . difficult, isn't it? Easier to stay asleep. I'll stay asleep. Let's get comfy . . . I rearrange myself and bury my face in the pillow when I'm suddenly hit with the strange and compelling thought that my pillow smells wrong. It's not that it smells bad, it just smells different, like a different kind of washing powder. The thought hits me so instantly that I open my eyes instinctively, and what I see is not only not my ceiling, but a ceiling I've never seen before in my life. A red lampshade is hanging above me that I do not know. The only thing I do know is that I'm not in my flat. That feeling that I got when the cable came loose at my first club night? That ice-cold horror? It turns out I had no idea what ice-cold horror really felt like. For a second I just lie there, too scared to sit up, too scared to turn my head and see who's in the bed next to me. But I know I have to start somewhere. Slowly, making as little noise as possible even though I feel like my heart is pounding so loudly you can hear it outside my body, I turn my head. But there's no one there. The bed is empty. That's something, right? That's a start. That's something, I tell myself. That's something. My whole body is shaking with . . . fear? Adrenaline? I make myself sit up.

And the first thing I see is Laurie O'Donnell, asleep on an armchair under two coats.

'Fuck!' I gasp.

'Shit!' he says, his eyes suddenly open, blinking, staring. He holds his hand against his chest and tries to catch his breath. 'You scared me.'

'Me?! I scared *you*?! Imagine how I felt waking up in a strange room! In a strange bed!' I say, feeling slightly on the verge of tears because the whole thing is so bewildering but simultaneously reassured to actually know where I am. I can't have slept with Laurie, can I? Why would I do that? Why would that ever happen? And why wouldn't I have any memory of it? Unlessssss . . . Did I . . . get really, really drunk last night? Is that possible? And even if I did get really drunk, and even if for some reason we did . . . you know . . . have sex, why would he be sleeping on a chair?

'It's . . . it's OK,' he says, holding his hands out like I'm a wild animal that he's scared of. He swallows. 'I didn't know what else to do . . . I couldn't figure out what to do with you . . .'

'What? Why?' I ask. 'Why . . . am I here?' When I hear myself say the words out loud I sound like a child. It's such a stupid question – how can I not know? But I don't. I just don't. 'All I remember is . . . starting to pack up at the end of the night . . .' I look at him, and my desperation to understand must be palpable.

'Yeah, the newspaper lot had just left, and I was about to head home but I thought I'd come and say bye, but you were acting really . . . weird, I guess?'

'Weird how?'

'Like, really drunk. Or just very tired, like you couldn't stand up. Which seemed weird because you were fine when I'd spoken to you a couple of hours earlier, not even on your way to a bit tipsy.' We just look at each other for a second, me waiting for him to say more, him waiting for me to ask something. Finally, he continues, 'And then I realised . . . you probably weren't drunk at all,' he says, swallowing again. 'I mean, I might be wrong, but it seems likely that someone spiked your drink.'

He says it so gently, but it's like being hit over the head. My night. My fucking night. What was meant to be fun and silly and flirty . . . being invaded like that by someone who wanted to . . . to . . . I can't even make myself finish the thought.

'Fuck,' I say.

'And I didn't want to leave you on your own, you know? I mean, I just couldn't, not with you seeming as . . . out of it as you did. And if I was right and someone had spiked your drink, then I figured they were probably around somewhere waiting to swoop in when you were on your own. So I didn't want you to be on your own.'

I nod.

'I couldn't really get any information out of you about where you lived so I thought the easiest thing to do was just bring you back here where I could keep an eye on you, I guess. If that doesn't sound too creepy.'

I shake my head. 'Not creepy.'

'Good . . .' he says, looking down at his hands. 'I really couldn't figure out what the right thing to do was. I didn't get to sleep for ages because I worried that there was some other option I hadn't thought of and that was what I should have done, but . . . whatever way I looked at it, I always ended up with bringing you back here being the safest thing.'

He looks up at me, his thick, dark hair falling across his forehead.

'Thank you,' I try to say, but it only comes out as a whisper. Not because I don't want him to hear it, but because I feel like if I exert too much effort then the floodgates will open and I'll be a weeping mess.

He shakes his head. 'It's what anyone would have done.'

'Not anyone. We know at least one person would have . . .' I begin, but then it's like the shutters come down and I can't make the thought go anywhere, can't make myself think, let alone say what the logical conclusion of spiking my drink would have been.

'Can I get you anything? Water? Tea? Something to eat?' he asks, standing up and wincing.

'God, Laurie, I can't believe you spent the night on that chair – you must feel like a pretzel.'

'There was no way I was going to sleep in the bed,' he says, like it's the most obvious thing in the world.

'But you're, like . . . six foot four; I'm surprised you even fit. No wonder you needed two coats to cover you.'

He shrugs. 'Tall-people problems. Nothing new there. I'm

going to make a coffee, but I actually only have instant so you probably don't want that.'

'Wrong,' I say, trying to summon a smile. 'That's exactly what I want.'

'Excellent, and I think I have some bagels, if that sounds OK to you?'

I nod quickly. 'That sounds OK to me. I just have milk in my coffee and a lot of butter on my bagels.'

He touches his right index finger to his head. 'I'll remember that,' he says, before padding off down the stairs.

Alone for a moment, I take in my surroundings. It's a small room, but tidy, and when I kneel on the bed to look out of the window I see we're in a low-rise ex-council estate surrounding a patch of scraggly grass on four sides where a group of children are playing football.

Laurie returns, somehow juggling two mugs of coffee and two plates with a bagel on each.

'What a skill!' I say, wanting to sound upbeat.

'Saturday jobs teach you a thing or two, I suppose.'

I take a sip of the coffee. 'Aaah,' I say, 'lovely, horrible instant coffee.'

Laurie smiles. 'I know what you mean. It's not fancy, but it's reassuringly itself.'

'Precisely,' I say.

We sit in silence for a moment, eating our bagels, both of us probably wondering what to say next, how to break the silence. At least, I definitely am. I swallow down my mouthful of bagel and realise there's only one thing I want to say. 'Why were you so nice to me? I've only ever been . . .' I pause, trying to phrase it as favourably as possible, 'a little bit rude to you.'

'I'd have done it for anyone,' he says without meeting my eyes.

I smile, for real this time. 'Glad to know you weren't being nice to me in particular.'

'Course not.' He pauses for a second. Sips his coffee. 'I also feel a bit bad about our first meeting. I have this . . .' He clears his throat, looks down at his feet. 'This bad habit of being on the defensive when I meet new people. I know it's not . . . not a good way to be . . . and I'm trying to work on it. Not always being on my guard. Not always trying to assert that I, you know, deserve to be somewhere or have something useful to offer. Sometimes it comes out a bit wrong.'

I don't know what to say to that. I mean, he was kind of obnoxious when we first met, but maybe I'm a little bit obnoxious too?

'Is your phone charged enough?' he asks, drawing the 'feelings' portion of the conversation to an abrupt close.

'Oh, yeah . . . my phone . . .' I say, looking around for it, feeling in the bed to see if it's there.

'I plugged it in for you; it's on the floor by the side of the bed.' He nods down to the carpet.

'Thanks,' I say, blushing at all the various efforts he's ended up making on my behalf. Him, of all people!

I lean down and feel on the floor for my phone. As soon as my fingers touch the screen I can feel it's all in one piece, mercifully uncracked, and when I lift it there are a couple of messages from my flatmates.

Morgan: *U gone to Felix's?*
Aleesha: *Could be some other mystery man.*
Morgan: *Let us know when you get this bc Aleesha is threatening to call the police and report you missing xx*
Aleesha: *Been listening to too many true crime podcasts init.*

I type a quick message, and as I watch my glossy red nails tap out the letters, I realise my hands are shaking. I have nothing to be scared of. Stop shaking. Everything is OK.

All good! Will be home in a bit, girlies, no need to call the cops xx

Another panicked thought enters my brain. 'Do you know where my laptop is? I did bring it with me, didn't I?'

Laurie nods to a little desk piled with books. Underneath is, blessings upon blessings, the bag I stash my laptop in for my DJing. I go over and unzip it, just to make sure, but he's right, it's there. Relief floods my body.

'Thank God,' I say, pressing a hand to my chest and feeling for my letter 'M' necklace. 'I don't know what I'd have done if I'd . . . left that somewhere.' I'm talking about the laptop, but I'm equally talking about the necklace.

'It's OK, I made sure all your stuff got rounded up,' he says, with a small, gentle smile, like it's all nothing, like he didn't save me from various calamities in several different ways.

I return to my perch on the edge of the bed. 'Thanks . . . once again . . . for doing that . . .' I say, looking around, not quite able to meet his eyes.

An awkward pause. 'Can I make you another coffee?'

'No, I should be heading off,' I say, mortified at the idea of outstaying my welcome in a place I shouldn't even be in to begin with.

When I turn back to say goodbye on the doorstep, it's like he fills the whole doorframe. A quite monumental person.

'Well . . .' I say, twitching my nose awkwardly. 'I suppose I'll see you around.'

Laurie nods.

'Thanks again . . . for . . .' I'm about to say 'rescuing me', but I realise it gives everything a veil of dashing and romance, and that's not the vibe really, is it? 'For everything. For the coffee.'

'It was nothing, really,' he says, his hand on the doorknob like he can't wait for me to get out of there.

'And if you ever find me in need of taking home again,' I say, though the thought is too horrible to contemplate, 'I live at Flat 2, Boston House, 247 Junction Road.'

'I'll . . . I'll remember that,' he says, as if he can't tell if I'm joking or not.

I give him one last look before turning away. I set off for home, and instinctively I walk to the main road in search of the bus stop. But I need to breathe outdoor air, need to buy myself some time just to think. So I start walking north, to the safe little cocoon of my flat in Tufnell Park, back to Morgan and Aleesha to tell them about the whole sorry ordeal (was it actually an ordeal, though? If nothing happened?). It's not long after I start walking that I realise the roads are familiar, and that I'm near Felix's flat. It wouldn't be such a bad thing for me to see him now, would it? I'm just passing by – there's nothing weird about that, right? I feel like a moth being drawn to a flame in search of comfort and familiarity. I wonder if I left Laurie's too quickly. Maybe I should have stayed for another cup of coffee. I'm sure Felix can make me one, can't he?

CHAPTER 18

It doesn't take me long to get to Felix's house, but I barely even know I'm walking anyway. It's like my brain is too buzzy and full of thoughts and distractions to register my steps from Laurie's to Felix's. As if by magic, I've made it to the corner of his street, and as soon as I turn the corner I start to wonder why I'm there, what I think I'm going to get from him. But I know just seeing someone familiar will make me feel a bit better, a bit more at home in the world. So I carry on, until I'm at the end of the gate leading up to the front door to the house where Felix lives with Oscar and Mitchell, that tidy garden and the paving stones a sharp contrast to the slightly neglected ex-council block I just left. And then I see them. It's like a huge cosmic joke. Of course. Of fucking course.

That stupid, floppy blond hair and that stupid, ugly, brightly coloured fleece and those stupid slippers can only belong to one person and that's stupid Felix shitting Balfour and he's kissing some girl with long red hair on the doorstep and of course that's exactly what would happen to me right now because why wouldn't it? Why would something good and nice and reassuring happen to me today when I needed it?

I can make it be like I was never here at all. It never happened. I spin around and start walking away so quickly I can almost convince myself I was never even here. I'm certainly quick enough to have managed not to be seen by either Felix or the girl, but that's not enough for me. I want to be able to erase it from my own memory, obliterate it all completely fuck fuck fuck why can't this be the thing that went into my black memory hole why did I do this why did I come here why did I think it was going to be different?

I need to go home. I need to get the hell out of here. I need to be with people who will actually make me feel like everything is vaguely OK in the world. I need to go home.

The whole way home on the bus I feel like I'm vibrating with unhappiness, like the fear and the anxiety and the disappointment are radiating off me and people can see it. This is the thought that shocks me the most: that I could feel like this about myself. It makes me wonder if I've just been completely deluding myself this whole time about who I am. I suppose I thought I was ... sort of invincible, and now I know I'm not. I didn't know I could be someone who people mess with and who gets messed around. A tragic, pink-haired clown girl. Pathetic.

My hand is shaking as I put the key in the lock when I finally make it home, like everything has built up inside me and has to come out somewhere. From the front door I can see directly into the kitchen, where Aleesha is painting her nails at the kitchen table (she's not been seen with naked nails since her trip to Le Salon de Mary-Elizabeth), while Morgan taps away on her laptop. A cosy Sunday scene. Two steaming cups of coffee sit on coasters, and I realise I want nothing more than this. To be home, with my flatmates, in the kitchen. Both of them look up as I disturb the serene tableau.

'There she is!' Aleesha says at the sound of me emerging into the flat. She sounds joyful, but also a bit relieved, like she was worried about me until I showed up.

'Where have you been, eh?' Morgan asks. 'Snuggled up with Felix?'

It's only then that the floodgates open and I properly let myself cry, in the safety of my flat, in the safety of my flatmates.

'Mate!' Aleesha carefully but quickly puts the top back on her nail varnish and stands up, holding her arms out, fingers awkwardly splayed, defensively guarding the wet nails.

'I just feel really stupid, you know?' I say into her shoulder.

'Why? What happened?' she coos gently as Morgan gets to her feet and comes over. She wraps her arms around both of us, a tight, warm hug that miraculously does make me feel marginally less like a piece-of-shit worthless person. 'Did something happen to you last night? I did have this . . . this feeling but just dismissed it. God!' Aleesha shakes her head.

'Too many things to explain,' I say, feeling overwhelmed with everything that's happened in the past twelve hours.

'Try us.' Morgan leads me to the little rickety kitchen table and flicks the kettle on. 'You can have mine. I just made it and haven't drunk it yet.'

'No, I can wait!' I insist, but my voice comes out high and shaky.

Aleesha slides the coaster and the mug in front of me. 'Drink up, girlie.'

Morgan hoists herself up and sits on the edge of the work surface as the kettle boils, crossing her arms over her chest, her fuzzy black jumper hanging off one shoulder. The sight of her sitting there, nibbling on one of her short, stubby, unvarnished nails, is so obviously the kind of comfort and familiarity that I needed that it strikes me as profoundly stupid of me to think I was ever going to feel this by going to see Felix. What did I think was going to happen? What kind of love and attention did I think he was ever going to give me?

'Did the night . . . go badly or something?' Morgan asks.

'No, it went really well!' I take a sip of coffee. Pure comfort.

'It felt like it was going really well! It was one in, one out by the time we left!' Aleesha says, which makes me glow with a little bit of pride, despite it all.

I nod. 'Yeah, it was great . . . Amazing attendance.'

'So then . . .?' Morgan lifts her eyebrows expectantly before busying herself with making herself another coffee.

All I can do is shrug. 'I don't know exactly, but I think someone must have spiked my drink. At the end. Because I can remember the whole night, but then . . . as soon as I'm starting to pack up, it's all just . . .' I wave my hands vaguely. 'Gone.'

'What the fuck?' Aleesha's face is ashen. 'Are you OK?'

'Did anything happen?' Morgan asks nervously.

I shake my head. 'No, thank God . . .' I swallow. 'Someone I know from *Quad* was still there at the end and realised I was acting weird, I guess, so took me home, back to his house, and put me in bed and he slept on a chair.' I realise in that instant that I don't want to talk about him at all, because

I don't know what to say about it. I want us to move on from Laurie.

'So nothing . . . you know, bad happened?' Aleesha asks resolutely.

'No, I promise. I would tell you if it did.'

'Insanely scary though. I'm not surprised you're upset about it,' Morgan says, before taking a sip of coffee from her replacement mug.

'I just can't get my head around it . . . this big black hole in my memory . . . It's really rattled me, even though I know I'm safe.'

'Thank God for your friend from the magazine,' Aleesha says, and I don't correct her that it was actually one of my newspaper rivals, and Laurie no less, who helped me out.

'I can't even think about what would have happened otherwise.'

'Don't,' Morgan says quickly. 'Don't think about it, that'll only make you feel worse.'

'Speaking of feeling worse . . .' I look down at the table, too embarrassed about the whole thing to be able to look at my flatmates. This is the part where I really should have known better. This is the part where I really blame myself. 'I made a bad decision.'

Even though I'm not looking at them, I can feel Morgan's and Aleesha's eyes meeting. 'Go on,' they manage to say in unison.

I let out history's heaviest sigh. 'Well, my friend who I stayed with, when I left there, I realised I was kind of near . . .' I pause, the shame burning hot on my cheeks. 'I was kind of near where Felix lives.' Morgan's face involuntarily rearranges itself into a grimace, like she can already see where this is going. 'And he hadn't come to the union last night because, well, he *said* he had a magazine emergency and . . . God, I just wanted to see him, you know? I thought it might make me feel better. To have a hug and some kind words.' They both nod silently. 'But when I got there . . . he was, like, kissing someone else on the doorstep, which is obviously fine because it's not like we're exclusive or anything, but it just really . . . made everything feel that bit more shit,' I say, and with every word my voice gets higher until it's basically audible exclusively to dogs.

Morgan sets her mug down, slides off the work surface and walks over to my chair. She slides her arms around me from behind and I feel her heavy blonde curtain of hair fall around my shoulders, resting her head against my candy-floss puff. 'He really is a shit.'

'I can't even figure out what I'm crying about,' I say, the tears sliding down my cheeks again. 'Because, like, nothing really happened after I got spiked, and then seeing Felix – it's not like he's my boyfriend or anything, so I don't really have a right to be upset.'

'It's everything happening at once, mate,' Aleesha says, her tone soothing and lovely. 'But the thing is . . . he did kind of lie to you about why he wasn't at your night, yeah? Like, that did actually happen.'

'I guess so,' I say. 'I just feel really stupid, and I hate feeling stupid because I think everyone already thinks I'm stupid, so when something like this happens I'm like, oh, so they were right all along, you know? Like I really am an idiot.'

'Babe, you're not an idiot,' Aleesha tells me, and it sounds like she means it, even though it's clearly not true: I clearly am an idiot. Only an idiot would get involved with Felix in the first place, despite everyone warning against it. How predictable! How pathetic! What a cliché! I thought I was above it, that I was better than everyone else, all the other girls he messed around, but it turns out I'm just like everyone else.

I go upstairs and drop my letter 'M' necklace into a trinket dish on my desk. In the absence of being able to think of anything better to do, I get into bed and stare at the ceiling. Then I decide on a change of scenery and roll over onto my side so I can stare at my bedside table for a bit. A text illuminates my phone. *How was last night? Sorry I couldn't make it, things are so hectic with* Quad *at the moment, but I know you'll have smashed it.* I let out a heavy sigh. I know that if I hadn't gone round there, I'd be so delighted to get a text from Felix, all fizzy with excitement even though it's really just crumbs rather than the whole cake.

Yeah, things got weird at the end of the night and I went by yours this morning but you were kissing some girl on the doorstep so that's all been fun, I reply impulsively.

I got what I wanted. I slept with Felix. Mission accomplished. If only I had been clever enough to leave it there.

CHAPTER 19

The pathetic thing is that, despite all of it, I do still want to see Felix. Isn't that sad? And yet I am what I am, so when he messages asking if I want to come over to his flat, I agree to it.

Pathetic that this is what it takes to rouse me from my misery hibernation. I haven't actually left the flat since I got back from Laurie's via Felix's. It's Thursday now so what's that? Nearly four days of full hermit-ing. Nothing but pyjamas, and certainly no make-up because I'm barely leaving my room. I don't feel proud to say that this includes lectures, and I am not usually one to skip school. Just as bad, I haven't been able to motivate myself to look at the problems that have been sent in for my next column. Grudgingly, I open the unread email in the problem page email account.

Dear M-E,

I feel like in general I'm pretty smart, but my boyfriend leaves me feeling kind of confused. We've been together since sixth form (where we were the only two out gay guys in our year) and now we're at different unis. He's in Leeds and I'm here. Since we've been doing long distance, I feel like things have changed between us. We fight a lot more than we ever did, which is not good obviously, but when we fight he'll bring things up, supposed bad things I did in the past, and I have no idea what he's talking about. I've racked my brain and I just have no memory of these situations, or, if I do, they're not at all how I remember them. And when I bring up things I know he did, he completely denies them and tells me I'm making them up to create conflict between us. Is it a question of perspective or is he lying to me? Long distance has been really hard because I miss him, but also because he hates knowing I'm going out with friends, going to parties, clubs and all that. But it's not like he's staying home when he's in Leeds! I love him and I want to be with him, but I'm finding the whole thing kind of a lot.

Love,

Gay-zed and Confused

My chest fills with compassion for this sweet person who's putting their trust in me, and thoughts start swirling in my head of how to answer, but the idea of sitting down at my laptop and typing out a response makes me feel a bit sick. I can't imagine having the confidence to dispense advice about anything right now. The magazine will have to make do without my pearls of wisdom this issue. I can't find them.

But if Felix wants to see me then who am I to say no, right?

'Well, don't you look cute!' Aleesha trills from the kitchen as I attempt to make a sneaky exit to Felix's. Busted. 'It's nice to see you looking more like you.'

'Thank you!' I say over my shoulder, putting my hand on the doorknob to signal my exit right that very second. But it doesn't work.

'Where are you off to?' she asks me over her shoulder, stirring something delicious-smelling on the stovetop. It would probably be nice to stay in tonight, be looked after by Aleesha and Morgan, but I'm not going to do that, am I?

I contemplate lying about where I'm headed, but Aleesha is too perceptive. Her face falls. 'Not Felix,' she says, the disappointment in her voice palpable.

I sigh, because I know I'm being pathetic and I can't hide it from her. 'Yes, Felix,' I mumble.

She doesn't say anything, just nods.

'I'll see you later. I can't imagine I'll be staying at Felix's.'

'He doesn't deserve a Mary-Elizabeth sleepover,' she says resolutely. 'Love you.'

'Love you too,' I call back.

* * *

Maybe it's that the temperature has taken a dive recently but I feel a chill when I approach the gate, like he could be there again, kissing another girl on the doorstep right in front of me. But of course he's not. I wonder if I'll think about that every time I come here. I wonder if I'll come here again.

I knock on the door and wait an almost interminable length of time before it swings open. 'Come in.' He holds his arms out to hug me. I let him, breathing in the luxurious, expensive scent of him. 'Oscar and Mitchell are out,' he says, gesturing for me to sit on the sofa (does he only invite me over when his flatmates are out?).

He flops down next to me, and I'm about to tell him about my weird, horrible experience and how silly I felt for coming here, but he speaks first. 'Look, I'm really sorry about you crossing paths with Dana – that was not my intention at all. But what happened to you? What do you mean, your night went weird?' he says, swiftly moving the attention from him to me.

I suddenly feel hot and panicked under this spotlight, because I realise I haven't actually thought through whether to tell him that I stayed with Laurie. I kept it from my flatmates for some reason, but with Felix I actually have a good reason to conceal it. On the one hand, I don't want to be . . . somehow tainted by association with this person that Felix clearly can't stand, but on the other I want him to understand that just because he wasn't there for me when I needed someone looking out for me, it doesn't mean no one was there for me. My life (despite my best efforts) does not revolve around him. 'I kind of blacked out at the end of the night,' I begin, since that is the beginning.

'Blacked out like . . . drank too much?' He grimaces.

'No, I definitely didn't,' I say quickly. 'I'm pretty sure my drink got spiked.'

'Wow,' Felix says with a frown. 'What happened?'

'I have no idea, all I know is I kind of lost control of, like, everything, all of a sudden, right at the end of the night.'

'Were you not keeping an eye on your drink?'

'I mean, yeah, but so many people were coming up to talk to me in the DJ booth while I was also trying to keep the music going that I guess my attention was a bit divided,' I say, because it's true, but as I say it I can see it all through someone else's eyes, that me not being 100 per cent vigilant 100 per cent of the time means that the blame fundamentally lies with me. 'But it's not like I did anything that . . . I don't know, that I *shouldn't* have done?'

'No, no, of course not,' he says, placating me. 'But, babe, there are posters all over the union about not leaving your drink unattended. We literally ran an article about it last month. I just don't get why you'd do it?'

'But I didn't,' I say firmly, feeling a lump forming in my throat. 'That's the thing, I never left my drink alone, but like I said, loads of people came up to the booth to talk to me so it could have been anyone, and I just have no idea.' The thought keeps hitting me that I don't know. That gaping hole again. That blackness. That blank space. That void. It's too big to think about, like a real black hole in space. Where do memories go? How can I have done things that I don't remember? How can there be a whole period of time that exists to other people, with me in it, but doesn't exist to me? It keeps running through my head, and every time I think about it too much I feel like I'm on the edge of a tall building and looking down. Instant vertigo. I take a deep breath. 'I didn't do anything wrong.'

He exhales loudly. 'I'm not saying you did anything wrong; I'm just surprised you would put yourself in that position, you know? You're too smart, right?'

'Clearly not.'

'So . . . then what happened?'

Maybe if he had responded better to the drink-spiking situation then I could have brought myself to tell him about Laurie taking care of me, but he didn't, and I don't want to be in the firing line of any more lectures from him. Not about leaving my drink unattended, not about what a bad guy Laurie is. So I skip it, and turn the spotlight back on him. 'A friend took me back to their place in Camden so I wasn't on my own, and then the next morning I thought I'd come see you since you'd missed the night because you were, you know, working so hard on this *Quad* situation and . . .' I throw my hands up in defeat.

Felix exhales heavily. 'Look, I didn't mean for that to happen. At all. But it's not like we're exclusive, is it?' He looks at me, eyebrows raised, as if he wants to properly check I understand this, which, on this one occasion, I do.

'No, we're not,' I say a little grudgingly.

'But that doesn't mean I wanted to hurt you by kissing someone else right in front of you. I wouldn't do that.'

I nod.

'So if you come by to surprise me, and you cross paths with someone else, that's sort of . . . out of my control, isn't it?'

I nod again. Because he's right. But that doesn't make it feel any easier.

'I don't want us to have to stop seeing each other, because I like you a lot, but . . . I need to feel like I have my freedom. That's the most important thing to me,' he says, looking at me earnestly through those pretty, light-blue eyes. 'Does that make sense?'

'I understand,' I tell him.

'Good,' he says, squeezing my leg. 'I knew I could count on you.'

I smile at him. Maybe we don't need to stop seeing each other? Maybe I can just . . . deal with it, the way he wants me to? Felix's hand is still on my leg. And now it's moving up my leg. Oh. Oh? I was so deep in my feelings that I hadn't even considered the idea of having sex with him again tonight. And I don't really think I want to. But . . . if I did, it wouldn't be so bad, would it? Sex with him has always been good, always been fun, so maybe I should just go with it even if I wasn't expecting it.

He kisses me, and I kiss him back, and we only make out for a few seconds before he pushes me backwards onto the sofa and starts removing my tights and unbuttoning his jeans, and pulling a condom out of his pocket and putting it on, and it's all happening quite fast this time, and then he's inside me, which should be fine and normal but right now I don't like it and I don't want him to be doing it but I find that I can't actually say anything so I just try to look at him like no no no please stop but even though he's looking in my eyes it's like he's not reading them, not picking up my silent message and really who can blame him because if I really wanted him to stop I would be saying so, wouldn't I?

Finally, he rolls off me and pulls his jeans back on. 'That was fun,' he says, flicking his sweep of blond hair out of his eyes.

I didn't stop him. But he didn't ask. But I didn't stop him. But he didn't ask. But I didn't stop him. But he didn't ask.

Or maybe he didn't need to ask. Maybe I should just be up for it. Up for anything. Say yes, enjoy the adventure. That sounds like me. So who can blame him for not expecting me to object? But I can't deny it didn't feel right. It didn't feel like the other times. No intoxicating pull, no balloon-light feelings of joy.

'Yeah . . . I think . . . I think I'm going to go now,' I say, with the distinct feeling that I'm on autopilot, like I'm just gliding over the surface of everything that's happening around me, like I can't quite touch reality.

He walks me to the door. 'It was good to see you. I'm glad we cleared the air,' he says, holding my gaze, and I can't help but wonder . . . did he really think I would like it? Or did he want to show me who's boss?

'Mmm-hmm,' I say, nodding quickly, wanting to get out of there, wanting to get back to my flat. Why do I ever leave my flat?

'I'll see you soon, yeah?' He smiles at me, and it's like nothing's happened at all. Maybe nothing did happen? Maybe I imagined it?

But as I walk down the manicured garden path, I can still feel the creeping dread, that stomach-drop of no no no I don't want this.

People warned me and I didn't fucking listen. Classic me. Classic stupid me, just thinking I can dance my way through life and nothing that bad will ever happen to me and 'don't worry, I can handle it', but it turns out I can't handle it at all. I'm an idiot. I'm a complete idiot for thinking that if I just kept it casual then Felix couldn't hurt me. Turns out expecting anything from him at all was way too much for him. I kept saying I didn't want him to be my boyfriend, it's not like I want to marry him, blah blah blah. Well, it turns out that even not being a total dick is beyond the realms of possibility for him. What an idiot I am.

CHAPTER 20

My first foray out of the flat was not a success, but that was Felix's fault. I should drag myself to campus and not miss any more lectures. I can't miss a whole week. Monday to Thursday is one thing, but missing Friday as well feels like a step too far. So I step into this cute vintage dress with a pussy-bow at the neck, throw on my favourite coat with the big faux-fur collar and pull on my boots. All I can do is try. Showing up is the first hurdle.

I rummage around in my trinket dish for my balloon-letter 'M' necklace. I like having it as a little protective charm. And I wasn't wearing it when I went to Felix's yesterday and he was a dick, so maybe things will go better if I wear it today. As soon as I pull it out, I can see it's all caught on itself, knots formed along the chain from being moved around in the dish. No matter how hard I try, I can't undo them, and I have places to be. This is not a good omen for the day ahead.

As soon as I make it onto campus, I realise we have a problem. My sense of safety and comfort has evaporated. As I tap my card in the café to pay, I make eye contact with the barista and wonder, Did you spike my drink? When I walk into the library, the guy ahead of me holds the door open and smiles at me as I pass through, and I wonder, Did you spike my drink? In my Considerations of Curation lecture I look around at the few guys on my course and think, Did you spike my fucking drink? It makes me wonder how I'm meant to be walking around out here in the world at all. And the thing I can't bring myself to think about is the fact that nothing actually happened, because then I have to think about what the alternative would have been, what their intentions actually were, and what I'd be feeling now if I'd found out. And when I make myself stop thinking about the spiking, I catch the eye of a cute boy reading on a bench, and though my usual response would be to return his gleaming white smile, today all I can think is, Do you want to have sex with me while inside I'm begging you to stop?

Nothing actually happened nothing actually happened nothing actually happened nothing actually happened nothing actually happened nothing actually happened nothing actually happened nothing actually happened nothing actually happened nothing actually happened.

So why do I feel like this?

I make it all the way to the door of my Contemporary Chinese Art lecture. I put my hand on the doorknob. And I can't make myself turn it. I can't make myself go in. I can't. I don't want to. I can't. What's the difference? Nothing.

Instead of going into my lecture, I leave campus and start walking down Tottenham Court Road, down Charing Cross Road, to the Portrait Gallery. I want to be in the soothing dark-green room surrounded by my saints. This time, the exhibition room is completely empty, and I get to sit in silence and solitude and just think. I can't do anything from here, but I can at least think. Besides, I always find I feel better once I've been here, like it's a weird sort of comfort blanket.

As I leave the gallery, I check my phone and see I have a message from . . . my dad. Not Stephen, but my actual dad.

Hello, I'm planning our Christmas trip back to the UK and thought I could take you for dinner on Christmas Eve if that works for you? If not, I don't know when I'll be able to squeeze you in so hopefully you're free. I'll make a reservation somewhere nice.

I'm free! I reply, before wondering if maybe I should have left it a bit longer to reply. Left off the exclamation mark. But that's something, isn't it? My dad coming to London, taking me for dinner on Christmas Eve? It's not all bad, I suppose.

Before I head home, I force myself to go back via campus, to check the Quad Media pigeonholes to see if anyone has sent in any new questions for me to answer. When I reach the top of the stairs, it's clear the pigeonholes are still being used as a bin, and I have to move a discarded takeaway coffee cup to see if there's anything for me in there. Amid other random paper junk, there are a couple of envelopes addressed to M-E. I open the first one, and it's a pretty standard question from someone about wanting to get with their flatmate but not wanting to disturb the domestic balance. I'll be able to bash out a response to that in no time at all. And then I open the second one.

Dear M-E,

My friend is going out with a guy who doesn't respect her at all, and I'm worried she has no idea. They're meant to be just 'casual', but I don't think that's any reason for her to be treated like shit. He's seeing other girls too, which is not the worst thing as I think she knows about that, but it's the way he talks about her that bothers me. He's known as a bit of a dick and definitely a player, and he makes a big deal out of how much he respects women and how he's a feminist, but everyone knows that's just a tactic to get girls to like him and trust him. I thought she could see through it, but I'm wondering now if he's managed to pull the wool over her eyes too. She doesn't know that I've heard him say things like, 'She just makes it so easy. It's harder to not sleep with her than it is to sleep with her so I might as well.' She's the most amazing, vibrant person and shouldn't be wasting time with someone who talks about her like this, no matter how casual the relationship is meant to be. Should I talk to her about it or just let the situation run its course? What would you rather someone did?

Concerned Friend

I read it. Then I read it again. Then I screw it up and twist the paper in my hands like I'm trying to wring out a cloth. I do all of this while I'm walking but I don't necessarily tell my body to walk, it just does it. Then I toss it into the recycling bin in front of the wrought-iron gates leading into Bedford Square. Was it about me? I don't know. Probably. By someone who presumably knows me and Felix at least a bit. Does it matter? Not really. If the shoe fits, right?

CHAPTER 21

From: Jessica.Bailey@qac.ac.uk
To: MBax2464@qac.ac.uk

Hi Mary-Elizabeth,

I hope you're well. I just wanted to drop you an email because Dr Schaffer mentioned to me that you didn't turn in your essay for Renaissance to Reformation, which surprised him (and me too!). I wondered if that was an oversight on your part or maybe if something more serious was going on? I also saw that your overall attendance has been very patchy in recent weeks, and while there's no actual attendance requirement for the course, it did worry me a bit because you're usually such an engaged, attentive student. Please do let me know if there's anything that I can do to help. As your personal tutor I'm always here to talk about things academic and otherwise. Missing your insights!

Best wishes,
Jessica

I take a deep breath and delete the email.

CHAPTER 22

I feel bad about how things went last time. Can we talk?

I don't know, Felix, can we? It feels like everything that's happened between us has happened on his terms, so why should now be any different?

OK.

Meet me for a drink at the White Hart on Camden Road?

Ha. He won't even come to me – I have to go to him. Why am I even a little bit surprised?

Feeling like a complete idiot for jumping when he says 'jump', but willing to jump nonetheless, I pull on my big, furry leopard-print coat and head out of the door. I decide to walk rather than take the bus so I have time to figure out how I feel, what I want to say, how much I'm willing to take from him. The walk passes in a blur. As I'm crossing the road to the pub, someone on the opposite side catches my eye, a large figure in a dark coat, walking quickly, head down against the bad weather. I see him but he doesn't see me. Laurie. I almost call out to him, but I don't know what I'd want to say. Probably something weird and rude and awkward. It's like we exist on these two different planes and can't quite connect.

I let him walk by. This evening is about Felix. Whatever the hell he wants to say to me.

The pub is loud, full of boisterous Friday-night energy, and it feels like there are bodies pushing right up against our little corner of the pub. Hardly the ideal scenario for a serious conversation. But I fight to make myself heard above the noise.

'So, what did you want to talk about?' I ask, my heart pounding in my chest. It's like I know things need to end between us, I know they're bad, I know they're wrong, but I just can't be the person to draw that line. It's like I'm just so intoxicated by the whole thing, how much I fancy him, how good it can feel to sleep with him, but I am me and I need to expect better. And the question is, am I going to get that from Felix?

'Mary-Elizabeth,' he says, looking at me very sincerely. 'I'm sorry about the whole thing. I really fucked up.' He shakes his head ruefully and I actually believe that he regrets it. 'Plus, the magazine wasn't the same without your advice column this issue . . . obviously I could move things around so there wasn't a gaping hole in the magazine, but it just didn't feel right.'

It got to the point where I was so late delivering it that I just thought . . . what's the point? It's too late now. And then I never turned one in. Not my proudest moment, but I've run out of steam.

'And obviously I knew that was at least partly because of me,' Felix continues.

I nod, not wanting to let him off the hook.

'So, yeah, I just wanted to say I'm sorry for how I reacted to . . . the whole drink-spiking thing . . . and the whole . . .

other girls thing. I like you and I want to keep seeing you and have you writing for the magazine.' He pauses. 'You're good for the magazine . . . and you're good for me, I think.'

'Well,' I say, not knowing exactly how to respond. 'That's nice.'

'And . . . we can keep this whole thing between us, right?' he says, fixing me with a soft-eyed stare.

'What whole thing?' I ask. My tone is weary but inside I can feel myself rallying, something of the old Mary-Elizabeth coming back.

'You know, me handling that situation badly, I guess.' This time his gaze wanders, like he knows he's obfuscating, knows he's not covering himself in glory.

'Are you asking me not to talk to my friends about what's happening in my life?' My tone, I can tell, is a little incredulous now.

'No, of course not, it's not that.' He shrugs, raises his hands defensively. 'I just . . . don't want you going around telling people I'm some kind of bad guy over all of this, you know?'

I nod slowly, trying to fully comprehend the shittiness of what he's asking of me. 'So it's not so much that you regret being a complete dick to me, it's that you don't want people to find out the precise variety of dick that you were, in case it affects your ability to get other girls into bed with your fake feminist posturing?' I say, my voice shaking a little. It's fine that my voice is shaking if my resolve is strong.

In an instant his face transforms from all soft and gentle

and apologetic to a disbelieving smile. 'What? What's all that about?' He frowns at me, like he can't possibly understand where I'm coming from.

'You talk such a big game about wanting to include female students in the magazine, have girls as section editors and all that, but it's just ... nonsense. It's just for your image, or because you want to sleep with them. It's based on nothing.' I can't believe I'm pushing Felix away but even I have a limit, and I've just about hit it.

'Come on now, that's a bit much, isn't it?' Felix scoffs.

I shrug. 'It's what it feels like to me.'

'Look, I like you. I do. But this was meant to be fun. You're a fun girl, right? That's your thing?' He looks at me, searching my face for agreement. Is that what I am? Is that my thing?

'I can't just be fun all the time!' I protest. 'Sometimes I reserve the right to be zero fun, because I'm a person and sometimes life isn't fun!'

He sighs. 'I thought we were on the same page about all of this, just a bit of fun, nothing getting in the way of the magazine or of uni, all time-limited by me going abroad next year, so I don't understand why everything has had to get so serious with you.'

'I think I understand you now,' I say calmly. 'After we slept together the first time you mentioned your year abroad, and there I was, thinking to myself, Oh, it's such a shame that we got together shortly before he goes on his year abroad! How unfair that we won't be able to keep seeing each other when he goes away! While, actually, the fact that you're going away is probably the only reason we could get together at all. A built-in time limit, a perfect excuse to get what you want but be able to walk away from it on your terms.'

'I think you think about this stuff too much,' he says, but I know I'm right. I can see right through him.

'And I don't think you think about anything nearly enough.' I get to my feet and leave the pub, the noise muffled but audible as soon as I close the door behind me, the windows fogged up against the cold from the heat of all the bodies inside.

As I walk home, I wonder how I got the whole thing so wrong. Was it my fault for wanting too much from him? And then it hits me that so many experiences we have exist in this weird grey area where you can't shout, 'Fire!' and point directly to the catastrophe that's happening, and have everyone instantly understand what's happening and why it's bad, why it's a problem. They exist in this nebulous world where we have this sense that something wrong has happened, that things are out of order in the world, that you've been on the receiving end of . . . something. But what? You get your drink spiked but no one assaults you (in fact, someone goes out of their way to help you) so does that mean nothing happened? You get into a casual thing with a guy you know is, in some way, bad news, and when it turns out he is, in fact, bad news, you're just meant to do what? Shrug your shoulders and move on because it was your fault for thinking it would be any different? Brush off any of the bad feelings you experienced because they were fundamentally your own fault, because he didn't promise anything other than what he was? Once again, you're left with nothing. Grey. Even though it doesn't feel like nothing. It feels like something. Resolve? Determination? Something like that.

I realise that just as I don't have anything left to give Felix, I don't have anything left to give the magazine either.

CHAPTER 23

As I stride with great purpose through the quad a couple of days later, a figure in a zingy Kelly-green scarf and cobalt coat waves at me from the main gate. Jessica, my personal tutor. I turn away so quickly that it's obvious I'm avoiding her, and I promise myself I will do something about all the classes and work I've missed recently. But one thing at a time! Rome wasn't built in a day and nor was me sorting my life out.

I've realised the whole thing about life getting on top of you is that it's like Pringles: once you pop you just can't stop. Or rather, once you stop going to lectures you can't . . . stop . . . stopping going to lectures. But at some point I have to go back. Today, though, it's magazine business.

Onwards and upwards to the Quad Media office.

'There you are!' Felix says so warmly when I walk through the door that I almost second-guess my decision. It's like he's genuinely happy to see me. Or maybe – and more likely – he just feels guilty about how our talk went. He wraps his arms around me in a way I'm pretty sure he's never done in front of the magazine lot before. But I must remain resolute. No backtracking. I don't respond, let my body go stiff until he lets go and looks away, clearly aware that something is up.

We get started, each section editor going around in turn and telling the group their plans for the next issue. When it gets to the music section, Felix is very enthusiastic that Tyler sends someone to review a Swedish feminist punk band at the union who are famous for taking their tops off. He says he'll even send a photographer if they don't already have one.

'Lucie?' Felix says, turning his attention to Lucie Hardy, the features editor. To be honest, Lucie is quite clearly much too good for us. She's got the potential to be a proper journalist, and probably will be one day soon. Last year she was on the newspaper, but then she broke up with her boyfriend who was the sports editor of the paper so told Felix the magazine needed a proper features section, and here she is. The paper's loss is our gain.

Lucie looks down at a battered spiral-bound notebook. 'I think we need to do something about the outsourcing of staff at Queen Anne's. I have a few people I can talk to on staff and at the union. I think it would make an interesting story that people don't necessarily know about,' Lucie says assertively.

'Yeah,' Felix says, nodding. 'I think students are becoming increasingly interested in what's going on with their lecturers behind the scenes, and I know some people at the University and College Union if your contacts don't come through.'

'Not lecturers,' Lucie says quickly. 'Cleaning staff.'

'Cleaners?' Felix says, with a little laugh.

'Yes.' Lucie's tone is brisk and confident. 'QAC outsources the cleaning work to a third-party company that only offers zero-hours positions, which means no holiday pay, no sick leave, unpredictable hours, which makes it basically impossible for them to do their jobs and have a normal life and know they're going to make enough money to support their household. We shouldn't accept outsourcing as a default way to provide this kind of labour and I think it's useful to get the students to see this side of the university that most of them miss.'

'I think it's a good idea,' I say lightly, because I do, and because I have absolutely nothing to lose by supporting Lucie. And as soon as one person speaks up, there's a murmur of agreement around the room.

'I'm just not sure it's very magazine? Doesn't it sound like more of a newspaper sort of story?'

'Well, I don't write for the newspaper any more, I write for the magazine, and there's nothing to say that the magazine can't deal with more serious stuff along with the lighter sections.'

'True . . .' Felix says grudgingly.

'Most of them are women,' Lucie says simply.

'And?' Felix asks.

'Well, you seemed so keen to get the magazine reporting on feminist causes, and I can't help but notice the Audre Lorde pin on your jacket . . . I just thought a story about a cause that disproportionately affects women on campus would appeal to you.'

Felix motions with his hands as if he's weighing something up. 'I mean, are they really on campus though? Like, are they part of the Queen Anne's College community? I'm not saying they're not; I'm just asking the question.'

'Er, what?' Olu asks, squinting at him. 'If lecturers are then so are cleaners.' She says this like it's the most obvious thing in the world, which it sort of is.

'Uh, OK, OK, yes, no, totally.' Felix is a little wrong-footed now. I don't want to put words in their mouths, but I have the distinct feeling that now more than ever the magazine staff is experiencing regrets at voting for him as the new editor. He literally ran unopposed, so make of that what you will.

Tyler glances at me across the room, their eyes bright with enthusiasm for Felix being unmasked as, let's face it, a bit of an idiot.

'Lucie, yes, definitely write the . . . the . . . cleaners' story,' Felix says, clearing his throat in a deeply awkward way.

And then it's my turn.

'Mary-Elizabeth?' Felix's eyebrows are raised expectantly.

'I'm out,' I say, fixing him with a stare, unblinking.

'Out . . .?' He cocks his head.

'I'm out. No more column. No more *Quad*. I'm done with it. I just wanted to come here to tell you that in person. I'm withdrawing my labour.'

One of his sly smiles creeps across his face. 'Come on, Mary-Elizabeth, be serious.'

'I am being serious,' I say, the irritation erupting in me like a volcano, and it's clear from the silence and the tension in the room that everyone around us knows I'm being serious. Finally, I think Felix does too.

'Well . . . if that's how you want to play it . . .' Felix says, breaking my gaze. This meeting is not going well for Felix. Such a shame.

'It is,' I say, keeping my tone light. 'I just thought it was something I should say in person.'

'I don't know if that was strictly necessary.' Felix's eyes flare with irritation. 'But I'm hardly surprised you would want to resign in such a dramatic fashion.'

Instead of feeling embarrassed or ashamed, I just put my hands under my chin in an angelic Shirley Temple pose. 'That's me, I guess!' A giggle goes up around the room. From everyone except Felix obviously. And now I've said what I came to say, there's no point in me staying. 'Well, I'll leave you guys to it. Good luck with the next issue,' I say over my shoulder as I make my way to the door. Murmurs of conversation are already starting in my wake as I make my way down the corridor, adrenaline pumping around my system. And then, footsteps behind me. It better not be Felix trying to change my mind, because I'm very much resolved to stick with this decision, plus, can you imagine how cringe it would be to backtrack after resigning, in Felix's words, in 'such a dramatic fashion'.

But it's not Felix. It's Tyler.

'Wait!' they call to me, and keep walking towards me with their quick step until they're right in front of me. They hold out a hand, rest it on my arm. 'Don't go.'

'Tyler, I'm not going to change my mind.'

'No, it's not that – I don't want you to change your mind. I mean, feel free to leave *Quad*, but don't go right now. Meet me for a drink in the Queen Anne Tavern after the meeting, yeah? I want to talk to you,' they say, looking me right in the eye.

'OK, I can do that,' I say, nodding, my curiosity most decidedly piqued. To be honest, I just wanted to make a dramatic exit from *Quad* and hadn't really thought about what I'd do when I stalked out of the office, so it's quite nice of Tyler to give me an idea for my next location.

'I'll see you there.' Tyler squeezes my arm and turns around to head back to the meeting.

* * *

When the dust settles, as I'm sipping on my large and refreshing, greeny-yellow pint of lime and soda, waiting for Tyler, I realise I already feel better for being out of there. Away from Felix. Untethered from *Quad*. No further business with him or with the magazine. A sense of calm settles over me at last. This is good, because it means that I really wanted to quit, I wasn't just doing it for dramatic effect – you never really know with me, so it's welcome to have that reassurance. Sitting drinking on my own in a public place is a weird sensation. I feel so conspicuously alone, but at the same time . . . it's kind of nice, just watching everyone doing their thing – big groups of guys, couples canoodling in the corner, people propping up the bar after work. No one cares that I'm alone. It's nice to have a minute to myself, not embroiled in some rigmarole or difficult conversation.

Finally, Tyler shows up, slinking their way through the busy pub, a few people turning to look at what a sharp figure they cut in their black leather jacket over a brilliant-white T-shirt. 'Can I get you another one?' they ask. 'I need something stronger after that meeting!'

'Oh, go on then – two lime and sodas never hurt anyone,' I say, shrugging.

'I'll be back . . .'

And when they return, setting our drinks back on the table, they have a naughty smile on their face. 'Well, wasn't that something?'

'I did what I needed to do!' I say a little defensively.

'I've never seen anyone put Felix in his place . . . or even say no to him for that matter.'

'I'm sure it's good for him.'

'Oh, absolutely. I just . . .' Tyler trails off.

'What?'

'Never thought it would be you, I guess.'

'Me either,' I say, blushing. 'I guess he was my kryptonite. I mean, when have you ever seen me chase after someone like that? Put up with nonsense, tolerate feeling anxious and insecure . . .'

'It's so not Mary-Elizabeth. But everyone's got someone like that, haven't they? Just this one person that makes you feel a little bit insane, you know? It's not some kind of personal failing on your part.'

I suck on the straw. 'It feels a bit like I've failed. At a lot of things. Like I'm not really cut out to be giving anyone advice if I've got such bad judgement, such bad taste in guys, you know?'

Tyler thinks for a minute. 'I suppose the thing is, it makes you more human, because it really does happen to everyone.'

'Maybe you should be the one with the column,' I tell them warmly. 'You can take over from me. There's a vacancy now, you know?' I wonder who will be the next me. The next M-E, in fact.

'Well, I was thinking . . . that's what I wanted to talk to you about, why I asked to meet you.'

'I'm not coming back.' I frown at the idea that Tyler would even ask me. It doesn't seem like them.

'No, it's not that.' They shake their head. 'You know I do stuff with Quad Radio?'

I nod, wondering where this is going. 'We're finally doing podcasts now rather than just live stuff, and I was thinking . . . maybe you could do your column as a slot on the weekly podcast instead of in the mag?'

I let out a heavy sigh and set my glass down on a coaster. 'Really?'

'Why?' Tyler asks, baffled.

'Because I feel like an absolute idiot right now, like I'm only capable of making bad decisions. I already told you – I feel like I don't have a leg to stand on and that basically no one should be taking my advice,' I say, feeling the embarrassment at all of it – getting messed around by Felix, the drink spiking, believing that Felix would be different – swirl around in my chest.

'I believe in you. I know other people do too. I get it, you're in a downswing right now, but this is just a temporary blip and you're going to be back on the upswing in no time, and you'll forget you ever felt like this.' They sound so sincere, so reassuring, that I almost believe them.

'I don't know . . .' I say, shaking my head. 'I sort of wanted a clean break . . .'

'This is a clean break! A whole new format! A new life! But still getting to do what you do best. I just hate the idea that you're having to give up something you're great at because Felix Balfour has messed you around. And the thing is, it's not even hard – I'll be right there on the other side of the glass while you record. I can take care of all the technical stuff, I just need you and your brain and your voice. But only if you think it'll be fun. Not if you think it'll make you feel worse. I'm trying to simultaneously communicate to you the idea that I really think you should do it because it'll be fun for you, and the fact that if you think it'll be horrible then you shouldn't say yes just because I think it'll be good.' Tyler pauses for a moment. 'Do you think people write to you for advice because you're perfect? It's because you think about things in a way that feels human. You have a way of looking at things that's yours.'

I nod. I think about my Saint Fabiolas. I've spent more time looking at paintings done by random people than I have any portrait by Rembrandt or Reynolds. And Tyler's right: I shouldn't have to give up my column just because of Felix. And if I really think about it, he is the main reason I wanted to jump ship from *Quad Magazine*. Sure, I'm generally not loving life at the moment, but without Felix adding that extra layer of shit to it all, I will probably be able to press on. He's the one who's dragging me down.

I hold out my hand to Tyler. 'I'm in,' I tell them.

'That's the spirit!' they say, slapping their hand against mine and grabbing it in an enthusiastic handshake.

'What shall we call the slot? Do I need a new name, or can I keep the old one from the magazine?'

'I think a fresh start is in order, don't you?' they say kindly.

'Yeah,' I say, already feeling that much lighter for putting Felix and the magazine behind me. The two are too intertwined, all part of the same messy scenario. This can be my own new thing. 'So . . . a name . . .' I mumble, rummaging around in my brain for a good idea to present itself.

'Not that I let myself get too into the idea before I even asked you if you wanted to do it . . .' Tyler says, raising their eyebrows at me.

'Ye-e-e-s?' I encourage them to go on.

'There's this song you've played before at your ThrowBax nights,' they begin, and I'm already suitably intrigued. 'And every time I hear it I think it's "Fantasy" by Mariah Carey, but it's not, so I googled what song samples "Fantasy" by Mariah Carey, and I found out it's called –'

'"Genius of Love",' I say with an instant smile – because I love the song, and maybe just a little bit because it makes me think of first meeting Laurie, when we had our silly little skirmish at the Quad party, when I poked at him to start his own advice column and he bloody did. It all feels like an altogether simpler time.

'I thought that was kind of a fun name for a relationships advice podcast feature,' they shrug modestly.

'Tyler, my friend, it is the name. You've done it. You've invented a new podcast, found the host and given it the perfect name. It's all tied up with a ribbon. You are very good at this.'

'I did think it was all very neat. So . . . you like it? "Genius of Love"?'

I nod. 'I don't really feel like a genius these days, but maybe I just have to fake it 'til I make it and get my vibes back.'

'The vibes will 100 per cent come back, I know it. You're Mary-Elizabeth Baxter. Queen of vibes. It's frankly criminal that a slimy posh-boy wanker like Felix would make you doubt it. But enough about him. He's in the past.'

I don't need *Quad Magazine* and I certainly don't need Felix Balfour. Onwards and, indeed, upwards.

I raise my half-empty glass of lime and soda and clink it against Tyler's.

'Fuck the past,' Tyler says. 'We're the future now, baby.'

CHAPTER 24

And so, *Genius of Love* was born, and your old friend Mary-Elizabeth is going to become a podcast girlie. By untethering myself from the fantasy of Felix, I'm taking control of my own shit. But there's some of my own shit that doesn't really have anything to do with him, and I need to get on top of that too.

I steel myself and open my laptop, type an email to lovely Jessica.

From: MBax2464@qac.ac.uk
To: Jessica.Bailey@qac.ac.uk

Hi Jessica,
    I feel like everything's got to be a bit of a mess and I would really appreciate your help in trying to un-mess it. I know that's not your job as my personal tutor, but . . .
    With hope,
    M-E
    p.s. Sorry for blanking you in the quad, very rude of me. Should have told you how gorgeous that green scarf was with the iconic blue coat.

She replies almost instantly:

From: Jessica.Bailey@qac.ac.uk
To: MBax2464@qac.ac.uk

Hi Mary-Elizabeth,

Really glad to hear from you. Would you be on campus tomorrow afternoon? I have a good amount of time then and will be in my office from 3 p.m. I would really love to help, and I know we can work something out.

Best wishes,

Jessica

I'm unquestionably nervous as I make my way to Jessica's office. I've never been bad at school or university before. I've always had good attendance, always turned my work in on time, always been trying even if I found some subjects hard. Tentatively, I knock on her office door.

'Come in? Ah! There you are!' she says, as if she's genuinely happy to see me.

'Are you still all right to . . . you know, talk now?'

'I am indeed! Take a seat,' she says, gesturing to an elegantly beaten-up sofa with a big check blanket draped over the back. 'So, how are you doing now?' She casts a searching look over my face and waits for my response.

'I'm doing better, I think,' I say, nodding.

'Do you want to talk about what's been going on with you?' she asks gently.

'Um,' I say, furrowing my brow. 'I suppose it all started when my drink got spiked while I was DJing. Nothing happened, a friend looked after me and everything was OK, but it threw me off a bit and I didn't, like, want to come onto campus. Didn't want to leave my flat really, so that didn't help. And then I was seeing . . .' I swallow, wondering how much detail you're allowed to go into with your personal tutor. 'I was seeing this guy, and I thought I could handle not being exclusive with him, but it turned out I couldn't and then he was kind of a dick to me about getting my drink spiked and then this thing happened where . . . I didn't really know how to tell him I didn't want to have sex with him and did it anyway. So I felt shit for a while and couldn't bring myself to do anything, stopped writing my advice column because I didn't know what to say to anyone, stopped coming to lectures because I knew I wouldn't be concentrating. Just stopped really.'

Jessica nods. Something has come over her. It's like she's trying to remain cool and professional, but the barely contained anger on my behalf is radiating off her. 'That's completely understandable.'

'I guess I just feel . . . a bit silly, you know? I should be able to deal with all this stuff and write essays and show up to classes . . . but I just couldn't.'

She shakes her head quickly. 'No. It's not silly. It's really easy for these things to snowball and get on top of you. You're not the first person whose life got a bit out of control and their studies took a backseat, and you won't be the last. But I was really encouraged by your email, and if you're ready to get things back on track then I want to support you in that.'

'I just feel so far behind, even a few weeks is like . . . an avalanche of work,' I say, burying my head in my hands, letting my pink curls fall over my face so she can't see me. It's not just uni either, I've agreed to do another ThrowBax in a couple of weeks and I just want to feel like myself for that again, too. 'I don't know if I can bring it back.'

'I'm here to help,' Jessica says, the perfect mix of businesslike and warm. 'As far as my classes are concerned, don't worry about attendance. That's not something I think is particularly important. I just think you would enjoy the material, so if you feel like catching up, I can send you some notes, and if you feel inspired, you can turn in an essay any time, just so you feel like you're on top of stuff but with no time pressure. Does that sound OK?'

I nod. 'But it's not just your classes . . . it's the others too.' I nibble my lip, which is something I never do because I'm always wearing lipstick and I don't want to leave a gross little blank patch where I've gnawed away the colour. 'Should I make an appointment to talk to John Schaffer about the essay I didn't turn in? It counts towards my final grade. The stupid thing is that I started it and it's just sitting on my computer half-done.'

Jessica shakes her head. 'I can talk to him; it won't be a problem. I think maybe it would be better for you to just start over when you leave this room. Consider the matter closed and the only thing left to do is finish that essay, send it to him when you're ready and then take next term as a new beginning.'

'That would be really helpful . . . thank you.'

She pauses. 'I know it's hard. And things have happened to you recently that shouldn't have happened. So I'm not surprised you reacted the way you did. I would probably have done the same.'

'Would you?' I ask, and I realise I'm crying. I didn't mean to cry, but it feels OK to do it here. Not like she'll think I'm weak and silly.

She reaches behind her and hands me a box of tissues from her desk, which I assume are there for this specific reason. Tearful undergraduates. 'Of course,' she says gently.

'I just . . . got it into my head that nothing that bad happened and I was overreacting.'

'No. Absolutely not. These things are less ambiguous than you think they are. What happened to you was wrong, on both counts, with the drugging and what happened with your boyfriend.'

'He's not my boyfriend,' I say, gently dabbing under my eyes so I don't disrupt my mascara.

'Was it that blond boy I saw you with in the storm? I sensed there was something between you two.'

I nod. 'Felix. He didn't look like he'd hurt me, did he?'

'They never do, that's how they get away with it.' She reaches across and gives my hand a gentle squeeze. 'Do you feel a bit better now? I always find doing something is useful, once I've got into a pattern of not doing things. It was brave of you to contact me. I appreciate it.'

'Yeah,' I say, my eyes finally dry. 'I do feel better. Thank you. I feel . . . I feel like I have things to be getting on with now. Not even, you know, just to distract me, but proper things to do. And that's what I needed, you know? I'm a doer. I like doing things.' The temptation to tell Mark at the Union that I want to cancel ThrowBax has been strong, but maybe I'm a bit stronger.

'I can see that in you,' she says, smiling. 'I think the world needs more doers. Please try not to let this steal your joy.'

I take a deep breath and get to my feet. 'I won't. I've got essays to write.'

Not to mention a new podcast to record . . .

CHAPTER 25

'This is fancy as hell,' I say, looking around the studio. Jessica's right. I'm a doer. I need something to do, and the podcast is exactly that. 'I can't believe I've never been in here before! It's so cool.'

'The new media landscape, init?' says Tyler proudly, surveying their domain. 'The uni gave us a bunch of money to drag the radio station into the present day.'

I take a seat in a swivel chair in front of one of the microphones and swivel around. 'Well, it's very cool. I feel honoured that you've asked me to be part of it.'

'I would have attempted to poach you from the mag if you hadn't jumped first. The time just felt right, didn't it?'

I nod. 'Definitely. I just hope I'm up to the challenge.'

'Well, you were certainly up to the challenge of running your own night, so you can probably do this with your eyes closed.'

'I appreciate your confidence in me,' I tell Tyler.

'It's literally not even that different to what you were doing before. You've written the script, right?'

'Right,' I say with an assertive nod.

'And you know how to talk, right?'

'Right,' I say again.

'Then you're basically sorted. Shall we get going?'

'Sure!' I say enthusiastically to cover my nerves.

Tyler sent me a question a couple of weeks ago that I've been answering, plus some extra chat to introduce the podcast, all of which I've written into a script that Tyler has approved, because of course they have. They show me into the recording booth, and I slip on the headphones. Everything is muffled but my voice sounds super-clear. Different. More . . . serious, somehow. Hearing myself through the headphones sends a little shiver of nerves down my spine. Everything just got very real. But I can do this. Tyler's right. It's not that different.

'We can do it as many times as you want until you feel like you've got it right. Until –' they look at their watch – 'like seven o'clock when I have a date with a cute Italian exchange student.'

'Tyler, if we're still here at seven o'clock, you have to shoot me.'

'Let's get started then!'

Tyler closes the door to the booth and gives me the thumbs-up through the glass.

'Hi!' I begin. 'I'm Mary-Elizabeth Baxter, the artist formerly known as Ask M-E Anything in *Quad Magazine*, now Genius of Love for Quad Media Podcasts. Or . . . Quadcasts, if you will. I'm going to be answering your questions in audio form rather than print, but still with my trademark brand of optimism and the pursuit of fun. Fortunately, we've already got a question to kick off the first mini-episode, but any future questions, please just write me a note and leave it in the Quad Radio pigeonhole. No emails for this one as we found with the magazine that people were much more likely to contact us with a question if they felt it was completely anonymous, so notes it is! Let's get started . . .' I clear my throat before thinking that no one wants to hear me clear my throat. 'Tyler, you can edit that out, right?'

Tyler nods enthusiastically at me through the window and I give them the thumbs-up. 'Great. OK, so . . . today's question: "Dear Genius of Love, I feel really silly even writing this, but I hate the fact that my boyfriend's best friends are girls. It makes me so uncomfortable and jealous, and I don't know what to do. I know that if I mention it to him, I'll sound crazy, but I already feel crazy so I feel like I might as well tell him that I hate him hanging out with them without me. Please help. I really like him and don't want to sabotage this, but it's really getting to me! Love, Outta Control Babe."

'Dear Outta Control Babe, I think jealousy crops up in more questions to me than any other experience or emotion. You're definitely not alone – this kind of feeling is something that people are experiencing all the time, whether from their partner's friends or from an ex or just someone you get weird vibes from. I completely empathise: I'm not at all immune to this myself and completely know the feeling. But I think this is something you need to work on in yourself, and you won't necessarily get the response you want by sharing those feelings with him straight away.

'I think the first thing you need to ask yourself is whether this jealousy is corresponding to something you feel is lacking within your relationship. Do you wish you saw him more? Does he give his friends something he isn't giving you? What is the thing that's missing, and is it something that you can achieve together? I find jealousy often flares most strongly in situations when we feel like we're missing out on something, or, to put it simply, someone else is getting something that we want. But what is that thing for you? Maybe figuring that out will help you navigate this situation.

'Have you thought about getting to know the female friends better yourself? I wonder if you're putting them on a pedestal because you don't know them, and you're able to project this idea of perfection onto them, invent ways that they're perfect for your boyfriend, create scenarios where you're threatened. Maybe if you spent time with them – with your boyfriend or maybe especially without him – you'd see that they're just people. You might end up with some new besties, but even if you don't, they'll at least seem more real and flawed, just like the rest of us.

'I would really advise against demanding that your boyfriend brings you along to all of their hangouts. I get wanting to spend time with him, but you have your dates for that, and just like you need time with your mates, he needs and deserves that too. I feel like the best-case scenario is them talking to him about how cool and great and hot and funny you are, and the worst-case scenario is them all bonding over something you said or did in the heat of the moment, or all giving each other looks because you turned up to their hangout unexpectedly.

'Communication is great, and generally what I would recommend, but as a first step I would definitely try to work on this in yourself, as figuring out how to sit with jealous feelings is a skill that will probably come in handy more than once in your life. Of course, if you try all of this and you still feel terrible and like you can't handle it, definitely talk to your boyfriend about it. But be prepared to hear things you might not like: don't go in expecting him to dump his friends for you and be shocked if you end up boyfriendless instead.

'I really hope that helps! Don't be ashamed of feeling jealous – it's completely natural but not something that has to dominate and control your relationship. Good luck! I believe in you! Genius of Love.'

I glance out of the booth to Tyler, who is once again giving me an enthusiastic and now double thumbs-up. 'I hope you enjoyed this first advice slot on the *Quad* podcast, and remember the more questions you send in, the more questions we can drop into episodes! I've been Mary-Elizabeth Baxter, the Genius of Love, and don't forget, if you want to get in touch, just drop your note into the Quad Radio pigeonholes in the union building. See you next time!'

'You're a natural!' Tyler says when I emerge from the booth. 'Is there anything you can't do?'

'Make good decisions about boys?' I offer.

'Can't help you there, matey,' Tyler says, clapping me on the back. 'But, seriously, you have such an empathetic way about you. Like you're really thinking about this person and trying to help them. I think that's going to come across even more in the podcast than in print. And . . .' Tyler pauses, 'I can't help feeling there's a new kind of . . . maturity about you. I don't know what I mean by that exactly, but . . . I think you're just getting better and better.'

'Thanks, Ty,' I say, blushing. 'Good luck with your Italian exchange student.'

'Don't need it, mate,' they say, squeezing me into a hug.

* * *

When I leave the studio, full of the kind of confidence and enthusiasm that I feared might be gone forever, I head to the Workshop for a silly little iced mocha. There in the corner, heads bowed and deep in conversation, are Charlotte Sherman and not Laurie this time but Felix. Ugh. I suppose there's no reason why they shouldn't be hanging out. They're both in the Quad Media machine. But that doesn't mean I have to like it, for either of them. Sort of makes me want to bump into Laurie now, for symmetry. And because he's quite nice.

Get a life, Mary-Elizabeth, you've got bigger fish to fry than either Quad or Felix Balfour. You're a strong, independent girlie, making content on your own terms. And you have another club night to prepare for! Not just any club night: this time it's the Christmas Edition!

CHAPTER 26

The one thing I'm not going to do is let the drink-spiking incident steal my joy for the club night. Yes, I'm still rattled by it, but I don't want to let it consume my every thought. Instead of leaving my drink at the front of the booth like I normally do, I'm extremely careful to put it right behind me every time I take a sip.

The union is in full Christmas mode: tinsel hanging off everything, strings of lights wherever they can be strung, paper garlands arcing across the ceiling. It's actually quite cute.

Morgan and Aleesha periodically come over to check in and report on the vibe, which, as I can observe from my perch in the DJ booth, is immaculate. I can't believe I nearly let some shithead ruin this for me. I can't believe I nearly cancelled the whole thing. (Don't think about the fact that the person who did it could be here right now and you'd have no idea, don't think about that).

Something that's nice about this particular night is that I'm devoting precisely zero brain space to wondering if Felix fucking Balfour is going to show up. I mean, it would be nice if he did, you know, to . . . pay tribute or whatever people do in mafia movies, but it's not like my levels of hype live or die based on whether Felix is there. What the hell was I thinking? Wasting that much time and energy on someone as pathetic as Felix? Deeply unchic.

When I look up from my laptop I see that someone's waving at me from the other side of the dance floor. A tentative wave, not a wild, enthusiastic wave like most of my friends would be doing. I can only think of one person who cuts such an imposing figure. Laurie. He makes his way across the dance floor towards the DJ booth.

'Hello, Laurie,' I say, and for the first time, there's no sharp tone. I feel happy to see him. I sound happy to see him.

'I didn't want to bother you while you were working, but . . .' He trails off.

'Oh, no, bother away.' I realise now that I should have contacted him since he took me home after the last club night. I should have thanked him properly. But there was too much going on in my brain and I didn't have room for Laurie. I hope he knows that I appreciated it. I hope he understands that.

'I just wanted to say . . .' he says, but his voice is too low and quiet for me to be able to hear him.

'Come in!' I say, gesturing for him to actually enter the DJ booth, which is something I haven't permitted anyone else to do tonight. Gotta have professional boundaries, right?

He smiles awkwardly but steps up into the slightly raised booth. Now he's towering over me even more. 'I wanted to tell you that I think your new podcast slot is . . . well, it's really great.' He clears his throat. 'You're a total natural.'

I feel myself blush at how completely straightforward the compliment is. No messing about. 'Oh! Thank you,' I say, looking at him.

'It's . . .' He trails off again, breaks my gaze. 'It's great to hear your voice.' Laurie swallows and I realise that he's exuding a strange, nervous energy. 'Just a shame not to be able to see your face at the same time.'

'Ha,' I say, 'I think video is maybe a level of effort I'm not yet willing to make . . . but maybe one day.'

'Anyway,' he says, 'I can't stay, I just wanted to swing by and congratulate you on your post-magazine life . . .'

'I've formulated a theory that the less time a person can spend with Felix the better,' I say with a bitter laugh. He throws his hands up as if to say 'you said it, not me', and I'm struck by this sharp little thought that they look really quite lovely, all big and soft, just like him. 'What nice hands you have,' I say, before I realise I'm saying it.

His eyes widen, and his cheeks turn pink as he looks down at them. 'Well, thank you.'

I clear my throat, wanting the whole thing to be over. Why did I say that? To him! 'Anyway, I'm sure you've got more interesting places to be. Thank you for coming, even just for a little bit.'

He gives me a small smile and puts a hand on my shoulder. It's like we want to hug but can't. Instead, he squeezes; his big, soft hand all warm against my bare skin. 'See you. Or . . . hear you, I suppose,' he says. While his eyes are still lingering on me, I see Charlotte Sherman approaching from behind him. The moment is nearly over.

'There you are!' she says, as if he's her lost dog. 'We were going to head out and go to the pub, are you coming?'

'Yes, sure,' he says quickly, like he's desperate to extricate himself from a situation he isn't quite sure how he got himself into.

'Well,' I say lightly, 'I'll see you around.'

Laurie nods and doesn't quite look me in the eye, and then he's gone.

I don't have much time alone with my thoughts because within about three seconds he's replaced by Patrick Denton. 'That was a close one!' he says, a naughty smile on his face.

'What do you mean?' I call to him over the edge of the booth.

Pat nods above my head. I turn to look, and see a little red ribbon hanging from the ceiling, a sprig of mistletoe dangling directly over me. 'Nearly had to kiss a newspaper guy. Can you imagine?'

'Ha . . .' I say weakly.

'Anyway, is it time for Mariah yet?'

I smile, trying to put the thought of the mistletoe out of my head even though it makes me feel a bit fizzy inside. 'I think so.'

'Iconic!' he yells over his shoulder as he dashes back to his group.

I'm so distracted by what Pat has said that I don't even think about what Laurie said until later in the evening. 'Just a shame not to be able to see your face . . .' Laurie wishes he could see my face. I queue 'Pony' by Ginuwine because we've reached the point in the evening where I know everyone wants to be grinding on each other, and Christmas songs don't generally lend themselves well to grinding. Someone comes up to the booth and requests 'More Than a Woman' by Aaliyah, presumably to facilitate even more grinding.

I look up at the mistletoe hanging above the DJ booth. I swallow down a rising uncomfortable feeling. The feeling that it might have been nice to have an excuse to kiss Laurie.

CHAPTER 27

'Knock-knock!' Morgan says brightly – a little too brightly, some might say.

'What time is it?' I ask, bleary-eyed after my late night.

'Oh, like, eleven o'clock. Aleesha has gone to Tesco Express to get Pop-Tarts and I didn't want you to miss them.'

'I would rather die than miss Pop-Tarts.'

'And I brought you a coffee,' she says, holding the milky cup of instant out to me and perching on the end of my bed.

'You're too kind,' I say, meaning it. I know I'm lucky.

Since the second I opened my eyes, I've had this strange but familiar fluttering in my chest. Oh no. I know what that feeling is. I let out a groan.

'What?' Morgan asks, leaping back up in fear that she's sat on me.

'It's . . . nothing. I'll tell you about it when Aleesha gets back.'

'Speak of the devil,' Morgan says with a smile, hearing Aleesha's key in the door.

'Honey, I'm ho-o-o-ome!' Aleesha calls from the hall, the sound of a plastic bag swishing away in her hand. 'Let me just rustle up a little something and I'll be right there!' We hear the sound of the box being torn open and the foil packet being ripped into and then, one after another, the metallic springs of the toaster being pushed down. Finally, Aleesha bounds up the stairs and comes to join Morgan on my bed, a familiar tableau of cosy weekend mornings.

'Two hotter-than-the-sun, molten-lava, burn-your-tastebuds-off chocolate Pop-Tarts for your delectation,' she says, sliding them onto my plate.

'There is nothing I want more right now.'

'Fun night? Too fun?' Aleesha asks, raising her eyebrows and grinning expectantly, before her face falls. 'Nothing weird happened again, did it?'

I shake my head. 'Nah, nothing like that,' I say, but I don't know where to go from there. How do I introduce the . . . the idea of Laurie?

I nibble the pastry edge of my Pop-Tart, trying to get my teeth as close as possible to the frosting without eating any, before moving on to the process of lifting off bits of frosting with my teeth so I'm left with just the chocolate sauce on the bottom layer. I know no other way.

'Guys . . .' I say very seriously, 'something terrible has happened.'

'What?' Morgan asks quickly, but I can tell Aleesha knows I'm being silly.

I take a deep breath. 'I think I have . . . an unwanted crush.'

'Not an unwanted crush!' Morgan grins. 'But you love having a crush. What was it you called it? Your animating life force or some shit?'

'This is where the unwanted part comes in,' I say. 'Do you remember . . . maybe I mentioned this guy . . . um, Laurie O'Donnell?'

'I'm going to level with you, babe, I find it hard to keep track of all your mans,' Aleesha tells me, grimacing.

'In your defence, there have been rather a lot over past year . . . but one . . . um, he works on the newspaper?' I say casually, lightly. But Morgan has the memory of an elephant. She never forgets.

'Laurie O'Donnell? You mean the guy who was rude to you and made you feel stupid and who you said was a demon and you accused of starting a rival advice column?' she helpfully supplies.

'Not that guy?' Aleesha says, disbelieving that the person that I spent most of a Big Shop, pushing a trolley with a wobbly wheel around Tesco complaining about is now the object of my affections.

I hold up a finger to pause their scepticism. 'There is a key piece of information that I think I neglected to tell you . . .' I say, swallowing, trying to remember why I didn't want to tell them in the first place. 'You know when my drink got spiked?'

Morgan gasps dramatically. 'That wasn't him, was it?'

'No.' I shake my head emphatically. 'He was the one who took me home and looked after me. Made sure nothing bad happened to me.'

'Oh . . .' Morgan's face softens.

'Not such a demon after all,' says Aleesha quietly.

'He contains multitudes, I guess.' Don't we all?

'Why didn't you tell us that?' Morgan asks, smiling, a little baffled. 'You know, at the time, when it happened?'

'I think . . . when I really dig deep . . . it was because maybe part of me knew I liked him in that way, but I just couldn't admit it? And I can never lie to you two, so I thought if I just didn't mention it then I wouldn't have to acknowledge it.'

'Are you sure you're not just looking for something or someone to replace Felix?' Aleesha asks me sagely, taking a sip of coffee.

'I don't know,' I tell her, because it's true. I don't know. I don't feel like I know anything any more. I used to feel like maybe I knew everything and had some sort of deep, useful wisdom that I could apply to myself and share with other people, and I'm wondering if actually the fun bits of life come from the not knowing, the uncertainty. And more to the point, I'm wondering if that isn't sort of . . . good? Better? To know that I'm just doing my best, trying to help other people have as much fun and joy as humanly possible? That maybe being curious about people is my superpower, rather than being certain about what I know?

'What do you like about him?' Aleesha asks, seemingly satisfied with my previous answer.

I think for a moment. 'I like that there's always this tiny bit of friction with him in some way, which is in itself sort of intriguing, but underneath the friction I feel like we're compatible. In a way that feels . . . real? I mean, yes, we like some of the same things, but it's more than that. He's calm and I'm never calm, but I feel calm when I'm with him, not like I have to be on my guard like I need to impress him or think about what I look like. And he's, well, he's quite nice-looking now I look at him properly. All big and dark and cute,' I say, feeling my cheeks heat up. 'Nice hands. And he came up to the booth and said he thought the podcast was good, and somehow a compliment just feels like it really means something coming from him?'

'Just be careful, that's all,' Morgan says gently. 'I feel like you've been through a lot of change recently and maybe it would be good to just . . . do less for a bit.'

Aleesha rolls her eyes. 'That's like asking the sun not to rise.'

I smile. 'Doing the absolute most is my default state . . . but maybe Morgan is right. Maybe not everything requires action. Or a reaction. Anyway, I might be projecting. It's possible he doesn't like me at all and was just being nice because he knows the last club night ended in a bit of a mess for me.'

The idea that I could just do nothing is very unfamiliar to me, but I wonder on this occasion if it's the correct path to take.

'At least you've got the Christmas holidays to give you a bit of distance from the whole thing.' Aleesha's right.

I nod. Maybe some time at home will give me the kind of break I need. No drama. Just switch my busy brain off for a bit.

THE CHRISTMAS HOLIDAYS

CHAPTER 28

I try to creep out of the house as quietly as possible. My mum is in the kitchen, wailing along to 'Last Christmas' by Wham! on the radio and doing what I have no doubt is an absolutely appalling job of icing some Christmas cookies (what she lacks in skill she makes up for in enthusiasm). The thing is, the creeping is as much for her benefit as it is for mine. But when I put my hand on the doorknob and check my bag for my house keys, the door opens towards me and Stephen emerges, carrying a bag clinking with bottles.

'Ah!' he says, as if he's surprised to see me. 'Just went on a Baileys run!' He holds up one of the shopping bags jubilantly. 'Where are you off to?'

I keep my voice low, even though he's not someone I'm naturally inclined to confide in. 'I'm meeting my dad,' I say through gritted teeth. I'm the nervous kind of excited about seeing Dad, something that happens vanishingly rarely since he lives in Singapore with his new (actually not even that new at this point) wife.

'Who?' he says loudly, wrinkling his nose and squinting at me through his goofy glasses. Bloody Mum and bloody

Wham! – what a racket.

'My dad,' I hiss a little bit louder.

'Oh!' Stephen finally catches on. 'Well then, I'd best leave you to it.' But before I can complete my creep into the cold December air, he catches my arm. 'It's one thing not to tell her who you're meeting, but one of us should at least know where you're going. You know, in case something happens.'

I suppose that's sensible. 'A pasta place in Covent Garden. So if they drop a nuclear bomb on the piazza, you'll have to tell Mum.'

Stephen nods and lets me go on my merry (Christmas) way.

I walk to the station, and when I take my phone out of my pocket to touch in on the card reader, I see a message. My stomach drops.

I'm so sorry but there's a huge crisis at work and I'm the only one who can sort it. I'm going to be chained to my laptop in the hotel room from now until Boxing Day. I'll send you some extra £ for Christmas and I really hope I can see you soon. Maybe you can come visit?

I feel that prickly shame feeling sweep over me. I just stare at my phone for a second, trying to decide what to do now. I could slink back home, pretend I never left. I could go and lurk at the Dog & Bell, drink a Guinness on my own and play on my phone. But it'll be rammed with Christmas Eve drinkers. Instead, without really deciding to, I find my hand tapping my phone against the card reader and going through the barrier. When the train pulls in, I get on it, and I change at London Bridge as if I'm still going to meet Dad. But I'm not. I'm on my own, and maybe that's what I need instead. Time to think.

Central London is heaving. Last-minute shoppers and tourists are thronging every street between Charing Cross and the piazza. Every café is spilling over with people, every pub has people standing outside, bundled in their winter coats. I know I'm meant to hate it, but . . . I kind of love it. It means I'm in a place where other people want to be. I can't imagine living somewhere boring that people want to escape. I'm already in the place they escape to. Strings of fairy lights zig-zag between the buildings that are close enough together, and the huge Christmas tree between St Paul's Church and the piazza is illuminated with what must be thousands of tiny bulbs. It's all a little bit magic. I pull my sky-blue fauxfur stole more cosily across my chest and buy a fancy hot chocolate to sip as I walk.

And that's all I do: I just walk. I've been let down by a man once again and this time it's actually worse because it's my literal actual dad, and I could let that send me off into a tailspin but I've decided the time for tailspinning is over. As I walk, through the busy streets towards Chinatown, then down to Trafalgar Square and Downing Street and to the river, I think. I think about the sense of shame I felt when my dad cancelled on me, as if it was something I should be embarrassed about rather than him. I can't control what he does, all I can control is how I react to it. I can't control how Felix treated me last term, but I can try to see next term as a fresh start. Work hard, get good grades, record good stuff for Tyler's podcast, spend more time looking at art. I've got a lot of time on my hands now I'm not occupied with chasing Felix, I suppose. It's really time to get things back on track.

After a couple of hours of walking, I decide it's time to go home. Dad tried to steal this evening from me but I wrestled it back off him by sheer force of will and I already feel a little bit more prepared for a new year.

On the train home, I realise that I hope Mum is still up when I get in, and when I see the lights on in the living room a sense of relief sweeps over me.

'Where have you been, darling? Did you have a nice evening?' she asks over her shoulder, all curled up on the sofa.

I feel a little lump in my throat, glad I'm here with her now. 'I just went for a bit of a walk. To see the lights and all that.' I glance over at Stephen who can tell something's off but knows better than to ask and will probably assume I just feel guilty for spending time with my dad.

'Lovely! There are cookies in the kitchen in the red tin!'

I smile, knowing they're going to look dreadful. 'I'll take one up to bed with me. See you in the morning.'

'On Christmas!' Mum says, gleefully, holding her arms out for a slightly tipsy hug.

New Year's resolution: maybe be a bit less hard on her.

THE SPRING TERM

CHAPTER 29

And a happy bloody new year. And now I'm being good. I'm getting everything back on track, like I told myself I would. Everything that I want to get back on track anyway. I'm properly back in the swing of going to lectures, accepting that it is, in fact, an integral part of being at university, and that I really did not enjoy my brief detour into my little pit of misery and avoidance. It's just not me. A new term feels like the right moment to very gorgeously commit to myself, and not to be distracted by boys and nonsense. New year, new me and all that! A more serious Mary-Elizabeth Baxter. More focused.

I've just been in the booth in the little studio to record a couple more problems for the podcast, and I didn't even need Tyler to hold my hand for it! There was a silly one about how to gently tell someone's partner you hate an item of their clothing ('History's Ugliest Coat', as they called it) and then another one about cheating, which required a bit more thought.

Dear M-E aka the Genius of Love,
  Is it ever right to get back with someone who cheated on you? I'm feeling the urge to get back with

my girlfriend even though I only broke up with her a couple of weeks ago for sleeping with someone else after a night out. She's been pleading and begging to get back together and she regrets it big time. I know she's not the only hot gay girl in the world, but I'm worried she's the only hot gay girl in the world for me. Can you rebuild trust in a relationship when someone's done something like that? Or is it broken forever?

Love,
Moping Lesbian

Dear Moping Lesbian,

I can't tell you what to do, only offer a range of things to think about while making your decision. Firstly, I know it's maybe controversial, but I think there are a lot of reasons people cheat and it's maybe worth excavating the 'why' of it all, and trying to figure out if it's something that's likely to happen again. I believe in the capacity of people to change, and I don't believe that 'once a cheater, always a cheater', like it's an ingrained personality trait. I don't personally believe that anyone is forever lost, irredeemable, whatever. I believe that people make choices. Is this a choice you think she's going to make again? Even if the answer is 'no', it's still OK to realise that she's hurt you too much and that you don't want to go back there, even though you really miss her. I think if you do decide to get back together, it has to be on the understanding that it can't ever happen again, and also that this can't be a stick for you to beat her with.

It can't be your 'get out of jail free' card, or something that you hold over her head. If you do reconcile, you both have to be on the same page about what happened, and approach the new attempt at being together as a team, not as adversaries. If you can't do that, then maybe it's best to start getting excited about one of the many gorgeous, gorgeous girls of the QAC campus. You didn't cause her to cheat on you, it's just something that happened, and I think it would be a shame to carry that fear into a new relationship and project it onto someone else. Approach anything you get into with an open mind and try not to take this experience with you too much, even though I know that's a lot to ask. I hope I've given you some things to think about, and that you're feeling a bit clearer and stronger!

Love,

Genius of Love

So here I am, striding across the quad that gives Quad Media its name, when I see someone waving very enthusiastically at me from the opposite side of the square. Not just waving, but properly barrelling towards me at great speed.

'Mary-Elizabeth!' Tyler leans forward, putting their hands on their thighs, bent double trying to catch their breath.

'I'm happy to see you too,' I say, a little baffled at being actually chased.

'You are literally the exact person I wanted to see,' they say between gasps. 'God, I really need to get a bit fitter – can't be on death's door after a little sprint.'

'How can I be of assistance?' I say perkily. 'My new podcast segment is in the can, as I believe is the technical term. It's scheduled for tomorrow afternoon,' I reassure them.

'It's not that, it's actually something else, something that just came up.'

'Intriguing,' I say archly and put my hands on my not insubstantial hips.

Tyler grimaces at me, which does not bode well. 'I was hoping you could do me a favour. Not just . . . any favour.'

I swallow. 'What?' I ask, more than a little warily.

'We've got this . . . this whole Quad Media party tomorrow night to kick off the new term.'

I shrug. 'I know, I'm not going.'

Tyler's face falls. I can tell this is some high-stakes shit and I'm intrigued. 'But you're not busy, are you?'

I squint at them, give them a slightly sideways look. 'Yes?' I venture, sensing I'm about to get dragged into something I do not wish to be dragged into. 'Very busy. Lots of plans . . .'

Tyler clasps my elbows, like the desperate grasping of a drowning person. 'Oh, Mary-Elizabeth, please!'

I sigh dramatically to signal how very above it all I am, whatever it is. 'What am I being asked to do exactly?'

'The thing that you do best,' Tyler says, finally releasing my arms from their vice-like grip. 'I just got a message from the guy who was meant to be DJing saying he's got norovirus! Well, obviously we can't have that at a Quad party, can we? So . . . I am very much in search of a superstar DJ, and it will come as no surprise that I thought of you.'

I let out an involuntary groan. I swear it was involuntary! 'I assume Felix Balfour will be there?'

Now it's Tyler's turn to give me a sideways look. 'Do you want me to say yes . . . or no? I'm a bit lost with this one, my friend.'

'I want you to say no, obviously,' I huff.

'Well, he is going, so there's no point lying to you about it.' I twitch my nose, deep in thought for a moment. Tyler raises a finger to stop me in my conversational tracks, lest I say no too decisively. 'One compelling reason to do it could be the fact that we have . . .' They raise their eyebrows meaningfully. 'A budget.'

'A budget, you say?' I reply keenly, but not too keenly. Got to play it cool, remember? Not that playing it cool has ever been my strong suit. Too earnest and too enthusiastic, that's me. But not today!

'We were paying him £200, but I can do £250 for you . . . an inconvenience fee, you know?'

'I want £275,' I say instantly, hoping I'm so fast that Tyler will just agree to it because they're so relieved I'm entering into negotiations.

'My final offer is £262.50,' they say even more quickly than I had, as if they had come prepared with this exact figure in anticipation that the conversation would go precisely like this.

The specificity of the number provokes a smile that I simply cannot suppress, which turns into a laugh, and finally an agreement. I hold out my hand. 'Deal,' I tell them, grasping their slim hand in mine.

'It'll be fun.' They nod reassuringly. 'I know you want to

put the whole thing behind you, but I do think this'll be a good opportunity for you to make some money, get some more DJing experience.'

'And show Felix what he's missing,' I say, raising a finger as if I'm making a very important point, which I suppose I am.

'Er, yeah, that too,' Tyler says, though I can tell they're not entirely convinced, and who can blame them? I'm not entirely convinced either, I've just got hyped up in the moment. I blame the prospect of an unexpected £262.50 on my horizon. 'I can't tell you how much I appreciate it, mate.' It feels quite nice doing Tyler a favour actually. And the podcast, which was totally their idea, has given me a nice sense of structure and purpose away from the magazine.

'Now I have to think of something cute to wear,' I say, already mentally rifling through my wardrobe in search of something suitable.

'If anyone can come up with the perfect look-what-you're-missing-out-on-you-total-fuckboy outfit, it's you,' they say with a smile.

'That is precisely the look I'm going to go for,' I tell them.

They take their phone out of their pocket to check the time. 'Shit, I'm late for my tutorial – been spending too much time negotiating this business deal with you,' they tell me.

I hug them goodbye and wonder if I should have stuck to my initial instinct to not go. But no, it'll be good to see Felix. Remind him exactly how cool and talented – not to mention devastatingly gorgeous – I am.

CHAPTER 30

If I didn't know better, I would say that Felix is completely ignoring me. Not that I'm looking, of course, it's just that every time I glance in his direction, he's deep in conversation with some other girl. But the thing is, the night is going so well that I can totally live with it, because in every way other than getting direct attention from Felix, my plan is totally working. I am showing him that I am living, that I am thriving, plus I get to make some money. Bish, bash and indeed bosh.

Or rather, bish, bash, bosh and ... smash. It seems someone on the dance floor has got too into the spirit of celebration, and cheers go up around the room as a pint glass makes contact with the hard floor, sending glittering shards spinning off in different directions. Wonderful. People cluster in little groups, leaving the site of the smash an obvious void that Mark from the union rushes to clear up. Before long the glass has been collected, the pint has been mopped up and the dance floor is densely packed once again.

I'm bopping away behind the decks, very nonchalantly swaying my hips and trying to remind myself that this isn't my club night so I can – and more to the point should – play music released since my own birth. It's kind of fun to be doing something different, and I tell Tyler as much when they come to check on me and offer me a drink.

'No, I'm good,' I tell them.

'You're better than good. You're everything,' they say, pressing their palms together in prayer and bowing at me. 'Also, I'm obsessed with your look tonight!'

I glance down at my outfit: a pink denim boiler suit that wouldn't look out of place on the Pink Ladies from *Grease*, but paired with a tough pair of gladiator sandals (yes, I am brave enough to do exposed feet in January). Tyler's right. It's an outfit worthy of obsession.

I'm just about to ask them if they would mind holding the fort for a second so I can make a quick bathroom trip when they do an abrupt heel turn to the sound of last year's big hit of the summer and make a beeline towards one of the pretty girls that never seems too far away from Tyler. Maybe Tyler should have a dating podcast: *Romance for the Non-binary Rogue*. I should suggest that. But more urgently, I will absolutely die if I don't wee soon.

'Pat!' I cup my hands and call across the dance floor to where he and his immaculately dressed crew of gorgeous boys are bopping away. One of them nudges Pat and nods in my direction. Pat duly spins around and sees me waving at him. I gesture for him to come over and he approaches, slinking his hips through the crowd. 'Could you do me a favour? Could you look after the DJ booth while I go to the toilet? You can –' I take a deep breath – 'play anything you want, because I know you're not going to take the piss and ruin the vibe.'

Patrick places a hand on his chest dramatically. 'Take the piss and ruin the vibe? Moi? I wouldn't dream of it,' he says as we trade places and finally I am released from my duties for the briefest of moments.

'Sorry,' I say, grimacing at the girls in the toilet queue, 'I need to get back to the DJ booth. Is it OK if I . . .' I ask sweetly, and one by one the line consents to my social faux pas of queue-jumping. The girl at the front of the queue just happens to be the person Felix has been chatting to all night, so I take extra pleasure in cutting in front of her. As I'm waiting for a cubicle door to swing open, I'm taken aback that she taps me on the shoulder, and when I turn around, says, 'This is really fun, you're doing an awesome job.'

'Oh! Thank you! That's really nice of you.'

She just shrugs and smiles, the interaction over as a cubicle becomes free. I guess the problem was never the girls, was it? It was always just Felix.

Just as I make it back to the decks, when I'm one step away from the little raised area with the DJ booth, I bring up my foot, set it down, and that's when I feel it. The pain is instant and overwhelming, and radiates so sharply that I actually let out a gasp. I look down. There is a shard of glass sticking out of the side of my foot. It takes all my strength not to faint right there on the spot.

'Oh my God,' I murmur, just looking at it. 'Patrick,' I say a little louder. 'Could you keep holding the fort for a while longer? I have a slight . . . situation to deal with . . .'

He gives me an enthusiastic thumbs-up and I wonder if

I'll ever get my booth back or if this Quad Media party has turned into an all-night Britney fest.

For a moment I just stand there, looking at it, not sure what else to do, not sure how to deal with this situation, but somehow sure that whatever option I choose will be the wrong one.

'Mary-Elizabeth?' comes a voice from over my shoulder. I turn only the top half of my body, too scared to move my legs lest I disrupt the fine balance that's stopping the glass from going any further into the side of my foot. Laurie.

'Oh, hello,' I say, and my voice comes out a little shaky.

'What's . . . up?' he asks, surveying me with intrigue.

'It appears –' I begin, feeling a bit cold and clammy – 'that I've trodden on a bit of glass.' I look down again. Laurie follows my gaze.

'It does appear that way, doesn't it?' he says, his voice lighter and less serious than I've heard him before. But it doesn't sound like he's trying to make fun of me, or make me feel silly. 'Would you believe me if I told you I'm not afraid of blood and decently proficient in first aid?'

'I really, really would believe you,' I tell him through a weak smile.

'Let's get you out of here. It seems like your friend is doing a decent job of covering you already.' He nods towards Patrick, who has his hands in the air, and then holds out an arm so I can hop on my uninjured foot towards the back exit, which is being vigilantly policed by a security guard called Mike. We are absolutely not allowed to use any of the fire escapes outside of an emergency, but Mike takes pity on me and holds the door open for us so I don't have to hop all the way across the dance floor to the main exit and out through the union building.

On the bench outside the back exit, I can still hear the pulse and buzz of the music from inside. Everything sounds like it's under control. And it's just me and Laurie. I catch my breath. First, he gently takes off my shoe and surveys the damage. 'Doesn't look like it's in too deep, so that's something,' he says. 'I'm just going to go back inside and get the first-aid kit. They should have one behind the bar. Don't go anywhere.' He fixes me with a very serious look.

'I don't know how I would, even if I wanted to,' I reassure him.

'You just . . . seem like a person who doesn't like sitting still.'

'I think I can make an exception for first aid.'

Laurie disappears back into the union building, leaving me alone on the bench, my foot elevated, the shard of glass still . . . disgustingly present. Fortunately, he's not gone for long, and returns with the green first-aid kit, crouching down at my feet again.

He reaches into his pocket and produces a single green pear. 'You eat this while I sort your foot out.'

'Do you . . . do you always carry pears in your pocket?'

'Er, no, I just . . .' He clears his throat awkwardly. 'I just came here from my parents', and they have a shop and they get these pears from this one specific farm in Kent and they're always perfect.'

'Perfect, you say?' I hold out my hand and he puts the pear

into my palm. I feel the slightly rough, scratchy skin and the satisfying weight of it.

'I'm not saying it'll cure all your problems, but it certainly won't hurt.' Laurie looks up at me from his seat on the floor. Maybe it's the slight vulnerability of his position. Maybe it's my vulnerability at being a literal wounded animal. Maybe it's the taste of the pear as I bite into it, perfectly and completely ripe, the proof that if you let a pear be a pear in January, rather than trying to make an out-of-season lychee taste good, then you will experience something truly delicious. Maybe it's none of those things, but I can't help feeling . . . something. Something like my heart fluttering a little bit, something like my stomach flipping over like a pancake, something like that warm, tingly feeling of a crush.

After he's got all his necessary equipment out of the first-aid kit and I'm merrily nibbling away on my pear, trying not to make too much of a mess, Laurie fixes me with a serious stare.

'This is going to hurt a bit, but it'll be over soon,' he says, his tone calm and reassuring. 'I'm going to pull out the glass, clean the wound and bandage it up. If it doesn't feel right tomorrow, please do go to the medical centre because, just to clarify this, I'm not actually a doctor.'

I gasp. 'What? Really?'

He rolls his eyes at me, a brief glimpse of the Mary-Elizabeth and Laurie who met at that event way back at the start of the autumn term. 'Do you understand?' he asks me.

'I understand,' I reassure him.

When he pulls out the glass, the pain is possibly worse and

more head-spinning than when it went in, maybe because I'm extremely aware of it happening. I try to keep my breathing deep, but the thought of what's going on in my body is making me feel nauseous and weak. If you couldn't tell, I'm a little bit squeamish. 'Oh God, oh God, oh God,' I murmur as he disinfects the cut, the alcohol stinging so sharply I see stars in front of my eyes.

'You're doing really well, I'm nearly finished,' Laurie says, his voice steady and focused as he doesn't take his attention off the task at hand. He neatly wraps a length of bandage around my foot, cutting it and taping it securely. It actually looks quite stylish, I have to say. Very respectably done. 'Wiggle your toes for me?' he asks, and I do. 'Great. Does the bandage feel too tight or anything?'

I shake my head, my pink curls bouncing. 'You should be doing medicine rather than maths,' I say lightly.

He shrugs as he gets to his feet, dusts off a little bit of gravel from his hands on his trousers. 'Too expensive.' He doesn't look at me as he says this.

I frown. 'What do you mean?' I ask, trying to figure it out.

'Medical school,' he says, clearing his throat, bending to pick up the first-aid kit. 'It's . . . too many years. Easier to get a maths scholarship.'

'Oh,' I say, feeling silly and clueless. 'Of course, that makes sense. I just mean . . . you have a nice, calm manner.'

His face softens. 'Thank you.'

'I suppose I should return to my workstation . . .' I say reluctantly.

'Yes, you're on duty, aren't you?'

'Tyler's paying me big bucks to be here. Can't let them down.'

Laurie sighs thoughtfully. 'I don't know Tyler well but whenever I run into them at a Quad thing they just seem . . . so much happier now than they did last year.'

I nod. 'I agree.'

He gives me a slight smile. 'Who knew that being able to be yourself was the key to happiness?'

I finally push myself to my feet, and as I'm hobbling back towards the door to the union, I say lightly, 'You should put that in one of your columns.' But Laurie doesn't reply.

I limp back towards my booth, trying not to put too much pressure on my bandaged foot, and thank Patrick profusely for his hard work. 'Any time, girl! This DJing thing is fun, isn't it? Like being in charge of Spotify at a party!'

'It's exactly like that,' I agree, before looking over my shoulder to say goodbye to Laurie. But when I turn my head, he's already disappeared. Over by the bar, however, I catch a glimpse of Felix with his arms around the girl from the toilet queue, and for some reason the sight of him with someone else riles me up that little bit less than it did earlier this evening.

The adrenaline from the injury pulses around my system for the rest of the night and I'm shivering like I'm freezing to death. I was only gone for – what? – ten minutes between the bathroom trip and the first aid, but everything feels . . . different now. When I talked it over with my flatmates before Christmas, I thought these slightly unwelcome new feelings for Laurie would pass, but they haven't. That's OK though. I'm a strong, independent girlie and I won't be distracted by another boy! I can keep my head in the game, my eyes on the prize! I don't have room in my life for another crush. I'm much too busy and important!

CHAPTER 31

If he's there then I'll ask him. If he's not there then I'll just forget about the whole thing. That's the bargain I make in my head as I climb the stairs to the *Quad News* office. I'll leave it up to fate to decide. It's not up to me! It's up to fate! I don't care either way obviously. I'm just doing a good deed, returning the favour, making up for the fact that I didn't properly thank him last time, after the drink-spiking situation. And now once again he has come to my rescue, so I can't let it pass by again unthanked. That's not scary, it's not a big deal. It's nothing. Just asking Laurie if I can take him out for something to eat sometime. Just casual, like. Because while I'm in the danger zone of developing and/or cultivating a crush on Laurie, I'm not, like, there yet. So it's all fine. All under control. Don't care either way.

The fact that I don't care either way is probably why I stop outside the *Quad News* office and reapply my lipstick, making sure my cupid's bow is looking extra-sharp, the line of my lips extra-defined. I look myself over in the little compact mirror I carry around with me, fluff up my candy-floss hair, take a deep breath and knock on the door. I half expect no one to answer, but –

A low voice I recognise answers, 'Come in?' And instantly I feel butterflies flapping around in my stomach. I could just leave, do a runner, pretend I wasn't there. Felix kissing that other girl on the doorstep 2.0. But I don't. This time I'm going to see it through.

I push the door open and am immediately greeted by three faces turned to look at me. One is a guy I know to be Josh Levy, the investigations editor of *Quad News*; another is, mercifully, Laurie, and the third is Charlotte Sherman, seated very close to Laurie. Josh Levy I could deal with, but the presence of Charlotte has thrown me right off course.

'Um . . .' I say, feeling like I've been pushed out onto a stage under a glaring spotlight in front of a huge audience with no idea of what I'm meant to be performing. 'I was just looking for . . .' I try to think of a random name of someone from *Quad News* that I could feasibly have business with, and can only summon up the names of three *Quad* people, which are Josh Levy, Charlotte Sherman and Laurie O'Donnell. What was Lucie's ex-boyfriend called, the sports editor guy? But then again, why would I be looking for him. Shit. I just stare at them for a moment, wondering why I hadn't actually planned for this potential situation. It's because I'm too bloody optimistic, isn't it? This is my problem! Every time! 'Sarah Al-Aziz!' I say triumphantly, remembering the name of the girl who takes their photos around campus. Why wouldn't I be looking for Sarah Al-Aziz?

'She's not around at the moment – I think she's got a

lecture now. Were you meant to be meeting her?' Josh asks politely, pushing his dark-framed glasses up his nose.

'No . . .' I say vaguely. 'Just wanted to ask her about . . . cameras,' I say, knowing my eyes are darting around wildly like a trapped animal but the whole time I'm avoiding letting them land on Laurie's face. 'Not to worry! I'm sure I'll run into her somewhere around campus!' I say, pulling the door closed behind me and extricating myself from the situation as fast as I can.

Well, that was a mistake! You live and learn! Time to get out of here and erase it from my memory.

But I barely make it to the end of the corridor when the door opens.

'Mary-Elizabeth,' Laurie says, and I can't help turning back. 'How's your foot doing?'

'Oh! It's much better, thanks to your expert medical care! No need to go to the medical centre!'

'Great,' he says, nodding, his dark eyes staying on me like a laser beam. 'Not to . . . dispute your version of events, but were you really looking for Sarah?'

'Are you trying to tell me I'm not very good at improv?' I ask, feeling my cheeks warm up.

'It could do with some workshopping.'

'Well, the thing is, I just wanted to talk to you about something, but . . . it's not important,' I say, shaking my head. Why am I making such a mess of this? I'm usually very smooth and in control! Not a bumbling idiot!

'What . . . what was it you wanted to talk about?' he asks me.

I look up at him, swallow down my nerves. 'I wanted to ask if you would be OK with having dinner with me sometime. To say . . . to say thank you for all the nice things you've done for me.'

'You don't need to do that,' he says instantly, his tone a little gruff.

'I don't think I need to do anything. It's more that I . . . want to.'

'Well, then,' he says, before clearing his throat, his gaze locked with mine. 'I suppose it would be rude not to, wouldn't it?'

'I think so. And we know you're never rude.' I can't help smiling, and my brain is already trying to figure out what to wear. 'Are you free tomorrow night? Or maybe that's too soon,' I say, blushing at my keenness. 'You're probably busy.'

'Not busy,' he replies quickly.

'Oh, great!' The relief in my voice is audible, and I want to keep the conversation going so we can establish a plan and then I can get out of there. 'So, how about we meet at Da Antonio at the top of Charlotte Street at seven-thirty?'

He nods. 'I know where that is – it was near my halls in first year.'

'But you haven't eaten there?' He shakes his head. 'I think you'll like it,' I say, and then I twitch my nose in thought. 'I don't know why I think you'll like it . . . I don't really know you at all . . . maybe you'll hate it . . . but it's very convivial. That's what my stepdad always calls it.'

'Sounds perfect.'

When I walk through the quad to the bus stop, I break into an involuntary little skip for a moment. I can't quite believe it, but I'm actually a bit excited! OK, so I know I said I wasn't there yet, but I am now forced to admit that I might be there now. But that's all right, isn't it? I can keep everything under control, can't I? I need to remember that I'm Mary-Elizabeth Baxter, and I can do anything I put my mind to.

CHAPTER 32

'Just checking, you told me it's not a date, right?' Morgan says drily from her position on my bed, leaning back against the wall, looking very cool and nonchalant.

'Of course it's not a date,' I say impatiently. 'But you know me, I like to look nice all the time, not just for a date.'

A smile creeps across her face. 'I don't know, man,' she says, throwing her hands up. 'It kind of feels like a date.'

'I'm just doing something nice for someone who was nice to me. Not once but twice. Double nice.'

'And also, you think he's cute, right?'

'Undecided,' I lie. 'I regret mentioning it to you if you're just going to shame me for maybe having a little crush on him!'

'I'm not shaming you,' she says gently. 'I'm just being naughty.'

'Naughty I can tolerate.' I pull a slinky slip skirt in a vibrant fuchsia pink out of my wardrobe. 'This with my turquoise top? Or is that too much? Too clown?'

'I don't know what makes me say this given that I've never met him, but this guy seems like someone who isn't going to judge you for being, as you put it, too "clown".'

Now it's my turn to smile. 'I think maybe you're right. Clown fashion it is.'

Before I head out the door, I pick up a bright red-and-blue crocheted hood from my pile of winter accessories as defence against the cold. It will serve the dual purpose of establishing whether Laurie is the kind of person who doesn't want to be seen in public with a red-and-blue crocheted hood, and therefore is not the kind of person I can have a crush on.

On the way to the restaurant, I keep checking my phone to see if Laurie has cancelled on me, and have to repeatedly remind myself that he doesn't even have my number. I mean, I'm sure he could locate an email address for me if he really wanted to flake, but that's how little we know each other, how unconnected we are. When I get there, though, I see his large, slightly awkward figure waiting for me on the corner.

'Hi,' I say, reaching up to him to give him a hug, and although he's a little awkward, there's warmth and enthusiasm too. He smells nice, sort of clean and comforting, like a basket of laundry. Not expensive and decadent like Felix, just . . . lovely. 'It's just here,' I say, leading us towards the warm glow of the front windows. 'I hope it's OK.' I smile at him over my shoulder in a way that I hope is confusingly seductive, easy to dismiss as friendly if needed, but also very cute and gorgeous. Overthinking it? Moi?

'It looks perfect. And you look . . .' He pauses. 'Well, I like your, er . . . balaclava.' He gestures at my headgear. 'Very avant-garde.'

'Thank you, Laurie,' I say brightly, holding the door open for him.

We're seated at a cosy table in a little alcove with a good view of the whole restaurant, perfect for nosy girlies like me, although on this occasion I sense my attention will be pretty focused on my dinner date. I'm actually quite excited to properly talk to him and look at him in unchaotic conditions. Not that it's a date, of course; I'm just doing something nice for someone who was nice to me. But I have to say, he is looking rather nice this evening. I covertly look at him over the top of my menu, watch him twitch his nose as he contemplates what to order, watch his thick eyelashes bat slowly, gently. Ah, yes, there it is. The unmistakable feeling of a crush.

I order us the cheapest bottle of wine because although Dad's guilt money goes some way, it doesn't go that far.

'Cheers,' I say, clinking my wine glass against his.

'Cheers,' he repeats a little stiffly, eyeing me with . . . not suspicion, but maybe caution, like he thinks I might be making fun of him, or the situation. But I'm not. I'm really not. I'm just happy to be here.

'Thank you for listening to my section on the podcast, by the way. I'm glad you think it's . . . good, I guess?'

'With a name like that, how could I resist?' He smiles, and that soft, sweet, lopsided smile makes me feel happy I suggested this.

'I forgot you liked that song,' I say, even though I hadn't forgotten at all.

'It's funny . . .' he says, clearing his throat. 'I can't help but think of you when I listen to it now, not just because of the podcast, but because it sort of . . . sounds like you, in a way. All . . . carefree and fun and exuberant.' He doesn't look at me when he says this, which is how I know he's giving me a very sincere compliment.

'Thank you . . . I aspire to be all of those things,' I say, trying to act cool and nonchalant when in this moment I am very much neither. Usually I like throwing myself into a crush with complete abandon, but Laurie feels so . . . serious, so high-stakes somehow, that it's giving me nervous butterflies as well as excited ones. 'So, how's the newspaper these days?'

'Oh, not so bad. I mean, there's some behind-the-scenes nonsense I don't entirely approve of,' he says, glancing at me but not elaborating, as if I obviously know what he's talking about. Probably some high-level Quad Media stuff, the kind of thing Felix was always stressing about. 'But I like it. It gives me something to focus on that isn't maths.'

'I can't imagine having to think about maths all day . . .' I say, feeling a bit sick at the prospect.

'Lots of people feel like that,' he says lightly. 'But I probably feel just as confused when I look at a painting or a sculpture as you do when you look at an equation. It's . . . it's not that maths is harder than what you do. It's just different.'

'I hadn't really thought about it like that.' I shrug, but I realise he's right. 'And anyway, you don't need to feel confused. It's just a question of different ways of looking at art. Different theories, different experiences, different tastes. And . . . well, at least with some contemporary stuff, I think some of it is about being comfortable with not understanding it. Knowing that there are some things you can't know, can't understand. That when people make art, it's sort of . . . for them, not for you. Does that make sense?'

Laurie nods. 'It does. I think maybe for me, being clever and knowing things was a way to defend myself against feeling out of place or awkward . . . socially, I mean. So it's possible I have a tendency to avoid anything that makes me feel like I'm on the back foot or a bit baffled.'

'I wonder if maybe . . . instead of being baffled, you let yourself feel curious . . . maybe that would be something?'

'Maybe it would,' he says, his big brown eyes softening, sparkling a little. 'I think maybe my new year's resolution should be to give in to curiosity more.' He flicks his eyes down so he's not looking at me when he says it. 'Like tonight, I suppose.' Oh, hello!

He raises his glass to his mouth, and I decide to use these few seconds of silence to ask something I've wanted to know for a while. For no reason, obviously. Just curious. 'So, is Charlotte Sherman your girlfriend?'

Instantly he coughs, covering his mouth with his big paw of a hand. 'Sorry, just wasn't expecting you to ask that right then . . . or so early in the evening.'

'Sorry!' I say lightly, with another shrug. Because of course I am just curious. No big deal to me.

'You're very, you know, direct . . .' he says, catching his breath. 'I can't say I'm used to that.'

'I am what I am.'

'And in answer to your question, no, she is not my girlfriend. Not any more.'

'So . . . she used to be?' I ask, my curiosity (nosiness) piqued.

'We gave it a go. It didn't work out. I think she's struggling a bit with that.' I brace myself for him to tell me about some 'crazy' thing she did, some 'insane' way she expressed her desire to still be in a relationship with him, because that's what boys do. But he doesn't. He just leaves it at that. Or rather, diverts the conversation onto yours truly. 'And . . . Felix Balfour?' he asks, giving me a meaningful look. 'Still not your boyfriend?'

'Decidedly not my boyfriend,' I say firmly. 'And never was. Just a . . . a silly fling. I thought it would be more fun than it was.'

'Hm,' he says tightly, in lieu of anything more illuminating.

'What's your beef with him anyway?' The more time I spend with Laurie, the surer I am that Felix's account of their past is not 100 per cent the truth, but I'd still like to hear it from Laurie.

Laurie shakes his head. 'I'm fed up of talking about him – he takes up too much social oxygen as it is.'

'That's one way of putting it . . .' He's certainly taken up a lot of my social oxygen this year. 'So,' I decide to quickly change the subject. I felt like we were really getting somewhere before. 'You were in Hatton Hall last year?'

'Yep,' he says, nodding his head in a way that denotes 'up the road', which is exactly where Hatton is. At QAC, Hatton Hall is the cool halls, the one everyone seems to be in except you. It's the only catered hall, and that communal eating lends itself to a greater feeling of sociability. It's also one of the cheapest, despite being catered, with the highest number of people to a flat and the fewest facilities.

I smile. 'That surprises me,' I say gently.

'Yes . . . it's not very . . . me, is it?' Laurie says, suddenly a little bit less serious. 'I can't say I loved it. Parties almost every night, almost never quiet – it felt like everyone was on a sports team except me. I ended up going home a lot, just to get a good night's sleep.'

'Where's home?' I ask, sipping my wine and realising I barely know a thing about him. In terms of facts, at least. But if we're not talking facts, I have to say, I feel like I do know him. Or maybe that I understand him.

'Uh, Camberwell. My family have a shop, and we live in the flat above it,' he says quickly.

'The pear.' I smile at the memory of it.

'Exactly. Sorry, I forgot I'd already told you that.'

'No, it's interesting! I like imagining people in their places, with their people. I'm nosy, I suppose, but I find you interesting.'

'Well, it's nice of you to say that, but I always had this sense that people found me, you know, too . . . different from everyone else, maybe too boring . . . until I started writing for the newspaper, and then I felt like I'd, you know, found people I got on with.'

'That's good,' I say, feeling a tug of sympathy for the old Laurie, all adrift at university. 'I think finding your people is the hardest part. Maybe harder than the classes . . .'

Laurie looks at me with surprise. 'I can't imagine you finding it hard to make friends.'

'It's not about making friends. It's about making the right friends.' I tell him. 'I know it's easy for me – someone who can and indeed will chat to anyone – to say, but that doesn't mean everyone is someone that I like or trust or want to have a deeper relationship with.'

He nods. 'That makes sense.' Our waitress sets down our pasta in front of us. 'So, yeah, it took me a while to find my feet at QAC, but that's . . . well, that's nothing new,' he says a little ruefully.

'Why's that?' I ask, spearing a tube of rigatoni. 'The nothing-new part, I mean.'

'Well,' he says, setting his fork down, 'I went to my secondary school on a scholarship.' I don't tell him that I already know that, from Felix of all people. 'And it was a real thing there, you know? It's quite an expensive, old-fashioned school, lots of money around, so obviously anyone who's there on a scholarship is looked at as a bit of an interloper. You have to really . . . want to fit in, and I just didn't want to play the game. There was some other stuff towards the end, but that was really just the icing on the cake. And then I thought maybe university would be different.'

'And it wasn't?' I venture.

'I mean . . .' He sighs. 'It was definitely better . . . there are more different people here. And it was a fresh start, so that was something. But in lots of ways it's no different. It's easiest for the people who have always found everything easy. Or had things made easy for them.'

I think of Felix's house, just sitting there waiting for him. His certainty that he'd get in to Queen Anne's, his dismissal of any suggestion that he'd be rejected from the university. 'I . . . I can see what you mean.'

'This is delicious, by the way,' Laurie says, clearly at his limit of talking about himself. 'I absolutely love mushrooms but often find people don't know what to do with them and they end up rubbery and tasteless. But not these.' He twirls some linguine around his fork with great enthusiasm, and I can't help but smile.

'I'm glad I chose an appropriate venue, and that you're enjoying your thank-you meal.'

'I . . . I really am.' He sets his fork down on the edge of his plate. 'So –' he raises his eyebrows and smiles – 'do you come here often?'

'Ha!' I say, blushing at the silly turn of phrase, and assuming he used it intentionally. That's good, isn't it? If that's, you know, the Laurie O'Donnell version of flirting? I flick my eyes away from his face, not wanting to look at him looking at me blushing and slightly wrong-footed. Instead of looking at Laurie, I cast my eyes around the restaurant, looking at the bustling room full of busy tables. 'But, yes, I've been here before with . . . my . . .'

And that's when I see him. Stephen, my silly, bumbling stepdad, on the other side of the restaurant, holding hands with . . . not my mum. Some other woman. But definitely not my mum, not least because she's wearing a yellow dress, and my mum has never worn yellow in her life. 'Fuck.'

'What's the matter?' Laurie asks, his brow furrowed.

'I'm . . .' I say, getting up as discreetly as I can. 'I'm really sorry but we have to leave right this second. Or at least, I do. You . . . you should stay. I'll . . . I'll pay on the way out . . .'

He laughs, slightly disbelieving. 'I'm not going to stay without you. What on earth is the matter?'

I feel hot and dizzy, the rush of panic at the sight of what I think is very clearly Stephen cheating on my mother passing through my whole body.

'I can't stay. I have to go.'

'Let me come with you then,' he says, abruptly getting up from his seat, the sudden scraping sound drawing the attention of diners nearby but fortunately not Stephen, who's clearly lost in the eyes of this woman in the yellow dress.

'OK,' I say, nodding quickly. 'But we have to be really fast. And discreet.'

'I'll . . . try not to knock any tables over?' he offers, finally understanding that something serious is going on.

As we creep as subtly as we can from one side of the restaurant to the other, I'm torn between not looking towards Stephen in case it makes him look at us and wanting to check if he's noticed me or if I'm getting away with it. Finally, we make it to the till by the exit.

'Everything OK?' our waitress asks, disturbed by our sudden appearance at the cash register, coats on and ready to bounce out of there.

'Yes, sorry, something came up and we have to leave quite urgently,' I say apologetically, but feeling even more apologetic towards Laurie, who I can't help feel I have seriously short-changed. But I can't stay here. I have no idea what to do. And if I stayed, I'd spend the whole evening watching them, rather than being present in the conversation with Laurie. Either way, we lose. So we might as well leave undetected.

'I'm sorry to hear that,' she says, pressing buttons on the screen and producing our bill, which I pay quickly.

'Thanks so much, we'll be back another time!' I assure her as we head out of the door, my cheeks burning at how things have gone, my head spinning with anger.

I take one last look back through the window into the bustling dining room. Stephen and this yellow-dress woman don't look out of place in the cosy, warm, loving atmosphere that included me and Laurie just a few moments ago. Of course, I look for just a second too long, and with his hands entwined across the table with this woman's, Stephen glances in my direction, and for one long moment our eyes meet. The look on Stephen's face tells me everything I need to know. It's like he's seen a ghost.

CHAPTER 33

Bleurgh. I regret to report that it's happening again: the inclination to slip into hibernation mode. But I really, really don't want to get back into bad habits, don't want to let life stress get on top of me and throw me off my studies again this year. So I decide to do something different, and just force myself to carry on as usual while I figure out what to do. Because, of course, I have to do something. Whether that's telling my mum or not telling my mum, both of those things are doing something. One is disrupting, the other is lying. I don't particularly want to do either.

The weight of responsibility is an unfamiliar feeling and I do not care for it, I have to say. Second year has been an absolute scam. First Year was so easy breezy, just bopping around and indulging crushes and finding out I'm actually quite good at art history and getting into *Quad Magazine* and making friends. Second year is altogether too real for me, I'm afraid.

Stephen is, of course, blowing up my phone with texts and calls and even emails – not sure he's emailed me before in his life, but so great is his consternation that he must try every possible line of communication. I'm letting him sweat, refusing to answer every call but not blocking his number because I want him to have the false hope that I might actually answer this time. I want him to listen to the ringing and think that maybe I'm going to pick up. I can tell from his texts that I have not, in fact, misinterpreted the situation.

Mary-Elizabeth, please talk to me.

We need to talk.

Please don't tell your mum.

Can we please talk?

Have you told her yet? I can't tell if she's being off with me today or if it's just a coincidence.

Oh, Stephen, you absolute idiot.

I'm home alone; both Aleesha and Morgan are out at lectures and I'm just lying on the sofa staring at the ceiling, wondering what to do, when the doorbell rings. It's never anything good. Always the Jehovah's Witnesses trying to convert me. But it might be a delivery for either of my flatmates, so I grudgingly trudge to the door in my polka-dot pyjamas and chic Moroccan slippers with a pom-pom on the toes.

I swing the door open, ready to receive whatever mystery item the girls have ordered, when –

'Ah, I did remember right,' Laurie says with a smile.

'Oh! It's you!' I say, more than a little taken aback. For a moment we just stand there, not sure what to do next. 'Do you . . . want to come in?'

'If you're not busy?'

'I'm not busy,' I say, fighting my natural urge to slam the door in his face and run to my room to change out of my pyjamas and put on a full face of make-up. Although something about him makes me feel like I'm allowed to be an unpolished version of myself.

'I thought maybe you needed someone to talk to.' Laurie steps into my flat and I close the door behind us.

'How did you know where I live?'

'When you slept at mine, before you left you told me your address in case you needed taking home again . . . and I remembered it. Or at least, I thought I did. Turns out I actually did. Sorry if . . . if it's weird, me coming here?'

I shake my head quickly. 'Not weird. Nice.'

He swallows and nods, relieved. I gesture for him to sit on the sofa.

'Do you want a –' I begin, but he cuts me off.

'Horrible, lovely, milky coffee?' he suggests.

I nod. 'Exactly.'

'Sounds delicious.'

Standing in the kitchen, waiting for the kettle to boil, a profound sense of peace comes over me. Laurie is here. Laurie will, if not help, then not make things actively worse. And more to the point, I don't need to perform for him, don't need to impress him, don't need to chase him. And I can't help but wonder what would have happened last night if we hadn't been rudely interrupted by stupid Stephen being a cheating dickhead. Would there have been a kiss? No, probably not. I think Laurie's too shy for that. But I'm not. Would I have felt it was the right thing to do? Or would I have sensed that was too much for him, too quickly? I'd like to think the evening would have ended on a hopeful note, rather than me dashing off to the tube station, leaving Laurie slightly bewildered in a hail of apologies shouted over my shoulder.

I hand him a steaming mug and sit down next to him on the sofa.

'How are you today?' he asks simply.

'I have been better.'

'Do you want to tell me what's going on?'

I sigh, but nod. 'I saw my stepdad cheating on my mum at the restaurant last night. That was why we had to leave.'

'God,' he says, shaking his head.

'And he saw me through the window and is now ringing me non-stop and texting me and emailing me, asking me to talk.'

'Do you want to talk to him?'

I shrug. 'I'm waiting to figure out what the right approach is.'

'And I assume your mum doesn't know?'

I shake my head. 'Nope.'

'Are you two close?'

I shake my head again, take a sip of the coffee. Perfectly horrible in its own special way. 'Not really. We have a bit of a difficult relationship, and I think this would absolutely tip it over the edge if I told her. Like it would be my fault, you know?'

'And do you think not telling her would damage your relationship too?'

'Exactly. I think if I didn't tell her, and she found out that I knew . . . I don't think she would be able to forgive me for that. I think she would think I was judging her or . . . mocking her, somehow, for having this knowledge about her that she didn't have. It's complicated.'

'No, I understand,' Laurie says gently.

'I think maybe . . . what's rattling me the most is that I don't know anything. Like I don't know anything about anything! All my life I thought my mum was the problem with all her flirting, but actually it's my stepdad who's . . . who's . . . the cheater,' I say, barely able to believe it myself. 'What's even the point of me? This whole year has just been one thing after another proving to me that I don't know the first thing about relationships and dating and romance, can't give good advice to other people and can't make good decisions for myself! I'm useless!'

Laurie's brown eyes soften. 'You're not useless. You're the least useless person I've ever met.'

'Really?' I ask pathetically.

'Really. You're so dynamic . . . always trying things. You don't need to know everything. You just need to keep trying. Doing what you think is the right thing to do.'

'The right thing to do would be Stephen telling her. Whatever way she finds out, it's going to be quite shit for her – they've been married for, like . . . ten years? So he's not just some random boyfriend. But him telling her would be the least shit approach.'

'Can't you tell him that then? That you'll tell her if he doesn't, and that will negatively impact your relationship with her, and this is something he could do for both of you to dampen the blow?'

'I . . . I had thought of that, but hadn't thought about it from the angle that it would be helping me as much as anyone else. Maybe that will appeal to him – if he thinks he's doing me a favour after putting me in this situation, you know?'

'It's worth a try,' Laurie says, nudging my knee with his, and amid all the anxiety and stress about my mum and Stephen, I feel . . . warm. Calm. Safe. Excited, too, by the feeling of Laurie's knee against mine, the warmth and the presence of him, being able to breathe in his clean, powdery scent, but mostly just . . . good.

'I think you're right. Thank you, Laurie. Thank you for coming over,' I say, and with a sigh I rest my head on his shoulder.

We sit in silence together, and the longer the silence lasts, the closer our legs move towards each other. This is not necessarily what I was expecting to happen when he came over today. But maybe it's happening. My heart starts beating fast and I'm overwhelmed with an urge. 'Laurie,' I say, my head still on his shoulder, very much not looking at him. 'For some reason I really want to kiss you now.'

'I . . . I think that would be OK,' he says, taking a deep breath.

I raise my head off his shoulder and lean towards him, our lips almost meeting when –

Bang! Bang! Bang!

Another knock on the door. What timing! What pure-evil timing! A confident, strong rap of the knuckles. I would be very surprised if that was Stephen – he doesn't have the guts to knock on a door so assertively – but I will be very pissed off if it is. 'Laurie, I'll be back in a second. Don't go anywhere, I'm just going to see who that is.'

He nods and I leave him sitting on the sofa. On the assumption that it's not Stephen, I pause in the hall for a second and send him a text.

Tell Mum TODAY or I will. And stop calling me, I don't want to talk to you. Got it?

Surely this time it's got to be the postman?

But when I impatiently open the door, my stomach drops.

'Felix?' I ask, trying to style out my surprise. What the hell? As if Laurie being here wasn't weird and unexpected enough!

'Look,' he says, 'I was in the area photographing some brutalist architecture and remembered you lived around here, and it made me think it was maybe worth a try coming to see you in person. I wanted to talk to you about coming back to the magazine. I know I fucked up, I know I hurt you,' he says, his eyes an approximation of softness and sincerity. 'And I'm not asking for us to get back together, not yet anyway, but the mag just isn't the same without you. You're so fucking good on that podcast and it drives me mad that we lost you, you know?'

'OK . . .' I say slowly, trying to take it all in.

'Can I come in?' He looks back over his shoulder, huddled against the rain.

'I don't think that's a good idea.'

'Come on,' he says, reaching out and brushing his hand against my arm. 'Just for a bit.'

I position my body defensively in the doorway, a sure sign of something to hide. 'No,' I say, shaking my head casually.

'Why? Is someone there?'

'What does that have to do with you?' I ask him, but the creaking of the floorboards in the living room pique his interest. Felix, the epitome of entitlement, pushes the front door open, unable to contain his curiosity. At the sound of the door banging against the wall in the hall, I hear Laurie walk out from the living room.

'Oh!' Felix laughs coldly. It's like a switch has been flipped at the sight of Laurie. 'Oh, this is wonderful, Laurie O'Doughboy swooping in for sloppy seconds? Of course he is, that's his trademark move.'

'What did you just call him?' I snap, ignoring the rest of what he said.

'Sorry,' he says sarcastically. 'Schoolboy nickname.'

'Felix, go,' Laurie urges him flatly, like Felix's mean words are just washing over him, like he's heard them a million times before. Laurie doesn't care about winning, about getting one over on Felix, about proving that he's superior in this situation. Laurie isn't interested in being the alpha, being the big name on campus. He just wants Felix to leave.

'As if you get to tell me what to do,' Felix says bitterly, pushing past me and towards Laurie, squaring up to him.

'Don't come any closer,' Laurie warns him.

'Or what?' Felix laughs. I just stand there, with literally no idea what to do and convinced, once again, that whatever I do will prove to be wrong.

'Felix,' Laurie says firmly.

Instead of listening to him and just turning around and leaving, Felix simply can't take being told what to do and everyone needs to know it. 'Or what?' he says again. But this time, he pushes Laurie in the chest. Just gently. But a push nonetheless.

Before I realise that Laurie has been stretched to his limit, he's already punched Felix. I gasp and cover my mouth with my hands, having never seen someone get punched before, much less right in front of me. Felix falls to the floor, but scrambles up quickly, keen to show he's not beaten.

'I'm going to fucking report you to the provost, you psycho,' he spits at Laurie, a trickle of blood running from his nose.

The punch was one thing but this, I'm afraid, is too much for your old friend Mary-Elizabeth. 'You wouldn't dare,' I say in a voice so icy that Felix literally does a double-take. 'There's more than one kind of violence and you're hardly blameless yourself.'

For just a moment, the veil slips and a flicker of recognition passes across Felix's face. 'All right, all right, I'll go,' he says, holding his hands up in mock defeat. 'You two can have each other.'

He slams the door behind him.

Laurie and I stand in silence for a moment. I'm completely shellshocked by the whole thing and have absolutely no idea what to say.

'I can't believe I did that,' Laurie says, looking at the ground. 'I . . . I don't do that. I'm not a violent person.'

'He provoked you!' I say, in absolute disbelief that Laurie thinks he was the problem in this situation.

'The temptation was always there, being so much bigger than the other boys, you know, when they would wind me up or bully me . . . but I never gave into it. And now I have,' he says quietly.

'Laurie,' I say sharply, pulling on the sleeve of his jumper. 'Look at me.' He looks up, his brown eyes mournful. 'If you didn't do it then I would have done. Felix Balfour is a menace, and someone needed to take him down a peg or two – it just so happened that it was you.'

Laurie shakes his head, pulls his arm away from me. 'I don't want to be this person, and now I am. I don't hit people, do I? But now Felix has made me a person who hits people, and I hate myself for it.' The bitterness is audible in his voice. He turns to the living room and re-emerges a moment later with his coat. 'Take care of yourself,' he tells me from the doorway, before opening the front door and stepping out into the rain.

In a daze, I walk back into the living room and sit on the sofa. I reach for my coffee cup. It all happened so quickly; the mug is still warm.

EXAM SEASON

CHAPTER 34

Here we are at summer term. Except it's not really summer. That still feels a long way off yet, since Queen Anne's College basically reserves the whole of the so-called summer term for revision, essays and exams. Much to do before *actual* summer.

Felix has been keeping his distance, which isn't surprising. Everything got so messy so fast with him. It was all meant to be a bit of fun and it's turned out not to be fun at all.

When it comes to Laurie, I don't want to be charging head-first into things like I always do, so I've been biding my time. I realise I really like him and I don't want to mess it up by accident before it's started. If anything will start . . . I don't want to mess up my exams either!

In the meantime, the club night and the podcast have kept me focused, along with a steady stream of questions. Here was one I really, really loved answering:

Hey, Genius,

Whenever I see you around campus, you always look so gorgeous and confident. You're always wearing something eye-catching, and the fact that you give out dating advice suggests you're not short of people interested in you. I just don't know how to achieve that for myself. I'm about the same size as you and I feel like my weight has always held me back from . . . pretty much everything. I guess I just have this voice in the back of my head that says, 'Why would anyone be into you when they have the option to go out with someone else who's thinner?' And I tell myself that I'll wear better clothes when I'm not so fat, but I don't know if that day will ever come, so I feel stuck! I just can't bring myself to believe that anyone would ever like me like that. How do I be more like you? Help!

Love,

Fat Girl in Limbo

Dear Fat Girl in Limbo,

Thank you so much for sending me this – I know it takes a lot of courage to talk about this stuff when it's such a source of anxiety. First, I have no doubt that you are wonderful, gorgeous and interesting. Simply no doubt about it in my mind. And second, I would hazard a guess that you really don't need to be more like me! You need to be more like you. What would you be wearing if you hadn't told yourself fashion was for other people? Who do you have a crush on? What would you be doing with the time and energy that you spend holding yourself back? I'm certain that dyeing your hair pink and wearing ostentatious clothes won't solve your problem, but I know that there's a version of yourself that you're not allowing to live fully, and she deserves to. What's the alternative? Holding her back for years, or even decades? Wouldn't it be exciting to find out what would happen if you lived the life you want now? It sounds fun to me, I have to say! I'm excited for you! In terms of your style, start by identifying the magic components of how you think you would dress if your body looked different. What excites you? What makes you feel comfortable? How can you adapt those 'comfort' styles to be closer to the way you want to dress? Would you dress more masculine? More feminine? More sleek? More playful? More daring? More minimalist? And if you can't put your finger on it and take action, maybe your style is fine but you're being bamboozled by the lure of thinness and the nebulous belief that you'll just wake up stylish if you get thin enough. Ain't gonna happen! Style comes from within, my friend, so you'd better start cultivating it now, on your own terms.

And now we come to dating, another area I simply love thinking about. One thing you need to understand is that the human mind and human sexuality is an unpredictable beast. It defies logic! I know we talk about people having a 'type', but really, if you delve deep into your brain and think about all the people you've ever fancied, were they all the same? Or were they kind of different? And can you always explain what you liked about them? I would guess the answers to those questions are 'no', 'yes' and 'no'. This school year I would say I've had two major crushes, and they couldn't be more different in terms of looks and personality. And yes, that extends to body size! Because there is nothing more gorgeous in the world than the sheer variety of humans. So to count yourself out of the running when it comes to romance is to deprive both yourself and other people of gorgeous, fun, thrilling experiences where you get to figure out what you like and what you want. I guarantee there is a long, cosmic list of people who have already fancied you in your life, but you had no idea because you weren't looking for the signs, because you believed yourself to be an undesirable person. I don't even need to see you to know that's not true. I could not be more excited for you, and I hope you take action ASAP!

Love,

Genius of Love

I felt like I was able to do a good deed with that one . . . it's sort of the point of why I do the podcast. But now exam season has crashed into me like a ten-tonne truck. Morgan and Aleesha have both gone back to their family homes to revise until the exams start, but I didn't think to do the same, and I'm . . . well, I'm sort of regretting it. I find I'm thinking about Laurie more than I want to, what with the weird silence since the stand-off with Felix at my flat. I've been giving him space; he's been keeping his distance. It's like we're both scared of making a move in case it . . . I don't know, *spooks* the other, like we're nervous horses. Anyway, I could do with a bit of company. And I think, with a little lump in my throat, my mum could probably do with a bit of company too. She's not used to being on her own either. Maybe answering that question for the podcast made me think of her. It made me realise that I was never brought up to feel bad about my body, and that this in itself might be a miracle. I can't help but wonder if I've been too hard on her. Alone in my living room, I take a deep breath and pick up my phone.

'Hello, darling, everything all right?' Mum says as soon as she answers.

'I'm fine, how are you?'

'Oh, you know . . . up and down, but this hallway won't paint itself!'

Instead of sighing and telling her off for embarking on yet another transformation, I ask, 'What colour?'

'A gorgeous hot pink – it was Stephen's one objection so I thought I should honour it while he was around. And, you know, he's . . . not around any more!' She says it brightly, but I can hear the pain in her voice no matter how hard she tries to conceal it. I was relieved that Stephen did decide to come clean to my mum and saved me the job. It was strange seeing this person who for so long I had just thought of as 'some guy' (even though he was technically my stepdad) wreak so much havoc on her. It was as if he had removed the wrong brick from the Jenga tower and her whole sense of self had come tumbling down. I've tried to see her more since then but never had the feeling that it was quite enough. All of which made this an even better idea.

'It sounds perfect. I'd love to see it actually. I was thinking . . .'

'Yes?' Mum says eagerly.

'I've got my exams coming up, and I could always come and revise at your house. Morgan and Aleesha are away, so I'm on my own here and –'

'Yes, do come,' she says, much too quickly. 'It would be so lovely to have you here.'

'OK,' I say, a feeling of relief washing over me.

'Do you want me to come and pick you up, darling? I don't mind driving.'

'No, that's OK, I don't mind taking the train.'

'If you're sure?'

'I'm sure. And maybe I'll come . . . this evening? If that's not too soon?'

'Well, that's just wonderful. I'll have a quick tidy up and I'll look forward to seeing you later. Bye, darling.'

'Bye, Mum,' I say before hanging up. I really hope this isn't a mistake, but deep down I'm pretty sure it's not.

* * *

Once I've packed all my notes and clothes and whatever else a girl needs for a couple of weeks of solid toil, I head to the tube station and cruise down to London Bridge to hop on the train. The whole journey literally takes me less than an hour, and the fact that I've made so little effort to go home and see my mum over the past month fills me with a shame so burning I feel my cheeks heat up as I stare out of the window for the mere ten minutes it takes to get from London Bridge to Deptford. But it's not like she has been desperately trying to make plans with me either . . . Then again, she's had a lot going on . . . but then again, so have I. Maybe I should cut myself some slack. Draw a line under it and try to do better. That's what I'm doing now, right? That's why I'm going, to keep her company.

'Hello, darling!' she says, drawing me into a tight hug as soon as I step through the door of the small but perfectly formed terraced house to the smell of fresh paint. 'Be careful! Don't touch the walls!'

The hot pink, I have to admit, does look extremely cool. But then again, so did the gentle duck egg before it, and the Yves Klein blue before that, and the stark white before that. It always looks good. There's never anything wrong with it.

'Looks great,' I say, skirting my way through the hall with my bags and into the little living room. 'Very chic.'

'Chic is what we aim for, darling!' she says, and I'm pretty sure I've said those exact words myself in the not-too-distant past. The thought of it brings a smile to my face. 'What are you smiling about?' she asks lightly.

'Nothing. Just happy to be here, I think.'

'Well, I'm glad! You need a break, don't you? You work so hard all the time.'

'I don't feel like I've been working very hard this year . . . that's part of the problem. Last year I felt much more on top of stuff by this point, but now . . .' I sigh.

'Had a lot going on?' she asks, sitting down next to me and stroking my hair.

I nod. 'A bit. How are you doing?'

'It's strange without Stephen but . . . not unpleasant, I must say.'

'I suppose he was part of the furniture really. He was just sort of . . . here.'

Mum nods. 'I hadn't really spent that much time thinking about how I felt about him, which is maybe a bad sign.'

'Not that it excuses what he did,' I say, lest we forget his crime to which I was a witness.

'Not at all,' Mum says, jumping to her feet. 'Have you eaten?' I shake my head. 'Well, we can't have that, can we? Let's order something fun.'

'Garlic beef pho?' I offer as a suggestion, as if there's any question of what we're going to order.

'What a great idea,' Mum says, as if it wasn't the exact thing she was thinking too. 'Oh, and some of that divine salt-and-pepper squid.' Again, we have never ordered garlic beef pho without salt-and-pepper squid.

* * *

When the takeaway arrives and Mum has pressed an incredibly generous tip into the delivery driver's hand, we sit in the living room, the strong scent of the food mingling with the not unpleasant smell of the paint.

'Mum . . .' I venture.

'Yes, darling?'

'You know all the . . . home transformations?'

'I do,' she says, before picking up a piece of squid.

'Is it . . . I mean, is it healthy? Like, are you maybe . . . chasing something with all the change, all the makeovers? Something you can never really catch?' I say gently, wondering about that question I had on the podcast the other week.

'Darling, the thing you need to understand is that I don't think these little makeovers are going to change my life. I think you've got it wrong there. I enjoy the act of doing them. The point isn't the fantasy, it's the doing part. Does that make sense?'

It surprises me, I have to say, that she has thought about this. Maybe I need to give my mother more credit. Clearly, I do.

'I guess so,' I say, shrugging.

'I mean this in the kindest possible way, darling, but . . . not everything is a problem for you to diagnose and solve in a column. Some things just . . . are.'

I smile. Ordinarily this is the kind of comment that would set off a sharp little skirmish between us. 'No, you're right,' I say, appropriately put in my place by my mum. 'But I didn't know you really knew about my advice column.'

'You told me about it when you got given it last year!'

'I know . . . but I thought maybe you'd forgotten. It's not like it's important, you know?'

'It sounds important to you. How's it all going?'

'Well, I've had a bit of a change of scenery and I'm doing it as a podcast rather than in the magazine.'

'Exciting!'

'Yeah, it's . . . it's been a good change. I had to get out of the magazine. Too complicated. Boy stuff.'

'It's good to know when to get out,' she says.

'It was definitely the right time.'

After we eat, we lie around watching TV. I could have been doing this all the time, but I'd been keeping my distance because, what, I find my mum a bit annoying? It makes me feel so silly and immature that I couldn't just get over it and hang out with her more.

When the random programme about Second World War air force pilots (that we were both too lazy to turn over) finishes, I get to my feet. 'I think I'm going to go to bed so I feel nice and ready to revise in the morning.'

Mum squeezes my hand before I head upstairs. 'Good idea. I'm glad you're here, darling.'

'Me too,' I tell her.

* * *

I spend the next week deep in my books (punctuated by little daydreams about Laurie), going for little walks down to Greenwich (wondering if Laurie has been in any of the places we go), helping my mum change the handles on a chest of drawers (don't think I thought about Laurie then), changing the configuration of a gallery wall that lines the steep stairs up to the bedrooms (again, DIY seems to be a Laurie-free zone for my brain) and just chatting to Mum and watching TV (contemplating what Laurie watches on TV).

One night, as we're eating a delicious pasta I've prepared, the fancy mafalde from the Italian deli all frilly and coated in spinach and goat's cheese and pine nuts, I remember something I've been meaning to ask Mum about. 'Whatever happened to that Sabor jeans shoot you were asked to do?'

Mum sighs heavily. 'I've been thinking about it, sweetie. It's not for another, oh, couple of months, and I haven't turned it down, but . . . it's hanging over me a bit.'

'I think if it's stressing you out then maybe you should just say no,' I offer.

'The thing is, darling, I want to do it.'

'So what's the problem?'

'It sounds silly,' she sighs, 'but I wish I was just . . . someone else. I wish I could do the shoot, but could have someone else's face. Someone else's body.'

'But there's nothing wrong with the way you look,' I protest.

'You have to say that,' she says, a sad smile on her face.

'No, I don't, you know I could be a rude little troll if I wanted to. But I don't want to, because it's true.'

'It's just hard,' she says, shaking her head, her curls bouncing. 'When you used to make money off your appearance, it ends up being the most important thing about you. And then it changes. And now I'm wondering if it's too late to bring it all back. I'm sure a little lift here and a little injection there wouldn't do any harm.'

'Are you really thinking about that?' I ask as neutrally as I can.

'I've been to see someone, a nice doctor that Laila Benayoun recommended on Harley Street,' she says, referencing one of her model pals. 'I'm giving it some thought. And if I really hit it hard, I could lose, what, at least a couple of stone between now and then, couldn't I?'

I shrug. 'That's not my area of expertise,' I tell her, my chest heavy. We sit in silence for a moment. Then I break it. 'There's something I don't . . . understand,' I say, trying to think it through in my head.

'What, sweetie?' she asks me as she takes a sip of rosé.

'If you're so critical of your own appearance, so worried about what people think about you, why have you never been hard on me about the way I look? Not that I want you to be, I mean. I'm just curious, I guess.'

She sets her wine glass down on the side table next to her end of the sofa. She turns to me and cups my face in her hands. I don't have any urge to wriggle away, to roll my eyes at her, to tell her she's being too much. I just want to hear what she has to say. 'Because you're perfect. Why would I want to change a thing about you?'

For all my mum's been hard work my whole life, one thing she's never done is try to change me or the way I look. I don't think I really understood until now how lucky I am – and given how much she struggles with it herself, it all seems even more miraculous. She lets go of my face and I feel my eyes prick with tears.

'I think that's why I . . . why I'm so against you doing anything to your face. Not on an ideological level, you know?' I say, trying to fight back the urge to cry. 'I don't really care what people do with their bodies, or how they want to express themselves. But . . . when I grow up I hope I look like you . . . and I want to know what that means. Does that make sense?'

I've never seen my mum look at me the way she's looking at me now. She's always been so touchy-feely, throwing herself at me, pawing me and pinching me. But I feel a greater sense of intimacy and genuine connection from this look than from any hug, any kiss.

'I've realised something . . .' I say, my cheeks burning with shame that it's taken me so long to get here. 'I've always been hard on you because I *could* be hard on you, because you're around. Whereas my dad always gets a free pass because he's . . . well, wherever he is . . . So it's harder to take my frustrations out on him than it is on you. And I think I understand now how –' I struggle to find a big, important word to describe it; there isn't one – 'wrong that is for me to do to you.'

'Darling,' Mum says, 'I think maybe we finally understand each other.'

And I realise that's what I've wanted all along.

CHAPTER 35

When my exams actually start, I return to the flat in Tufnell Park with Aleesha and Morgan. I can't be commuting to do my exams now, can I? Not when there's a perfectly good flat with perfectly gorgeous flatmates waiting for me on the Northern Line. And when I leave my mum's house, I feel lighter than I have in a very long time. Between properly committing myself to revision with no distractions, and feeling like me and my mum are actually on the same page for the first time in my life, everything looks that little bit brighter. More possible.

'This was a good idea,' Aleesha exhales, breathing in the calming scent of the tea cooling in the cup in front of her. I forced the pair of them to participate in a Salon de Mary-Elizabeth with me, on the grounds that we can't spend literally all day every day studying and that it'll be good for their brains to switch off for a couple of hours. So far we've done massages on each other that we learned on YouTube, I've given them both manicures – Morgan's mostly so she doesn't bite her nails down to tiny little jagged stumps – and I've been using a gua sha stone on their faces, which allegedly promotes 'lymphatic drainage' and I don't know what that is but I do know that it feels sort of nice.

'Yeah, man,' Morgan concurs. 'I heard you scraping around at like two o'clock in the morning last night. You need a break.'

Aleesha sighs. 'I know. I just . . .'

'What?' I urge her.

'It's a lot of responsibility, that's all. Being the first person in my family to go to uni and all that. Shit's expensive too.'

I squeeze her shoulder, what with her hand being out of action due to my manicure skills. 'Honestly, I don't know how you do it. Natural sciences is no joke.'

'I guess the weight of my family's expectations is how I do it.' She chuckles darkly.

'I hear you . . . but I've seen how consistently you've worked the whole year. Do you really think staying up late to study is going to make that much of a difference at this point?'

'Or maybe a good night's sleep would be more useful?' Morgan offers gently.

Aleesha nods. 'Maybe you guys are right. I mean, I already feel a bit clearer-headed after taking this time away from my laptop. If I got a good night's sleep, who knows what miracles I could accomplish?'

'Rest, hydration and a sense of zen. That's what we need to get us to the end of the year.'

'Rest, hydration, zen,' Aleesha repeats after her.

Of course, the energy on campus is not zen and is, in fact, totally manic: people bumping into each other in the quad because their noses are buried in reams of notes; queues for the library starting forty-five minutes before it even opens, so desperate are people to get a seat near a plug socket. Unlike at some other universities, every year of every course at Queen Anne's College 'counts' towards your final degree classification. Back in first year, I had no idea what friends from school were even talking about when they said they didn't care how they did in their end-of-year exams because it didn't make a difference. We have to be on our guard for the entirety of our degree. How's that for rigorous?

On the last day of exams, as I'm emerging, blinking into the gorgeous summer sunlight from my two-hour Sculpture in Space exam, in which I've written a blinder of an essay about land art, I'm once again pounced on by one Tyler Shaw, fresh from their penultimate history exam.

'Mate, did you hear?' they ask, their eyes full of that manic exam-season energy.

'Hear what?'

'*Quad* mag is –' They draw a line across their neck with a finger.

'Oh my God, what? It's finally happened?'

'Finally,' Tyler says, nodding. 'The axe has fallen.'

'I guess Felix couldn't save it in the end,' I say, shrugging. 'The end of an era.'

'I mean . . . within the magazine there wasn't much will for it to continue. By the end it was sort of his vanity project. Most of us wanted it to end, or at least for Felix to fuck off.'

'I didn't know that . . .'

'Well, you leaving was sort of the beginning of a downward slide. You brought the good vibes, plus everyone could tell

Felix had wronged you somehow even if they didn't know exactly how, and I think there was a lot of . . . defensiveness towards you, in a way? So with you gone, everyone's resentment towards Felix just . . . grew, so the only one fighting for the magazine's continued existence was him.'

'It's nice that people think of me like that . . .' I say, my eyes flickering to the floor, unable to meet their gaze.

'Oh, yeah, for sure. Plus it's like, "whatever" for me, because I've got you on the cheeky little pod, haven't I?' they say with a smile, but I'm still lost in my thoughts about *Quad Magazine* disappearing.

'So it's just . . . gone?'

'Eh, sort of. Bits of it are being subsumed into the paper. We're having an end-of-year party that's sort of a farewell to the magazine. You should come,' they say cheerily.

'Ty . . .' I say grudgingly.

'What? You're invited – I'm inviting you now.'

'I don't know . . .'

'You were an important part of *Quad Magazine*! People will want you there!'

I nibble my lip for a moment, thinking about it. As much as I don't want to see Felix, I really, really do want to see Laurie, and this might be a good excuse to do it without having to make a move of my own. 'OK, I accept your invitation,' I say finally. 'Let me know when and where and I will be there in my swishiest dress, with absolutely zero chat for Felix.'

'That's the spirit! You never know, he might not even turn up.'

'We live in hope.'

I head to the studio to get a couple of problems recorded that Tyler can drop into podcasts over the summer. My brain is exam-fried, so I choose a nice one first, something to which I'm sure I know the answer.

Dear Genius of Love,
I've been feeling really down since my break-up a few months ago and just want to feel like my old self again. How do I bounce back after living in a little depressed troll hole for months?
Love,
Lost Soul

Dear Lost Soul,
Well, the good thing is, it sounds as if you like your old self, so that's something. There's nothing worse than suffering a setback or a big drama and realising your whole life is just rubbish and you don't know where to go from there. So! We need to focus on getting you back on track. I'm so sorry that you've been feeling so down. Break-ups suck. Big time. There's no sugar-coating it and the only thing that can really get you through that is time, so I'm glad you're a few months out from the break-up itself. Basically, everything you're saying to me leads me to believe you are in the perfect position for the comeback after the setback. Now, for the practical steps: first, how would you identify your old self? What did you like about them? What did that person do, on a daily or weekly basis, that you've stopped doing? Make

a list of things you know have dropped out of rotation since the break-up. Is it a hobby? A place? A group of friends? Something to do with your image, like wearing make-up or doing your hair? Are you less interested in what you're wearing these days when you used to be well into fashion? For example, I'm a very sociable and extroverted person, and I knew things were not going well for me when I wanted to avoid everyone and hide in my room. The next step is choosing one of those things to do tomorrow. What would be an easy win? Pick the low-hanging fruit first. If you used to love painting your nails but haven't done it for ages, do that. Then, if you've been avoiding going to football practice or to LGBTQ+ Network meetings or whatever, build up to that. Try to remember the things that made you the person you are, the things you loved, and get them back in circulation. And once you've done that, maybe think about a new thing you've always wanted to try, like playing tennis or learning to knit or whatever, and adding that into your life when you have time. Because you're not just the old you, you're also a new you, and that's exciting! Treat this time like a new, exciting gift: you're ready to get back out there and be part of things! How exciting is that?

Love,

Genius of Love

CHAPTER 36

Hot-pink lipstick. My most obnoxious false lashes. My favourite babydoll dress. Some silly little strappy shoes. This is all I need for the *Quad* end-of-year/end-of-magazine party. I want to wear my initial necklace, my little symbol of sparklier times before it all went a bit shit, but have I done one single thing about untangling it? No. I have not.

'Felix can't make it,' is the first thing I hear when I walk through the door of the union. Tyler is right up on me, reassuring me that it's actually completely fine for me to be here.

'Oh?' I say, my nerves calming a little bit at this news.

'Yeah, he's stuck at the . . . Guadeloupean Embassy sorting out his visa or something.'

I check the time on my phone. 'At this hour?'

Tyler shrugs. 'Might be an excuse, who knows?' they say. 'Let me get you a drink. They're trialling some weird pink lemonade shit that's got Mary-Elizabeth Baxter written all over it.'

'Sounds like a bit of me,' I say, scanning the room for Laurie. But no Laurie yet.

'Cheers,' Tyler clinks their glass against mine when they bring the drinks over. 'End of an era.'

'End of a bloody era.' I take a sip of the pink lemonade and, to my delight, it is truly delicious. 'Ten out of ten, would drink again.'

'Ooooh, watch out, your nemesis is about,' Tyler says, raising their eyebrows and looking over my shoulder. When I turn, I see Laurie sloping in and my heart does a little backflip. The crush is, unfortunately, inescapable and embedded at this point. While I was revising for my exams, I would use daydreaming about Laurie like a little holiday. I would take a break from reading Clement Greenberg's essay 'Avant-Garde and Kitsch' and let my brain try to conjure up his face, his hands, his smell, the way he slept all pretzelled up in that chair and, more than anything, that kiss that almost was.

'Oh,' I say, smiling. 'I'd forgotten he was my nemesis.'

'He copied your column! You were fuming! What are you talking about?!' Tyler exclaims dramatically.

'It's a long story.' I sigh, and it strikes me how much my and Laurie's story has played out in private, how it wasn't something I shared with everyone in gossipy gasps and silly little vignettes about my life. It's like I knew he was something different. 'I'm not even that bothered he stole my column any more,' I add. 'I've achieved serenity, or something.'

'You're such a dark horse,' Tyler murmurs, as Katie Jones, the magazine's lifestyle editor, who is not making the cut for the newspaper staff next year, and esteemed features editor Lucie Hardy, who is returning to the newspaper now that her ex-boyfriend is about to graduate, slide up to us and join our chat. I participate as well as I can, but my attention is hovering around the room, trying to pick up on Laurie's location, mood, vibe, who he's chatting to, whether he's flirting with someone (ha ha, as if). Finally, the anticipation has built up inside me like a Coke bottle that's been shaken, and I can't keep it in any more.

'Sorry, guys, I'll be back in a second,' I tell Tyler, Katie and Lucie, who nod and get back to their chat, but when I scan the room again, I can't see Laurie anywhere. The panic sets in that I've missed him, that he's come and gone, and my chance to speak to him has evaporated until, what, the autumn? As romantic as it feels, this would be the downside to a whole crush played out in person, where we don't have each other's numbers, don't message back and forth between seeing each other. And then, finally, I spot him, ensconced at a round table with various people from the newspaper, including the ubiquitous Charlotte Sherman. The relief floods through me like a wave, the knowledge that he's not gone, that he's right here in front of me, at once comforting but also now something I have to act on. I take a deep breath, stand up straight, put my shoulders back and walk extremely confidently over to their table. I don't look at anyone else, not even Charlotte, and say directly to Laurie, 'Hi, Laurie, I'd love to chat to you if you've got a second?'

A murmur of intrigue goes up from around the table, but Laurie just nods and gets to his feet, extricating himself from the cosy corner.

'I'll be back in a minute,' he says over his shoulder. Charlotte is looking at me with the utmost disdain, whether for my general existence or specifically for my fake eyelashes.

I don't want to talk here with all these people around, so I lead us out of the union, round the back to the bench where he bandaged up my foot. Everything about tonight is different. I'm not injured. The air is warm. I know how I feel about Laurie.

Before I can begin, Laurie speaks. 'Mary-Elizabeth,' he says, not looking at me. 'I really want to apologise for what I did at your flat. I'm not proud of myself at all. It's really been weighing on me and I don't blame you if it's changed the way you see me.'

'Look, I can't stress enough how much I wish I'd punched him myself,' I say gently.

'I don't know if you know this, but . . . me and him, we have something of a history.'

I nod. 'Felix mentioned something.'

'Did he?' Laurie's voice is sharp. His head jerks up swiftly to look at me.

'Yes, but after I got to know you a bit, I didn't believe it.'

'What did he say?'

'Well, that's the thing, he was never very specific, just said something about . . . about you and a girl at school, and you being a creep?'

'God, he's such a piece of shit.' Laurie's tone is bitter in a way I've never heard it before.

'So what actually happened?'

'What actually happened is that Felix Balfour assaulted a girl at a party we were at. I found her afterwards, crying in a wardrobe – I could hear her, you know? Hiding and crying. I went into this spare bedroom just to decompress a bit – it wasn't my natural habitat, a massive party like that, but I went anyway because some of my mates were going, and there I was in this spare room and I hear this noise coming from a wardrobe and she's just in there. So I talked to her and she told me what had happened, and she was terrified I was one of his friends and I assured her I absolutely was not and that I wouldn't let him near her again, and we just chatted until she'd calmed down and felt a bit safer, and I asked her what she wanted me to do, and she said she wanted me to walk her to the bus stop. I told her she should get one of her parents to pick her up, but they were busy so she had to take the bus, and she was still crying, you know, and shaking? She clearly wasn't OK and I didn't want to leave her, so I asked if she wanted me to take the bus with her and she said yes, if I didn't mind. So I went with her, but one of Felix's mates saw us at the bus stop on his way to the party, so Felix decided that was the perfect way to deflect from what he'd done, to make it about me cosying up to her and trying to, in his words, "get in there", when it wasn't like that at all.'

It all sounds so very much like Felix, doesn't it? And, I think, with a lump in my throat, so very much like Laurie.

'What happened to the girl?' I ask.

'She's OK now, mostly. It rattled her a lot, I think, but she's at uni in Manchester and seems to be doing well. We chat every so often.'

'Is that why you were so . . . careful to take care of me?' I ask.

He nods.

'There was briefly some suggestion that Felix wouldn't be allowed in to QAC, but of course his daddy sorted that out.' I remember how easily Felix dismissed any suggestion that he wouldn't get in. 'I was basically ostracised for the rest of the year for taking her side, for accusing him of doing what he did when everyone else had already decided she was just a . . . you know, a slut, I suppose.'

'Oh, Laurie,' I say, reaching out to put my hand on his. It twitches, the instinct to pull away so clearly there and so clearly being fought. 'I'm so sorry.'

He shrugs, pulls his hand away, runs it through his thick hair. 'I'm not the real victim in all of this. Just collateral damage.'

We sit in silence for a moment. My hand feels oddly cold and lonely without his there. I want to feel him close to me, want the warmth of his skin, the comfort of his physical presence.

'Thank you for telling me all of that,' I say quietly.

Finally, he smiles. 'You are rather easy to talk to.'

'I regret that our dinner got cut short that time. I was enjoying it. I was . . . enjoying being with you, in that way, I think.'

Laurie clears his throat a little awkwardly, like maybe he can sense what's coming, but he doesn't interrupt me.

'And I was thinking, maybe if you're in London over the summer, we could . . . we could do something sometime?'

I pause, wondering if that's too ambiguous. 'Maybe . . . even . . .' I swallow, my heart pounding away inside my ribcage. For someone who shoots their shot as often as I do, I feel very nervous indeed. 'Maybe you could even call it a date?'

It's like the shutters have been pulled down on Laurie's face. In an instant, his expression changes. He breaks my gaze. 'Um, actually, there's been a slight development . . .'

I don't need him to tell me. I can already guess what it is. 'Oh,' I say simply.

'Yes.' He clears his throat again but doesn't say anything else for a moment. 'It just felt . . . like the right moment to give it another go.'

Look, I'm not actually upset, it's just a little bit of cringe, but for some reason, as well as my cheeks flushing, I can feel little needles stabbing at my eyeballs. But obviously I'm not upset. It's fine. Just a bit embarrassing, that's all. Nothing I can't survive.

'Of course,' I say, and before I can stop myself, I add, 'Lucky her.' It comes out high-pitched and scratchy.

'I'm . . .' He shakes his head, looks slightly bewildered. 'I'm sorry for all of this.'

'It's OK,' I say, reaching out and putting my hand gently on his arm. But it's not OK. I'm just pretending, for Laurie, for my own dignity. Inside I'm furious, hot with embarrassment, regret, resentment. It's not pretty and I don't like it about myself, but it's what I'm feeling. Why have I been able to get every boy I've ever liked except for this one? The only one who's got more depth than a fucking puddle, who has an actual backbone, who isn't just someone I like because they're hot but someone I like because they're kind and interesting and surprising.

'We've come a long way since the last time we were in the union with you wearing that dress,' he says, smiling sadly.

'You remember I was wearing this dress?'

He nods. 'I remember thinking, Why am I being so rude to this very pretty girl? It was like I couldn't stop myself, like it was self-defence or something.'

'And then you thought, Let's take this to the next level and really rile her up by copying her column?' I say, nudging him with my knee.

'What?' he says, frowning.

'You know, the No Nonsense column,' I say, frowning right back.

'That . . . wasn't me,' he says slowly. 'I mean, it was sort of my idea – I said it as a joke in the first meeting of term – but I never wrote them.'

'It's fine, Laurie, you can admit it. I'm not even annoyed about it any more!' I say, but part of me already knows he wouldn't admit to it being his idea but lie about writing it.

'But really, it wasn't me,' he says, fixing me with a very serious look. 'I didn't know you . . . didn't know that.'

'Well, who was it then?!' I say, feeling completely on the back foot but equally inclined to believe him.

'Mary-Elizabeth,' he turns to look at me, 'Felix wrote those columns.'

It's like all the wind has gone out of my sails. 'What?'

'Like I said, I sort of mentioned it as a joke, that maybe

we needed an advice column, and Charlotte really ran with it as an idea and then all of a sudden there it was, and when I pressed her about it, she finally admitted it was Felix. Something about how he wanted to get in with the newspaper in case the magazine folded. But it would be under the radar, you know? Not like actually writing for them openly.' He runs a hand through his hair, not looking at me. 'I told her I didn't like it but couldn't bring myself to tell her about the whole ... situation between me and him, and I figured I couldn't object too forcefully without having to air all the dirty laundry.'

I nod. 'I can't believe how wrong I got it.'

'I didn't realise you still didn't know,' he says, shaking his head. 'But it makes sense. You'd say things sometimes and I'd think, What does that mean? And now I get that it's because you thought I was the one writing that column,' he says, nodding thoughtfully.

'We've made a bit of a mess of this whole thing, haven't we?'

He nods again. 'I think so.'

I think of that little silver knot in the trinket dish on my dressing table. 'It feels like a necklace that's got tangled in ways you can't even really figure out, let alone untangle.'

Laurie smiles. 'Yes, I suppose it does.'

'You haven't got any delicious fruit in your pocket as a farewell gift, have you?' I ask, my voice cracking.

'Would you believe me if I told you', he says, reaching into the big pocket on the front of his jacket, 'that I am in possession of some of the finest lychees money can buy?' He produces a small brown paper bag. 'They travel surprisingly well.'

'For me?' I ask.

'For you.'

We eat them in silence, and both understand that this is an ending.

THE SUMMER HOLIDAYS

CHAPTER 37

It's funny. Even a couple of months ago, my mum would have been the last person I wanted to see in a difficult moment. I'd tell myself she would only make things worse, say something that would irritate me and leave me dwelling on our conversation for days afterwards. But now . . .

She gazes out of the train window, the verdant fields and forests rushing by. 'Oh, look, darling! A little Bambi!' She gasps with delight, pointing at a baby deer grazing in a field.

'Cute,' I say with a smile. The train route to Hastings is much prettier than I was expecting, once you get past the suburban London blob.

'Isn't this nice already?' Mum says enthusiastically. 'Our little trip to the seaside!'

I nod. Mum wanted a change of scenery and to celebrate the end of my exams, so we're going to spend the weekend in a little house in the Old Town. We've been blessed with the weather – you'd think late June would be a dead cert for sunshine, but a key thing to remember is that we live in England, so good weather is absolutely never guaranteed.

Once we're safely installed in the house, we wander out in search of a drink, and settle on a cute pub with seating outside.

'How are you really doing, darling?' Mum asks once we've got ice-cold drinks and a steaming bowl of chips in front of us.

'I'm fine!' I say breezily. 'Why?'

'You're just very quiet, that's all. I want to make sure you're having a nice time.' The idea that my mum would think I'm being quiet because I'm not enjoying being here with her tugs at my heartstrings. Which leaves me with no option but to tell her about Laurie. The first meeting, the misunderstanding over the column, the ways he was kind to me (skirting around the spiking incident because I don't want to rehash that right now), how my feelings changed over time and where we left things the other night, that final, grudging, ambiguous loss.

'And . . .' She pauses, thinking. 'What would you say to someone who wrote to you and told you about this situation? How would you deal with it if it was someone else?'

I think for a moment, sipping on my straw. 'I guess I would say . . . that it's good nothing really happened between you and that should hopefully make it easier to just move on and put the whole thing behind you. To confine it to the past and not dwell on it too much since it clearly wasn't meant to be. That there will be someone else out there for you . . . lots of other someones, in fact. And definitely don't chase him, because he's seeing someone else and has imposed that boundary.'

'And does that sound like advice you can follow?'

'I guess so. I don't think I have much of a choice.'

'I think that's always the hardest part. Not feeling like you have a choice, or feeling like the choice has been made for you.'

'I always want to feel like I'm in control. Like anything that's happening is happening because I want it to – I'm the master of my own destiny and all that. But this whole situation feels like such a mess,' I say, shaking my head. 'I think you're right. I think I need to just put it behind me and move on.'

Mum smiles. 'Darling, I didn't say that. You did.'

'Ha,' I say, blushing a little. 'So I did. It's like I'm trying to give all the power away to someone else so I don't have to be responsible for how I'm dealing with the situation I'm in.'

She squeezes my hand across the table. 'You're very wise. I think you'll do the right thing.'

'I hope so.'

Mum thinks for a moment. 'You brought your swimming costume, didn't you?'

'Yes, I thought I'd pack one just in case,' I say, though I hadn't actually thought of using it. 'Why?'

'I saw an inspirational quote on Instagram once that said, "The cure for anything is salt water – tears, sweat or the sea," and I thought, Do you know what? You're onto something.'

'Do you think the sea has warmed up enough?' I ask, pre-emptively wincing at the thought of plunging into cold water.

'Oh, maybe not,' Mum says. 'Silly me. Probably not a very good idea, is it?'

'No, it's not that,' I say quickly, realising that this is probably something she needs more than I do. 'I think it's a good idea. I want to do it. Shall we go tomorrow morning before we walk to Bexhill? We'll feel so smug all day.'

'We don't have to stay in long, darling! It's more . . . the act of doing it.'

'I'm in.'

* * *

The next morning, we wake up early with a mission, walking along the seafront promenade to St Leonards beach.

The pebbles shift underfoot, the click-clack sound oddly satisfying against the low, rhythmic sweep of the waves. Mum stands, hands on her hips at the top of the beach's slope. 'Are you sure you want to go in?'

'Positive,' I say.

'Good.'

We walk down, closer to the water, and put our bags down, slip off our shoes and take off our clothes.

'God, I wish I'd brought flip-flops!' Mum says, hopping from foot to foot as the pebbles press into the soles of our feet.

'Next time,' I say, smiling. 'You live and learn.'

Mum grimaces. 'There might not be a next time!'

'Come on.' I hold my hand out to her, something I can't have done for many, many years. She takes it, and I wonder if she's thinking the same thing. One day a long time ago I held her hand for the last time, and the next day I didn't, and then I never did again, until today. It's as if we never really know what's happening to us until it's in the past and we can look back on it. We're always too in the thick of it to really understand it in the present. That's just something we all have to live with, I suppose.

Hand in hand, we dash into the sea, separating to raise our arms over our heads, which only prolongs the initial discomfort of the cold as it hits each body part from our feet up. And finally, we're in, submerged.

Maybe it's the knowledge of Mum's quote about salt water, maybe it's the shock of the cold, maybe it's thinking about her, maybe it's how much I already miss Laurie, but within seconds of the water touching my skin, I feel warm tears on my cheeks. When I look at Mum, I realise she's crying too.

'See, sweetie? I told you it would be fun!' she says, sniffling, which makes us both burst into uncontrollable laughter.

We don't stay in long. Mum was right: what we needed was just the act of doing it.

'Now, we breakfast,' Mum says, stomping off in the direction of the café on the beach, so clearly infused with a zeal for the new day that it's almost radiating off her. 'We need fuel for our walk to Bexhill,' she calls over her shoulder.

When we get there, people are already sitting on benches, eating breakfast while their cute dogs pant next to them, morning runners basking in the warm glow of their achievements with a coffee on a deckchair.

We order and take a seat on a picnic table looking out to sea. Mum seems lost in thought, and I take the opportunity to cast my eyes over her. Not a scrap of make-up, damp hair, and she's still the most beautiful person in the world.

The breeze lifts her curls, sends them across her face. 'Darling, I really loved the time we spent together while you were revising for your exams. It really meant a lot to me,' she says, looking out to sea, the morning sunlight glittering on the gently undulating waves.

'Me too.'

'And I've been thinking a lot about what we talked about . . . the Sabor shoot . . .'

'Oh, yes?' I say, feeling like a fist is gripping my insides, so desperate am I for my mum to do it but knowing very well that she's reluctant.

'And I decided I'm going to do it . . . and I'm not going to . . . you know . . .' She mimes injecting something into her face. 'Or do a mad diet or anything like that.'

The relief floods through me so swiftly I actually let out an audible sigh. 'That's great news. Thank you,' I say, before backtracking. 'I don't know why I just said that. I meant to say . . . I think it's the right decision . . . and I'm proud of you . . . but it came out as "thank you" . . .' I furrow my brow, taken aback by my ability to misspeak.

She shrugs. 'Maybe I'm not just doing it for me.'

I nod. 'Maybe not. Who knows, maybe this will be the start of a new career moment for you?'

Mum shakes her head. 'I'm happy with my yoga classes, darling. It's just . . . the act of doing it, I think. And I wouldn't be doing it without you, so thank you.'

'Any time,' I say casually.

The sun beats down on us as we walk along the coast, a gorgeous, radiant warmth against our skin, the exact opposite of the cold shock of the sea. As we walk up to the top of the coastal path, the highest point before making the descent into Bexhill, I feel beads of sweat break out on my forehead. Surveying the landscape on either side from this vantage point, I'm grateful for all of today's salt water. But I miss Laurie.

CHAPTER 38

'Oh my God, have you heard?' Olu's clutching me in the home goods aisle of Sainsbury's before I even realise I've bumped into her.

'Er, hello, Olu!' I say, blinking at the unexpected encounter. I'm trying to avoid the tedious task of packing up my room so volunteered to go to the supermarket in search of cleaning products. 'What have I heard?'

'Felix,' she says, raising her eyebrows.

'What about him?'

'Maybe it hasn't escaped the French group chat yet, but . . . he's been kicked out of uni.'

My heart starts racing. 'What? Why?'

'Well, we all knew he was a bit of a shit and a total player, but it seems as if it all went a bit further than that.' She widens her eyes suggestively.

'What do you mean?' My throat feels dry.

'You know how hard it is for anything like this to actually stick against anyone, let alone a rich white boy like him – no offence; I know you used to be mad about him,' she says, holding up a hand to pause my objections, not that any would be forthcoming. 'So I guess it must have been something pretty compelling for him to actually get kicked out. People are saying it was multiple credible allegations of sexual assault.'

'Fuck . . .' I say.

Olu pauses. 'Was he ever –' she cocks her head – 'like that with you?' I guess I didn't do a very good job of keeping our 'relationship' under wraps from the *Quad* lot.

'No,' I say, shaking my head. But that's not true, is it? I let out a sigh. 'I mean . . . yes. It was one of those things that . . . I kept telling myself had to be OK because Felix wasn't like that . . . but it wasn't OK . . . and he was like that.'

'I'm sorry . . . and I'm sorry for being the one who had to tell you about this . . . I didn't know you didn't know.'

'I've sort of avoided him as a general concept as much as possible since I left *Quad*.'

'Probably a good idea. I'm just happy he's not going to be unleashed on the female student population of Guadeloupe. If he felt empowered to behave like that here, who knows what he'd get up to there?'

'You're right,' I say, feeling a bit sick.

'Anyway, enough about him – what are you doing this summer?'

'Um . . .' I say, decidedly discombobulated. 'I'm doing an internship at a gallery in Bermondsey. My sculpture lecturer put in a good word with a friend who works there.' Jessica has really saved this academic year for me, and I'm going to be history's best intern to her mate by way of thanks. 'How about you?'

'Just working before heading to Paris.' Olu says, as if getting to move to Paris for a year is so totally casual and not something I would *love* to do.

'That's so exciting, I'm so happy for you,' I say with a smile. 'Well –' I brandish my bin bags and bleach – 'I've got a flat to pack up and clean. It was . . . good to see you.'

'You too,' she says, and draws me into a hug. 'He was always the problem. Always. I know we were never close, but I often found myself really wanting you to know that.'

A thought crosses my mind suddenly. 'Olu!' I call after her and she turns back to look at me.

'Mmm?'

'Did you once write into my column . . . about, well, about me and Felix? I got a letter once in the magazine pigeonhole and I never knew who it was from.'

She closes her eyes and shakes her head. 'I'm sorry, I shouldn't have done it. It wasn't the way, you know?'

'But it was you, right?'

She nods, chewing her lip.

I now draw her into a hug. 'Thank you.'

'You're not mad? We're hardly, like, close so I thought maybe it would come off as weird or rude.'

'No. It's . . . sort of nice to know that good people are thinking of you even when you don't know it. It sounds silly to say it, but . . .'

'What?'

'But maybe it's like we all have these little invisible networks of people doing good things and we hardly know about any of it.'

Olu smiles wryly. 'You? Being an eternal optimist? I'm shocked! See you when I'm back from Paris, I guess.'

I walk back to the flat in a daze. Felix kicked out of Queen Anne's College for multiple sexual assault allegations? Olu's right – things like this don't stick to guys like him, so it must be inescapably bad. I don't know how to feel. I mean, obviously I'm glad he's experiencing some consequences for his actions, but now he's just . . . gone. Cut loose. Free to go and be the same person he'll always be, just somewhere else. It should feel like a win, but like so many things with Felix, it's ended up being so much more tangled.

I have packing to do, but something about this encounter with Olu makes me want to go and see my saints. I drop my purchases off at home and hop on the Northern Line down to the Portrait Gallery. I tread the familiar route to the little dark-green exhibition room, but when I get there, there's a sign blocking the entrance.

THIS GALLERY IS CLOSED

WHILE WE PREPARE THE NEXT EXHIBITION

I give a little gasp of horror. My saint! She's gone! All 450 of her! I feel as if the rug has been pulled out from under my feet. Of course I knew it was a temporary exhibition, but I realise now I'd never really thought it would close. I miss her already. It really is the end of an era.

I go for a wander around the National Gallery instead. I come across one painting on its own, with a crowd of people around it, transfixed. It's a painting on loan from Naples, one

I've heard of but never seen in person. I wait for the crowd to thin a little and make my way forward. It's gnarly. Dark, both visually and thematically. A woman cutting off a man's head complete with spurting blood, while another woman holds him down. Artemisia Gentileschi's *Judith Slaying Holofernes*. I read the card next to the painting, read about the Biblical story the painting is based on – a beautiful widow who saves her people from an oncoming army by beheading its general – and, maybe more interestingly, how this painting is understood to be a way for the artist to metabolise her own rape by her mentor, who was tried and convicted.

I look at the painting for a long time. At the long streaks of blood. Good for her, I think.

CHAPTER 39

My room is pretty much packed to move out. Just my dressing table to clear. Obviously, my make-up and jewellery have to be the last things to go because, heaven forbid, I can't express myself. I wrap my perfume bottles in scarves, and then move on to my jewellery, packing things into boxes. Then I spy something I don't want to pack away: my letter 'M' necklace, a thorny tangle in a shell trinket dish. Just looking at it provokes an audible sigh. It doesn't deserve to be in a box, all snarled up. It should be around my neck, where it belongs. Somehow the tangles have got worse since I last saw it, but there's nothing for it. If I could get through this weird mess of a year, I can get certainly do this. As I've discovered, the only way out is through. I take a deep breath, tip out the contents of the trinket dish in search of a safety pin, sit down at my dressing table and get to work.

Loosening what looks like the worst of the knot in one place seems to make it worse in another, so I move on to a different tangled clump instead, working away at it until I've cleared one patch and the chain can move more freely.

Slowly, slowly, I chip away at the mess until it's nearly done. I'm holding my breath, so desperate to get it over and done with, when –

'Knock-knock,' Aleesha says, poking her head around the bedroom door.

I look up, flustered. 'Hi!' I say, slightly manic.

'You look like a person in need of a pizza . . . Morgan and I are going to order from that new place in a bit if you want to join?'

'Of course I want to join,' I say, my eyes now back on my task, even more incentivised to finish it now. 'I'll be down in like . . . two minutes.' Optimistic, but that is the Mary-Elizabeth Baxter way.

'Good luck with . . . whatever it is you're up to,' Aleesha says curiously, before disappearing downstairs.

And then, all of a sudden, it's done. The sensation of slipping the chain through itself, back through the final knot, is almost ecstatic. I nearly shed a tear. When I fasten it around my neck it feels like a hard-won prize. I truly earned this.

'We're starving!' Morgan yells up to my bedroom as I'm admiring my reflection in the mirror, the necklace glinting against my chest where it belongs.

'Coming!' I call back to my flatmates as I head downstairs.

Before I even set foot in the living room, Aleesha says to me, 'We need a new QAC email address for our new-student customer discount scam. We've used all of ours already.'

'We can use my old advice column email, that's got a

.qac address. I always use that for random marketing junk now.'

'They actually send you a code to use to the email so you can't even make one up – how rude is that?'

'So rude. Lemme get my laptop . . .' I say, trotting back upstairs to my almost-packed room. The bed is still made because I'm sleeping here tonight, but everything else is in laundry bags and suitcases. I grab my laptop and head downstairs, where Aleesha and Morgan look just about ready to gnaw their arms off. 'Let's hope Felix hasn't somehow taken command of this email address and I can still get in . . .' I say, settling down in the armchair and typing in my email address and password. 'I'm in – pizza scam is go,' I tell them. 'Put in askmeanything@quadmedia.qac.ac.uk as the email. I'll have the pepperoni one.'

'Weeeey!' Morgan lets out a cheer.

'I've forwarded you the code,' I tell her, my role in the pizza scam fulfilled.

As we wait for the order to arrive, I cast my eye over the neglected email inbox, overflowing with spam marketing emails from all the brands I wanted to score a discount from, plus a couple of 'Ask M-E Anything' emails from people who clearly are not up to date with the internal politics of Quad Media and didn't know a) that I'd jumped ship, and b) that the magazine is now dead. I'm about to set the laptop aside and go to the kitchen for some water when something catches my eye at the top of the unread emails. Suddenly, I can't hear anything around me except the pounding of my heart. My throat goes dry. I forget to breathe.

From: LOdo0894@qac.ac.uk
To: askmeanything@quadmedia.qac.ac.uk
Subject: Advice needed

Dear Mary-Elizabeth,

I doubt you check this email address any more, which is exactly why I'm sending it here. I suppose I do need advice, but more than anything I just need to get something off my chest and out of my system. My problem is this: I don't know how to deal with the unhappiness I feel about you. I liked you from the first time I met you, even if I had a funny way of showing it. Every time I've seen you since then, I've felt more and more in awe of you, your confidence and your style and your charm – all of these things that felt so different not just from me, but from everyone around us. But you were so set on Felix and, well, for better or for worse I'm nothing like Felix, so I told myself I didn't stand a chance and reverted back to the old pattern of being on-again, off-again with Charlotte. Then we got to know each other, and I can't help thinking that underneath it all, underneath you being so sparkly and shiny and fun, and me being so . . . well, myself, that actually we would be good together. Charlotte's just like me in many ways, so I thought we were a natural fit, however hard it was to make things work between us, and finally we've admitted that it just won't work. No more trying. But maybe what I need is someone who isn't like me at all. Maybe what I need is someone who's just like you, and the unfortunate reality is that no one is like you except for you. So, as you can see, I'm a bit stuck.

I think what I need to learn from someone as wise as you is how I'm meant to just go about my business knowing you're somewhere in the world, somewhere not that far from me, and we're not together. I'm sure you're dealing with it better than I am, so any help in this area would be gratefully received. As I said, I know you're not checking this email any more, but I thought writing it all down might make me feel a bit less lost in this whole thing. It hasn't really helped at all. Although I understand there's a lot of 'mess' (your word) to sift through, at this point I can't quite believe that the act of sifting would be worse than not having you around.

Missing your shine,
Laurie

I read it once. And I'm about to read it again when I realise I DO NOT HAVE TIME TO READ IT AGAIN. When did he send it? Maybe this is old news, maybe he's over it by now? I check the date. He only sent it yesterday. I have to find him. I have to find Laurie.

'Guys . . .' I say, my voice shaking, 'I've . . . I've got to go . . . there's something important I have to do . . .'

'But what about the pizza?!' Aleesha looks crestfallen.

'You two have the pizza . . . I'll . . . I'll explain everything later . . .'

'Are you OK?!' Morgan asks, looking at me wide-eyed, but I think she can tell this is a good kind of stressed, not a bad kind of stressed.

'I'm fine!' I shout from the hall, pulling on the most sensible shoes I can find – some gold lamé Converse sneakers. I literally do not have time for uncomfortable shoes right now.

I've got somewhere to be.

CHAPTER 40

I dash to the bus stop, checking the bus-times app as I stride, but there isn't one going my way for . . . six minutes? What is this, the countryside? Ugh! I've got places to be, and I cannot be waiting six minutes! Instead of relying on the bus, I begin my speed walk down the main road, looking over my shoulder in case a mystery bus appears after all. I walk and walk and walk, and after a while I forget to look for the bus and I'm just locked into this mission, walking at great speed towards Laurie's. I'm walking so fast that at some points both of my feet are off the ground at the same time, which I believe is what they call running, something I am most unfamiliar with. God! I can't believe I'm literally running after Laurie O'Donnell of all people! So undignified! But for some reason, I just don't care about dignity any more, or playing it cool, or holding back. I don't have time for it!

The evening air is warm, and all the pubs are spilling over with people infused with the good summer vibes, but here I am, stomping wildly in the direction of Camden, getting a right sweat on. God, I won't even want Laurie to see me looking like this by the time I get there, will I? But then I think about my mum and her inspirational quote about salt water. Sweat. Will it cure this?

Finally, I make it to his estate, and then to his building, and then to the winding concrete stairs that divide the terraces of front doors on their outdoor walkways. By the time I get to the third floor, I'm properly out of breath, but I don't have time to stop. I dash towards where I remember his flat being, but then I'm suddenly gripped with indecision – which flat is it? I know it's one of the two on the end . . . but which one? As I approach, it's obvious which one it is. My heart sinks. The curtains are open and everything but the furniture is gone from the living room. The flat next door, by contrast, is a hive of activity – a children's birthday party is in full swing and a weary-looking woman comes outside to vape.

All dignity gone, and not even feeling that bothered that I have a witness, I peer through the glass into Laurie's flat, desperately searching for any sign of life, but there is none.

'I think those boys moved out today,' the woman says, hitting the vape and nodding in the direction of their flat, 'if that's who you're looking for.'

'Oh,' I say, as lightly as I can, as if really it doesn't matter at all, despite the fact that she just saw me with my nose pressed against the glass.

'Your mates, were they? They were all right. Bit quiet,' she shrugs, hitting the vape again.

I nod, feeling the lump in my throat get bigger, more insistent. 'Thanks for letting me know,' I manage to croak out as I turn back towards the stairs.

Today. They moved out today. Of course they did.

I don't know how to explain it other than that it had to be now. If it's not now, one of us will change our mind or lose our nerve or start seeing someone else and the whole process will begin again, and I can't do it. I just want to be with him.

I drag myself to the hulking concrete spiral staircase and slowly begin my trudge down. I got to Felix's and he was kissing someone on the doorstep. I get to Laurie's and no one's there at all. Why can't people just be where they're meant to be, doing the things they're meant to be doing? Just my luck. I hope Morgan and Aleesha haven't eaten my pepperoni pizza. I suppose I have that to look forward to, don't I?

Finally, I reach the bottom of the stairs. Children are playing out on the estate, the sounds of shouting and laughter and music from the open door of a flat, dashing little footsteps and the dinging of bike bells in the air. Just how a summer evening should be spent. I pause for a moment to just listen, to be in the moment, rather than trying to be in the past or the future. Then I head for the bus stop. I'll wait six minutes this time, I'm not in a rush any more. As I set off, another sound layers on top of the bike bells, the music from a nearby party, the giggles, and I'm struck with the certainty that someone is shouting my name. Why would those children know my name? But it doesn't sound like a child's voice. It sounds like –

When I turn around, I am face to face with Laurie. Or rather, face to chest, because I have to look up at him.

'Oh!' I say stupidly.

'I . . .' He blinks at me. 'I thought it was you. I mean, you are quite . . . distinctive.'

I just stare at him for a second, completely wrong-footed.

'I thought you were gone,' is all I can manage.

'My flatmate forgot to leave his keys, so I said I'd drop them through the letterbox for him,' Laurie says, his voice a little shaky. Thank God for forgetful flatmates. Thank you thank you thank you.

'Laurie, I . . .' I begin, and realise I don't have a plan at all. Everything has happened so fast that I have no idea what I'm actually doing here. 'I read your email.'

Laurie swallows. 'I didn't necessarily mean for you to –'

'I read your email, and I don't want you to have to get over me. I don't want you to have to find a way to move on without me. I'm completely obsessed with you, and I want to be with you, and I don't want to be with anyone else. So my advice to you would be . . . just love me.'

Laurie says nothing for a moment, just looks down at me with his big, brown, bewildered eyes.

'Does that sound like good advice?' I ask him.

Laurie's answer is to wrap his arms around me and kiss me – properly, not tentatively, nervously, like it would have been if we'd actually kissed in my living room before Felix showed up. This is the real thing. It's had the time and space to become the real thing.

'There's nothing I'd rather do,' he says.

And that, dear friends, is how you end your second year at university.

CHAPTER 41

Audio transcript of Genius of Love, from the Quad podcast, Episode 10, a Quad Media production.

Hello, gorgeous friends, I am Mary-Elizabeth Baxter, also known as the Genius of Love! I know term has officially ended, but podcasts wait for no man. Or woman. Or person who has transcended the gender binary. And today I'm coming to you in this special bonus episode to send you on your way over the summer holidays until we meet again in September.

This academic year has been really strange and hard for me. I thought it was going to be all fun and games, just flirting and dancing and writing essays, but unfortunately that wasn't the case. So I thought maybe I could write a letter to myself about how I felt this year, and then I could answer the letter. So instead of answering a question from one of you, I'm answering a question from . . . well, from me. Maybe it's a silly idea, I don't know, but let's just roll with it and see what happens. Worst comes to the worst, I just delete this before it ever goes live and no one except Tyler – that's the person who sort of . . . makes the podcast – has to hear any more of my nonsense until the autumn term. OK, here goes.

Dear Genius of Love,
My confidence got really knocked this year for a few reasons, but mostly due to feeling like sex and romance and dating was just going to end up with me getting hurt. How do I ensure that making bad decisions, or having bad things happen to me, doesn't stop me from approaching my romantic life with joy and excitement? How do I preserve my sparkle?
With love,
Sparkle-free Zone

Dear Sparkle-free Zone,
I completely understand where you're coming from, because I literally am you. So here's what I've learned between being you and also being me, while always, fundamentally, being . . . me and you.
After your trust was broken in different ways, for a while you wanted to stop engaging with the world because it felt safer. You had this fear pricking at you and couldn't help but wonder if maybe all boys were equally awful, equally likely to hurt you, that there must be something in their composition to make them want to do these things to girls (girls like you, in particular, whatever that means), but the thing that will take your breath away is the realisation that this is not true at all. It's not inevitable. It's a choice that some of them make.

All of which is to say, you're not wrong for trusting people. You're not stupid or naive. They're the ones making a choice to abuse your trust. Do not lose your sparkle. Do not lose your ability to trust. Do not let them take that away from you. By all means, if someone gives you actual reason to doubt them, listen. And I don't mean listen to every silly thing you hear about someone (consider the source!), I mean listen to how they treat you, how they treat other girls, how they talk about girls and whether how they talk about girls matches up to their actions. It's easy for someone to call themselves a feminist, but are they still interested in a girl when she disagrees with them or confronts them or says no to them?

Flirting is fun and sleeping with someone new can be thrilling, and it's fine to want the excitement of a new crush, to seek out the thrill of the chase, but if it still feels like you're chasing them once you've 'got' them, when will that insecure feeling ever end? Think of the feeling of being in your kitchen with your flatmates, drinking instant coffee and listening to the radio. You are going to find someone who makes you feel like that. The excitement and the thrill are going to come from actually spending time with them and getting to know them, rather than from the scarcity mindset that comes with a person who won't commit to you.

And know that while you are, by your nature, a boy-crazy little flirt, you will get so much out of deepening your love and connection with people in ways that aren't romantic. Learning to love people on their own terms, without trying to fix them or figure out what's going on with them, is a really powerful and beautiful way to engage with someone. You tend to think of your sparkle as something that exists in relation to romantic partners or someone you're flirting with, but it's something you have in all your relationships. Don't save that gorgeous attention and curiosity only for your new crush. Turn it towards your friends and family too. God knows they deserve it!

Know that you can't know everything, as much as you want to. Some things will have to remain a mystery, and you have to be at peace with the not-knowing. While you can't let the not-knowing consume you, you can let it inform you.

Finally: think about yourself slightly less. Think about other people slightly more. That is where the magic happens.

I love you. You are gorgeous, you are wonderful, you have so much to learn, and you are always deserving of care.

With so much affection,
Genius of Love

Acknowledgements

Thank you first and foremost to Jenny Jacoby for being a dream of an editor. Thank you to the Hot Key team, including Pippa, Jas and Holly for all your hard work. Thank you to Sarah Long for the wonderful cover. Thank you to Rachel Mann and Daisy Arendell at CAA for tolerating my emails.

Thank you to the Royal Literary Fund for their support.
Thank you to Paul, to my family, to my friends.
And finally, with great love, thank *you* for reading.

Bethany Rutter

Bethany is a writer and personal trainer. She writes books about women, bodies and clothes. She lives in South East London.

Thank you for choosing a Hot Key book!

For all the latest bookish news, freebies and exclusive content, sign up to the Hot Key newsletter – scan the QR code or visit lnk.to/HotKeyBooks

Follow us on social media:

bonnierbooks.co.uk/HotKeyBooks